# FALLING FOR HER

Geonn Cannon

Supposed Crimes LLC • Matthews, North Carolina

www.supposedcrimes.com

This book is typeset in Goudy Old Style.

FALLING FOR HER

## CHAPTER ONE

THE WIND gusted and blew trash and dirty snow over the toes of Kim Greer's boots. She kicked off as much as she could before stepping onto the sidewalk. The front windows of the convenience store were obscured by sale announcements and lost pet posters, lit from behind like the shadow boxes they used to make in elementary school. The bell over her head jingled as she pushed through the door and went directly toward the cooler at the back. Her knit cap was pulled down to her eyebrows, and she blew into her cupped hands to try and warm them.

She didn't notice the quiet of the store until she heard a shuffling step on the old linoleum. She caught movement out of the corner of her eye and jumped back, eyes wide with shock as the man stepped out from behind the display of chips. "Wrong store, whore," he said, and fired once, twice, three times.

Kim's body jerked with each impact. One in the right shoulder, two in the stomach. She slipped on the melting snow on her boots and fell backward into the cooler. The glass shattered under her weight, and she grabbed at the rack in a futile attempt to stop her fall. It was too late. There was no way to save her. She stared blindly across the store where another man in black was filling a bag with money from the register.

Her eyes went blank, her muscles relaxing as she sagged against the broken bottles of beer.

"And cut!"

Kim blinked, wiped a hand over her face, and tried to stand up. The shooter extended his hand, and she took it, hoisting herself up. People swarmed around her, making sure the broken glass had fallen away from her, that she wouldn't be hurt by one hanging loose in her clothing. Kim took off her knit cap, added to keep the glass from getting into her thick hair, and shook it out to one side.

The director had come out onto the set, standing next to the shooter. "'Bitch' might be better," he said. "'Store, whore' rhymes and it sounds unusual. Give it a try on the next go." He turned and said, "Kim, we'll do the coverage with a close-up of Daniel. Don't worry, we won't make you get shot again."

"Appreciate that." She looked down at her blouse, the fake blood smearing the white front of it. "How'd the squibs do?"

"Perfect, I was terrified for your life," the director said blankly.

Kim smirked. "Thanks. You need me to lie around for a little while?"

The director scanned his script. "No, we're going from the reaction shot of Kevin, then cutting to outside loading the van." He flipped a few more pages. "And the cops refer to the shooting off camera. Sorry, Kim, you don't get to play a corpse today."

"There's always tomorrow," Kim said.

She left the grocery store and stepped off the sidewalk. She took off her costume jacket and draped it over her shoulder. As she walked, the snow on the sidewalk began to thin, and then disappeared completely in a patch of bright sunshine. It was far too hot in the real world to walk around bundled up like her hapless shopper character. Shooting at a real location meant their trailers were lining the side streets and clogging up traffic like crazy. The things people would tolerate for their entertainment, she mused. As she passed a twenty-something with a headset, he nodded casually at the blood drying on the front of her shirt. "Need me to call a doctor?"

"I think I'll try to walk it off," she said.

"Stay strong."

The wardrobe trailer was at the end of the street, near the sawhorses that held back pedestrian traffic. A few people were snapping photos with their cell phones, and she felt the urge to tell them not to bother. It's not like she was Somebody. It was a one day job, a call to be a fall gal for a quick stunt. She didn't mind it; jobs like these were like being paid to play war. Instead of a neighborhood kid pointing a finger and saying bang, someone held a gun and small compressed gas packets blew holes in your clothes and spilled fake blood.

The costume designer looked up as Kim entered the trailer, putting aside what she was working on to make her way over. She was a plump, joyful ball of energy named Susan, and her eyes wrinkled when she smiled. "How'd everything go, dear?"

"I'm covered in blood." Kim held her arms out to show it off. "It was a good day."

Susan laughed and took Kim's thin fingers in her plump hand, guiding her toward the changing area. Kim stood behind the screen and stripped out of the borrowed clothes. Susan stood on the other side, taking each item as Kim handed it over the top of the screen. "So was it terribly exciting?"

Kim laughed. "Faking surprise and then falling backward into a sheet of breakaway glass. Typical day."

She took off the spent gas packets and disposed of them, checking to make sure none of the fake blood had gotten on her undershirt. She took her street clothes off a hanger and quickly changed into them. "Sorry about messing up more of your clothes."

"Feh. You should have seen what they did to my clothes on that science fiction program that used to shoot here." She shook her head. "So much slime and goop."

Kim said, "Yes, I try to keep the goop to a minimum." She tucked her blouse into her jeans, and flipped her hair out over the collar. She leaned down and kissed Susan's cheek. "Hope to see you soon, Susan."

"I'm doing costumes for that werewolf movie they're shooting. Will you be in that?"

Kim winced. Werewolves could be a lot of fun, stunt wise. "Sadly, no. I have a position on a new spy show. *Neutral Ground?* They got picked up for a series, but the network wanted to make some changes that included adding a female regular. So they hired me to be their stunt coordinator, and I get to double for the new lead. Should keep me pretty busy, but you never know. I might be able to fit in a werewolf on my slow days."

"I'll keep my eyes out for you, dear."

Kim waved her fingers over her shoulder as she left the trailer, returning to the street. Shedding the costume and hitting the street in her own clothes helped her break the spell of movie magic. Now she was just Kim Greer, not Grocery Store Victim. She put on her sunglasses and slipped past the barricades, the throng of spectators hardly paying her any attention now. Her Jeep was parked with the rest of the production's vehicles in a garage two blocks away, protected by a group of stone-faced security guards.

Kim put her hands in her pockets as she walked, lifting her head to the sun. She had gotten into character before entering the store, so a part of her mind had actually believed it was winter. To feel the sun shining down on her, and the cool breeze blowing her hair, were like miracles. She showed her ID to the security guard outside the garage and slid into her Jeep. The script for the pilot of *Neutral Ground* was on the passenger seat, and she smiled down at it.

The show was based on a series of books featuring Special Agent Thomas Templeton and his sometimes partner, CIA agent Simone Lethe. The producers had put together a thirty eight minute presentation for the networks to view before committing to a full series, and the gamble worked. The networks loved it, but they had several changes they wanted made before the series went to air. Lethe had been a guest star in the original pilot, but the networks wanted a strong female lead as a foil to Templeton. The original actress couldn't commit to a full series, so the character was recast and the title was changed from *Temple* to the more appropriate *Neutral Ground*. Now they had to completely reshoot the pilot for the new actress and to set up the new series premise of FBI and CIA agents working together.

Kim was more than happy with the change, since it meant she got to be the boss *and* still got to play rough. Besides, it had all the things that made being a stuntwoman fun: spy games, espionage, covert ops... she could hardly wait to get started.

She left the garage and drove away from the shoot, passing a street sign with a piece of paper taped to it. "Filming Today," the notice read, "HONOR AMONG THIEVES." An arrow pointed back the way from which she'd come. She knew people often kept track of those notices, hunting around for the names of their favorite TV series in the hopes of seeing something being filmed. If they only knew how much time actors spent in their trailers, waiting for the lighting and the costumer and the director to get everything perfect before any acting took place.

Kim turned onto Brewster Avenue and hung her hand out the window. She was happy, she decided, at that very moment. It was an unusual feeling after close to a decade of fighting her way up the ladder of her profession, paying her dues. And now, at thirty-four, she was more or less financially secure - a fact which sometimes depended on the outcome of her weekly poker game - and she had just been hired as stunt coordinator on a show with very good buzz. She managed to quit smoking a year ago, six months since falling off the wagon or whatever it was that smokers fell off, and she was getting steady work throwing herself around movie sets. The sun was out, the wind was blowing through the open top of her Jeep, and Pink was singing on the stereo. Life was good.

She parked in front of a video store called Reel Heroes and took the pilot script off the passenger seat, rolling it into a tube and cautiously peering out the window. She had spent her entire life on this street, but the steep angle still made her nervous. Sometimes it seemed as if it sloped eighty degrees straight down. She always felt like she was sliding for the first few steps, resisting the urge to cling to the side of her Jeep as she walked to the sidewalk.

The display window of the shop displayed the movie poster of some superhero movie or another. She went inside, the bells over the door reminding her of being shot an hour earlier, and hooked her sunglasses on her shirt. The check-out counter was to her left, in front of the display case, and aisles of DVDs stretched out to the right. They lined the walls from floor to ceiling, and stood at attention on both sides of wire racks. A big screen TV hung on the wall opposite the counter, quietly playing the first *Back to the Future* movie.

There were hardly any customers these days, but the store was still able to get most of the new releases. The big business came from film buffs who wanted the novelty of actually renting a physical copy of their favorite movie from the eighties or nineties. There were even a few VHS tapes on a shelf behind the counter, more display than anything else.

"Good afternoon, Auntie Em."

"I told you not to call me that," the frail woman behind the counter said, clicking her knitting needles together. Her name was Mabel Stern, and she was Kim's aunt. Combined with the fact she was a movie lover, the nickname made perfect sense to Kim. Mabel, however, hated it. She put aside her current project, a bundle of blue and white yarn that would probably end up somewhere in Kim's closet in some form or another.

Mabel picked up a handful of DVDs and laid them on the counter like a winning poker hand. "Here. Which ones?"

Kim moved to see the covers. "That one," Kim said, pulling

one from the stack and setting it aside. "I flipped Kate Beckinsale's car. And this one, I did all the stunts for the main actress. Tumbling, fighting, all that. But the others are safe."

Mabel put the two Kim picked out aside, and made a note of the other titles. Kim didn't mind running interference. Mabel hated watching a movie and seeing her niece get punched, thrown, shot, dropped, kicked, stabbed, or whatever mayhem directors were thinking up these days. She would skip an entire film just to avoid the shock of it all.

"So what did you do today?" she asked as she put the 'safe' movies away under the counter.

"Nothing heroic," Kim said. "They just needed someone to be knocked down when the bad guy tries to run away."

Mabel squinted through her glasses, but decided to accept the lie. "Don't know why you have to do this sort of thing. You're a very pretty girl. You could be an actress in movies, too, you know. Let someone else be tossed around like a rag doll for a change. Drink lattes in your trailer."

"Yep, that's me, auntie. The safe road." She winked and said, "I'll be upstairs."

"Maybe you can be a body double," Mabel said as Kim headed for the office. "You'd be naked, but you wouldn't be getting hurt. Not like you're getting laid anyway."

Kim twisted at the waist as she went into the office. "Ouch, Mabel. That was just hurtful. Besides, you'd rather see me all naked and sweaty than being hurt?"

"Nothing wrong with naked and sweaty, dear. Sex is beautiful."

"I remember," Kim said. "Vaguely."

"Do yourself a favor and refresh your memory while I'm still young enough to enjoy the juicy details."

Kim laughed and went through the curtain into the shop's office.

It was a narrow space, split down the middle thirty years ago to make room for a public restroom. Kim paused at the desk and looked down at the open books. From a quick scan, she confirmed the store really was doing okay. Not spectacular, but enough to keep the doors open and the lights on for another month.

The stairs were crammed between the office and the back wall of the store, following the corner of the building. Kim's arms brushed the sides of the stairwell as she went up, as they had since she turned fifteen. She unlocked the door to her apartment, her home. It was the only place she had ever lived, and the only place she could imagine living.

The couch stood against the kitchen counter, facing the window seat where she ate breakfast. The north wall of the apartment had three doors, leading to the bathroom, bedroom, and a closet. The drab green walls were mostly covered by framed movie posters, all of her favorites represented. She got them for free when Mabel rotated the stock downstairs, so she was able to keep the decorations from becoming dull. Currently the only ones that were permanent fixtures were *High Plains Drifter*, *The Princess Bride*, and *The Long Kiss Goodnight*. She eyed Geena Davis as she walked past, and smiled at the Dread Pirate Roberts as she dumped her coat and sunglasses on the couch.

The video store had been under their apartment for as long as she could remember, first run by her parents and then, after their death, by Aunt Mabel. She used to watch at least three movies a week growing up, taking the tapes after the store closed and watching them before bedtime. They had been a ubiquitous part of her life growing up, and it was hard to break the habit once she became an adult even though she had seen first-hand how the magic was made. Staying in the apartment kept her obsession going without killing her pocketbook.

She went to the desk in the corner and unrolled the script. As the stunt coordinator, it was up to her to make all the crazy stuff in the script come to life without actually killing anyone in the process. She flipped to the front page and began her third re-read of the story.

It was time to find out who she was going to be next.

## CHAPTER TWO

THE GUARD smiled as he stepped out of his little cubicle and approached Kim's Jeep. "Uh-oh. What are we doing today?"

"Nothing spectacular," Kim said. "First day on the set of my new job." She showed him the badge.

"*Neutral Ground?* What is that?"

"New show for TBC. Should be huge. International intrigue and sexual tension." She widened her eyes and pursed her lips, feigning excitement.

The guard laughed and handed the badge back to her. "Try not to hurt yourself too badly this time, eh?" He checked a clipboard and said, "You're in Soundstage Two. You know where that is, right?"

"I should be able to find it. Thanks, Jimmy."

He saluted two fingers from the brim of his cap as he went back into the guardhouse.

Kim drove through the gate, angling immediately to the right. The studios looked like regular warehouses from the outside, complete with plain white garage doors. A sea of white trailers and Winnebagos stood next to the building. Kim found a parking space in front of the chain link fence, underneath a sign that said "Reserved for *Neutral Ground* Cast & Crew." She released her seatbelt and picked up the script. She had spent most of previous evening filling the margins of the script with notes to herself, blocking fight scenes and stunts. She expected to spend the morning explaining to the director what needed to be done.

The access door was propped open with a milk crate, and she stepped into a completely different world. The studio was much darker than outside, and several degrees cooler. But if she kept her eyes forward and ignored the exposed wall of the studio, she could almost believe she had just walked into a foreign outpost. The main room of the complex stood before her, with a sea of desks all dressed out to look real. The windows looked out on backdrops that revealed a forested nightscape. A second floor ringed the walls on three sides, and she could see offices through the open doors.

Various crew members were busy setting up lights and bounce boards, kneeling to tape down wires so the actors wouldn't trip over them, calling out last minute instructions to people she couldn't see hiding in the shadowed catwalks overhead. She assumed she was standing in the "CIA offices" indicated in the script.

The plot of the pilot was simple: FBI agent Thomas Templeton finds evidence of a militia being built on an island in the Florida Keys. In the midst of his investigation, CIA agent Simone Lethe breaks into his office and, when caught, reveals that the militia group has ties to an Argentine dictator. Since the CIA doesn't have jurisdiction inside the borders of the United States, and the FBI has none outside the borders, they decide to work together to bring down the militia group. They are successful and, in this version of the script, decide to work together and share information whenever possible. Hopefully for at least one hundred episodes worth of cases, for the syndication bucks.

Kim spotted Kenneth Swift, the director, standing by his outpost of monitors near the cameras. He was easy to spot; a middle aged guy who looked like a grizzly bear wearing a human disguise.

She made her way over and whistled to get his attention. "Ken, you got some actors for me to abuse?"

He twisted at the waist, smiled, and took off his headphones. "Kim, great." He slipped off his chair and murmured something to the assistant sitting next to him. He gestured at the monitor, then at the crowd of people wandering on the set, and then turned to give Kim his full attention. He was a brute of a man, wide at shoulder and hips with ursine hands that Kim felt could crush her head if he had the mind. "Have any trouble with the script?"

"No, it all looks good. I just need to go over some of the routines with the stars."

"Easter isn't here yet, but I think Larkin is right next door in the FBI set."

Kim nodded. "All right. Thanks, Kenneth." She slapped his arm as she passed and he went back to his monitors.

She walked through the office set, through a door and past a backdrop to find a second set of offices. The differences were night and day; the first office set was bright, high-tech and polished. This office looked like a refurbished basement den. Old, scratched desks covered with bits of paper and out of date computers.

Marisa Larkin sat with her back to the door, bent over a script. Kim hesitated in the doorway. Despite the years she had worked in the business, she still got a bit of a thrill whenever she met a celebrity. Marisa wasn't exactly top on Kim's favorite list; she had only actually seen two of her movies and thought they were just all right. But she was still an actress. A celebrity. Kim politely cleared her throat. "Miss Larkin?"

The actress turned, and draped her arm across the back of her seat. "Yes?"

Kim was momentarily struck dumb. Seeing this face on TV was one thing, but it was completely different to be in her presence.

Marisa's eyes were steel blue, her eyebrows arched like a Renaissance aristocrat. Her features were similar enough to Kim's that they might be mistaken for each other during the insanity of a fight scene or from a strategic distance, but up close no one would ever confuse the plain Kim for the beautiful Larkin. The actress wore a white blouse, unbuttoned halfway to reveal the scooped neck of a grey tank top, and black trousers. Her legs were crossed at the knee, her body twisted so that her shirts pulled taut across her breasts.

Kim finally found her voice and said, "Kim Greer. I'll be your stunt coordinator and your stunt double for this production."

"Oh!" Marisa put down her script and climbed from the seat. She was only about an inch shorter than Kim with her high heels on, and she extended her hand. "You can call me Marisa. I figure we're going to be working together a lot, we might as well be friendly."

"Makes sense." Kim shook Marisa's hand. *Wow, her skin is soft.* "Do you moisturize?" she asked, immediately kicking herself for such a stupid question.

Marisa laughed. "I think it's mostly Purell."

"Right." Kim had no idea why she was acting like this. Usually she was star struck for about thirty seconds before her professional side took over and she was able to function. Something about Marisa Larkin was preventing her from making the leap. She licked her lips and held up her script. "I thought we'd go over a couple of the stunts we'll be doing."

"By 'we,' you mean 'you,' right?"

Kim smiled. "Right."

"Sorry. Don't mean to be a wuss, but—"

"Don't worry about it. That's why I'm here." She walked to the nearest desk and put the script on the blotter. She let Marisa have the seat, and bent down over the desk to point at some of her notes. "Okay, the first one we have to deal with is the fight between you and Temple. I'll choreograph that for the two of you, but I think Kenneth wants me to stand in for you during some of the wide shots."

"How come?"

Kim shrugged. "I know capoeira."

Marisa raised an eyebrow. "You know who?"

"It's a Brazilian fighting style. It looks very impressive on camera." She winked, smiled, and looked back down at her script. *Am I flirting? No. Definitely not.* She chewed on her bottom lip and said, "Okay, um... the next one. You and Temple are in the back of a Jeep being taken to see the militia leader. You overpower the guard. You'll have to do that, since the back of the truck will be tight and it'll be too hard to hide my face. Then you jump from the back of the truck, roll, and run into the forest."

"You'll be doing that?"

Kim grinned. "Yeah, I'll do that. So do you want to go over the fight, just to see what you'll be doing?"

"Sure."

"Okay. I'll be you, right now. You can be Temple."

Marisa smiled. "Works for me."

Kim rolled her shoulders and said, "First, get loose. Warm up your muscles a little." She worked her head back and forth, shrugging her shoulders and letting her hands dangle a bit in front of her chest before she squeezed them into fists. "We're going to go through it slow until you feel comfortable. The scene starts when Temple finds you in the basement offices. You're at the desk, and he comes up behind you." She turned her back, bending over the desk. "Temple walks in, you spin and throw a kick."

She turned and brought her leg up, aiming for Marisa's chest.

"Temple grabs your foot." Marisa grabbed Kim's foot and looked down at it. Her boot had three straps on the side, held by gold buckles. "These are great boots."

"Thanks," Kim said. "Okay, Temple holds on to your foot, you…" She gripped the edge of the desk and swung her other foot up, twisting her body as she did. Her other foot came within centimeters of hitting Marisa in the face. Marisa released Kim's foot and Kim dropped acrobatically to the floor. As soon as her feet hit, she spun to face Marisa again. "Temple comes at you. This will be you, so watch carefully." She waved her fingers and Marisa advanced. "Swing at me."

Marisa telegraphed a wide swing. Kim brought up her right arm, blocked the punch, and moved in. "Use your whole body, bury your shoulder in his gut and run him back." They walked slowly across the room, Kim's side pressed against Marisa's chest. When they reached the wall, Kim straightened and looked into Marisa's bright blue eyes. It took her a heartbeat to get over how great Marisa's body felt against hers, barely noticeable but alarming to Kim. "Uh, box his ears," she mimed that, "and twist to get out of his grip." She twisted, her back to Marisa. "He grabs you."

Marisa wrapped her arms around Kim and pulled her back. Kim was momentarily distracted, the simple act of having a woman's arms around her throwing her mind off-track.

"And then what happens?" Marisa asked, her voice very near to Kim's ear.

Kim said, "Uh… then, uh, you stomp on his foot." She lightly stepped on Marisa's foot, pulled free and threw her elbow over her shoulder. "Be sure to pull your punch here. Don't want to break your costar's nose on the first episode."

"Yeah. We can wait to see if he's an asshole before we start injuring him on purpose."

Kim laughed. "Okay, after that he'll let go of you and you run for the door. That's when he stops you, you know, 'Let me help you,' all that."

"And so begins a beautiful partnership."

Kim smiled and said, "Yep. So it begins." She put her hands on her hips and looked at the office set. She couldn't help wondering if Marisa meant a partnership for the characters in the show, or something else entirely. "Uh. Look, I hate to assault you and run, but I should probably go find the other actors and~"

"Yeah, go ahead. I'm still trying to get a handle on my lines."

She stuck out her hand. "Thanks for coming to find me."

"Sure," Kim said. She shook Marisa's hand again, a little reluctant to let it go, and said, "See you around."

"Hope so."

Kim chuckled and left the office, shaking her head as soon as she was in the hallway. *Stop being ridiculous. You're acting like this is the first time you've ever met an actress.* She scratched her eyebrow, risked one last glance into the fake office, and then went to find see if the guy playing Temple had shown up yet.

## CHAPTER THREE

KIM MANAGED to survive the horror of the make-up trailer, forced to sit still while some woman dabbed sponges on her cheeks and another woman teased her hair into a completely new and unflattering style. It was a necessary evil on every set, to make her look more like whoever she was doubling, but even years of experience hadn't taught her any tricks to endure it. When they finally released her, she fled the chair as quickly as was polite and hurried to the costume trailer.

As much as she hated the make-up routine, she loved the costume trailer. It was filled with uniforms from various foreign and domestic armed forces and various suits for Temple. Kim checked out the rack marked Simone and saw that Agent Lethe would be dressed predominantly in black and camouflage outfits. The scene where she broke into Temple's office required that she wear a black sweater and black jeans, both of which were set out on a chair with a tag that read "Lethe - Stunt."

She took it behind a screen and started to take off her street clothes. She was down to her bra and undoing her pants, when the door opened and Marisa stepped inside. The screen covered Kim's body, exposing only her head and shoulders, but she felt the need to cover up regardless. "Oh. Hey."

"Hey, Kim Greer," Marisa said.

Kim nodded. "Marisa Larkin."

Marisa picked up a costume identical to Kim's and carried it behind another screen. Kim heard zippers being pulled down and cloth rustling, and tried not to think too hard about it. She cleared her throat and said, "So, how have the preparations been going? Did you get together with William?" Kim had found William Easter, the actor hired to play Temple, and gave him the same run-down she'd given Marisa.

"I did. He and I have been running through the fight together. We think we've got a pretty good rhythm. I think I'm about ready to kick his ass."

"It's good to establish that in the pilot. Who wears the pants," Kim said, as she dropped hers and stood in her underwear.

"Well, I'll do my best not to embarrass you when I'm the one doing the fights."

Kim finished dressing and came out from behind the screen. She went to the mirror and looked at the job the hairdresser had done on her. The style was completely different than her usual; it was like a bad haircut. But it was just for a part, thank God.

Marisa came out from behind her screen, still tugging her sweatshirt into place. Kim looked at her reflection in the mirror and felt the horror of high school. To see someone not only wearing the same outfit as you, but wearing it oh, so much better. Marisa brushed some invisible lint from the stomach of her sweater and joined Kim at the mirror. "They look alike, they talk alike," she said, and hummed the rest of the song as she leaned closer to the mirror to check her makeup.

"Yeah, right," Kim said. "You show me someone who thinks I look half as good as you, and I'll drive you both to the optometrist."

Marisa chuckled. "Oh, you're one of *those*."

"One of what?"

"One of those beautiful women who talk bad about themselves to get other people to say how beautiful they are."

Kim opened her mouth to protest, but instead dipped her chin and shook her head.

"You're blushing," Marisa said. She looked at Kim and said, "Which means… you really *don't* know how beautiful you are. I hope you know that just makes you more adorable."

"All right," Kim said. "You can stop now."

Marisa chuckled and said, "I'll track down the hairdresser and let you know where she is. See you on set."

"Yeah," Kim said, watching the mirror as Marisa left the trailer.

When she was alone, Kim rested her hands on the edge of the table, hung her head, and hissed, "*Fuck*. Pull it together Greer." She chuckled, and then full-out laughed, and shook her head before she followed Marisa back into the sunshine.

They practiced in the office set, going through all the moves in slow motion so Marisa could do them regular speed during the filming. "Let me know if there's any move you're uncomfortable with," Kim said. "Last thing we need is for you to twist your ankle."

"Don't worry. I played a dancer on one of the *NCISes*."

Kim grinned and went through the motions again. "Think you've got it?"

"Yeah. Hard to believe this will look like a fight on-screen."

"That's why we do it." She spotted William Easter standing off to one side of the set, talking to a production assistant. "All right. I think you've got it down pretty well. I think I'll go through it a few times with William so it's not a total beat down."

Marisa sighed. "If you must." She reached out and gently slapped Kim's shoulder. "Thanks for the assist."

"No problem." Kim walked across the set and waited for William to finish speaking with the assistant.

Industry wisdom said that most actors who played tough guys were tiny in real life, some of them a full six inches shorter than their wives. William was the exception. He was as imposing in person as he was on screen; broad shouldered with a lantern jaw, his brown hair swept back away from his forehead. His eyes were bright blue, sparkling even in the darkness of the soundstage. Kim was impressed by his pre-make up glamour, but it was nothing like the knocked on her butt feeling she got from Marisa.

As the other man walked off, William turned toward Kim and flashed the smile that had graced so many teen magazines as the former lead of the high school drama *Landslide*.

"Hello again, Mr. Easter."

He stared at her for a moment before his smile widened. "Oh right. The stunt coordinator." He shook his head. "Sorry, I've met about a thousand new people today. You're the one who is going to make sure I don't really hurt myself."

"Well, I'll do my best." He wasn't using a stunt double in this scene, so she had to make extra certain he knew what he was doing before he did anything even slightly dangerous. She glanced off-stage and saw Kenneth standing next to a camera and watching them. "I think they're ready to roll, Ken."

He clapped his hands together, the sound louder than a gunshot in the small office space. "Excellent. Kim, I want you to go through the fight on your own first. We'll get the wide shots of the fight, and then bring Marisa in for the close ups."

Kim nodded and gave Kenneth the thumbs up and waited as the cameras and lights were moved into position. She gathered the facts of Simone Lethe in her head; secret agent on a covert op. Trained in martial arts. By the time Kenneth yelled action, she was already in the special agent's mind enough to play her for the next fifteen seconds.

She rifled the papers on the desk, closing out the crew hovering on the periphery. She was a CIA agent looking for information that could bring down a very bad man. She had broken into a federal building just to get a look at another federal agent's files. It would be a very bad thing to get caught. So, naturally, Templeton came back just as she found what she had been looking for.

"Hey, what the hell...?"

Kim turned and swung her leg at him. William caught it and held tight. Kim planted her hands on the desk for leverage and swung her other foot up to kick him in the face. William twisted to the side and let go of her foot, falling back. Kim hit the ground and spun to face him.

"Cut!"

Kim relaxed, and William dropped character to smile at her. "Nice moves. That kick thing was impressive as hell."

"Well, they didn't hire *me* for my looks."

"Ouch, ouch," Easter said. He narrowed his eyes and then said, "Although, since you have to double for Marisa... they kind of did hire you for your looks."

"Only fifty percent," Kim said.

Marisa joined them and shook her head. "I'm going to have a hard time living up to that."

Kim reached out and brushed her hand down Marisa's arm. "Just remember what we practiced. You'll be fine." Marisa surprised her by reaching up, taking Kim's hand, and squeezing it briefly before she let it go. Kim went to stand behind the monitors with Kenneth.

Kenneth glanced up before turning his attention back to the screen. "You're such a badass, Kim. Remind me never to mess with you."

"Big strapping guy like you? I couldn't even reach your head. In real life I'd probably just kick you in the balls and run."

Kenneth crossed his legs and said, "Action!"

Kim always felt like a mother watching her kids in a school play. She had done what she could to show the actors what to do, and she could only hope they managed to pull it off. Marisa blocked William's punch and threw her weight against him. She bulldozed him toward the wall, and he hit with enough force to shake the picture frames on the wall. Kenneth whispered, "Nice," as Marisa leaned back and boxed William's ears.

When Marisa twisted to get away, William wrapped his arms around her and lifted her up. Kim immediately saw a problem; the foot stomp wouldn't work. Marisa was too short, and being in William's arms had lifted her feet off the floor. Before she could mention it to Kenneth, Marisa grabbed William's thumb and twisted it back. William cried out and let her go, and Marisa scrambled forward.

"Improv," Kim whispered to Kenneth.

"Nice."

Marisa ran to the door and William, cradling his hand against his stomach, shouted, "You know you could have just asked for my help."

Marisa stopped in the doorway, silhouetted by the light from the hall. She considered his words and then turned to face him. The camera moved in on her face, held it, and Kenneth said, "And that is a cut. Beautiful work, everybody. William, how's your hand?"

"Fine," he said, holding it up to look at it in the light. "I was just startled. It wasn't in the script."

Marisa held her hands out apologetically, looking at Kim. "Sorry. I couldn't reach his foot and I thought–"

"No, it was great," Kim said. "It definitely works."

Kenneth clapped his hands together. "Excellent. Let's reset and try and get the next scene done before we break for lunch."

Kim fell into step next to Marisa as she walked off the set. She looked back and saw William was still shaking his hand and rubbing his thumb. "I thought you were going to wait and see if he was an asshole before you hurt him."

"Call it a preemptive strike." She winked. "This way he knows not to get out of line."

Kim laughed. "Good philosophy."

The next scene was just dialogue between Templeton and Simone, so there was no real reason for Kim to stick around. But she took a seat behind Kenneth's position so she could watch Marisa at work. Her usual method was to stick around just long enough to teach the actors their stunts, make sure they went off, and then focus on the next stunt. She almost never bothered to pay attention to the actual plot stuff. But something about the idea of watching Marisa act was very appealing to her. She settled into the seat as the director called for quiet, and then shouted, "Action!"

Kim spent the rest of the morning going over the stunt list with Kenneth. He promised her he would arrange the shooting schedule to get the majority of the stunts out of the way as early as possible, and let her know which ones needed to be reworked. When they broke for lunch, she said, "I need to speak to the other stunt people. Have you seen Break?"

Kenneth grunted. "You hired Break?"

"He keeps the other people in line. I need three other stunt guys for this episode alone, and he's a good wrangler."

Kenneth shrugged. "If you say so. Keep him in line."

Kim said, "You heard about the incident with the keg in Barstow?"

"I heard about a motorbike in Burnaby. What happened in Barstow?"

Kim held her hands up and refused to answer, backing away before Kenneth could get an answer out of her. Despite his problems, Jake "Break" Ransom was the best man for the job. With a wig, he looked close enough to William Easter to fool the camera. Not to mention the fact he was one of the best stuntmen Kim had ever worked with. She would just have to make sure he behaved himself while he was employed by the show.

She found him on the FBI set, sitting at Templeton's desk, feet up and hands laced over his stomach. He had the script open on his thighs, reaching down to flip to the next page as Kim approached. He had the same build as Easter, and to her surprise, he actually had hair. It was obviously dyed to match Easter's, since she had last seen him with rusty red hair. He wore a suit identical to the one Templeton had been wearing earlier, and Kim knew immediately she'd picked the right man for the job. He looked up when she approached and they smiled at each other.

"Don't get too comfortable, Break," Kim said. "If Kenneth had his way, I'd be firing you right now."

"If directors had their way, I'd never work in this town again." He smiled and added, "They hate what I do to their insurance statements."

Break earned his nickname by breaking both arms, both legs, almost all of his ribs, and eight fingers, all in the pursuit of perfecting his craft. Kim, with only two broken arms and one broken rib to her credit, felt like a safety warden compared to him.

"'Sides, I'm just getting into the character," Break said. "Getting a feel for the man." He reached into the jacket and withdrew a cigar in an aluminum cylinder. Kim's eyes widened at the sight of it and her fingers itched to grab it. "Still having those poker games?"

"Still playing the game. Not smoking anymore, though."

"Aw, that's a shame."

Kim snatched the cigar before he could take it back. "Doesn't mean I don't like the smell. I'll keep it, just to test my resolve. Anyone can be on a diet when there's no food around, right? It'll be good." She unscrewed the top of the cylinder to take a long, loving sniff of the cigar, and sighed happily before closing the cylinder and sticking it into the pocket of her jeans. "So, the poker game. This Friday, above the video store, as always."

"I'll be there."

Kim leaned against the desk. The cigar poked against her hip, preventing her from not thinking about it. "I was thinking, since you're here, we could go over some of the choreography for Templeton's big fight scene."

Break spread his arms to her. "I'm your punching bag."

Kim chuckled. "Good to know." She pushed away from the desk and slapped the back of Break's head when she left the room.

At the end of the day, Kim stopped by the director's lair to let Kenneth know she was going. "I'm heading out," she said. "Try to refrain from beating up on the real stars."

"Great work today, kid," Kenneth said. "Listen, we're not doing many stunts tomorrow, but I want you to be here anyway. Simone has a big fight at the end of the episode, and I want her to do as much of it herself as possible. You'll need to walk her through it."

"You got it. See you then. Bright and early?"

Kenneth nodded and turned to the production assistant that

had been trying to get his attention.

She was almost to the studio door when she spotted Marisa crossing to the craft service table at the edge of the room. Kim hesitated, glancing at the open door. It was the middle of the afternoon, but still before rush hour. She could hit the roads before everyone else, get home at a reasonable time. Or...

She crossed to the table as Marisa picked up a cup of fruit yogurt. Kim was closer to the pile of plastic spoons, so she picked one up and held it out. "Little snack?"

Marisa jumped and then chuckled nervously. "Oh, hi. I didn't see you there." She took the spoon. "Yeah, they're doing a scene with Templeton and his girlfriend, so I have time to snack. You?"

"No, I'm done for the day. I just thought I'd sneak a little something before I go."

"I've been known to leave a set with my pockets full of craft services swag. These guys cook way better than I ever could."

Kim smiled. "Listen, I wanted to tell you... you did great in that fight earlier."

"I had a good teacher."

"Kenneth wants me to show you some moves tomorrow. Get you ready for that big fight at the end of the episode. If you'd like me to teach you some of the capoeira stuff, I would be happy to."

Marisa chuckled and held her hands out in surrender. "Oh, I could never do what you did. I'm just not that flexible."

Kim exaggerated a sad face and said, "That is very tragic for your... love life." She had almost said boyfriend, but didn't want to have her fantasy destroyed just yet.

Marisa laughed and waved her spoon. "Oh, hardly. Hardly." She ate another spoonful of yogurt and looked down. Her face contorted into a weird expression, and she tilted her head to the side. She licked her lips, furrowed her brow and pointed at Kim's midsection. "You're, um... there's something..."

"What?" Kim looked down at herself. The cigar Break had given was her pressing lewdly against her pocket. Her cheeks flushed, and she quickly changed her stance. "Oh. It's just, ah..." She pulled the cylinder free and unscrewed the top to reveal the cigar. "Gift from a friend."

Marisa laughed. "Oh, my God. I'm sorry, I just..." She cleared her throat.

"No problem." Kim stuck the cigar into the pocket of her shirt. Out of sight, out of mind.

Marisa flipped her hair over the collar of her blouse and said, "Getting back on topic, um... if it wouldn't be too much trouble, I would love to learn a move or two. Like that kick you did, stuff like that, so they wouldn't have to pull camera tricks to hide that it's not really me."

"I'd be happy to teach you some basics."

Marisa nodded. "Okay. Great. We'll set it up sometime. I should probably go see if they need me for anything. Nice talking with you, Kim."

"Same to ya," Kim said. She leaned against the table and again watched Marisa walk away. She couldn't help where her eyes ended up, not with the way Marisa was swinging her hips, and she grunted quietly. "Good God, the ass on that woman."

"You noticed too, huh?"

Kim jumped and turned to see a teenager with a paper cap loading more food onto the table. Kim forced a smile, nodded her chin at him, and slipped away from the table. She pushed her hair out of her face and groaned at herself. Day one on the set and she'd already been caught leering. She was going to have to pace herself. She had worked with any number of beautiful women in the past. Obviously straight actresses, closeted lesbians, she'd seen all kinds. But none of them had distracted her to this level.

She turned when she was almost to the door and watched Marisa slip into a chair behind the director. Something made Marisa different from all the other actresses in the past. But damned if she knew what. Kim sighed and left the building, hoping things would be easier after a good night's sleep.

## CHAPTER FOUR

KIM TRIED to keep her mind on the pounding of her sneakers on the indoor track of the gym, listening to the pounding of her heart in her ears instead of the voices in her head. She had changed into a pair of shorts and a plain white T-shirt as soon as she arrived, driving directly to the gym from the studio. Her hope was that a nice, intense workout would help get Marisa out of her mind. Unfortunately it didn't seem to do anything for her one-track mind, which kept rerunning Marisa calling her beautiful. She tried to listen to the sound of people working out on machines all around her, but the clank of weights kept transforming into the sound of Marisa grunting when they rehearsed the fight scene.

She finally gave up after a mile, pausing to get a drink of water before she retreated to the lockers. She was sweaty, panting, sore, and frustrated that the thoughts of Marisa Larkin were still as strong as ever.

She showered quickly and changed back into her street clothes, catching glimpses of her reflection in the locker room mirror as she dressed. How many costumes could she wear in a single day, she wondered, and were any of them close to who she really was? What were the odds Marisa would ever see the real Kim Greer? If she even cared about Kim Greer at all, that is. Kim slammed the locker door and turned away from the mirror.

When she got home, her legs and back ached. She hooked the

strap of her satchel around her shoulder and let it bounce against her side as she went into the video store.

"You look wiped."

"I am wiped," Kim snapped. "I work for a living."

"Feh," Mabel said, waving her off the insult. "What do you need now?"

Kim sagged against the counter. She was determined not to dump her bad mood on Mabel. "I'm sorry. You work very hard." She looked toward the movie aisles and got an idea of how to erase Marisa from her mind. "Do you have any movies with Marisa Larkin?"

Mabel went to the computer and typed. "Used to, we had a big book. Actors and actresses listed by last name. Like a Bible, only bigger. Harder to find anything. This way, though..." She shook her head. "Larken, with an 'E'?"

"With an 'I.'"

Mabel scrolled down and said, "Like I said, this way, much easier. Quick, quick. Okay. Larkin comma Marisa. We have two. *Special Operations* and *King of Thieves*. Drama on the first, and the other is action."

"Thanks."

Kim left the counter and went down the drama aisle. Given the title Kim expected something about spies, but *Special Operations* was apparently about a surgeon. Marisa was on the cover, dressed in surgical scrubs. Her dark hair was tied back, her expression haunted. The picture behind her was a hospital operating room and a team of surgeons working hard to save the life of their patient. She picked it up and read the back, carrying the case up to the counter.

Mabel said, "What if one of my customers wanted this movie?"

"My money spends just as well as theirs."

Mabel pursed her lips and scanned Kim's card, then the bar code on the back of the movie. "It's due back by Saturday, or tomorrow for a one dollar credit."

Kim took two dollars from her wallet and dropped it on the counter. "I could just come down here after you close and take whatever I wanted. For free."

"Yes, but you are much too honest."

Kim made a so-so gesture with her hand, winked, and said, "Good night, Auntie Em."

"Enjoy your movie, Toto. See? How you like nicknames from old movies, huh?"

Kim carried her movie and bag up the stairs, forced to turn sideways to make room for her satchel. She put the DVD on the coffee table and carried her dirty clothes into the bedroom.

She'd slept with women she worked with before. A fellow stuntwoman on *Rock House* and the director of *Barnhart's Legacy*. If she wanted someone, she let them know, and she either slept with them or got blown off. No big deal. Her last crush was Katie Lynch, in high school. She didn't have crushes anymore, she had conquests. And if one woman didn't want her, well, hell, the next one would. Pining was for teenagers.

She returned to the living room after showering, brushing her teeth, and changing into her pajamas. She put the DVD in the machine, pressed play, and sank onto the couch. She sat through the FBI warning, and skipped to the main menu when given the chance. She pressed play, rearranged the pillows underneath her, and made herself comfortable.

Kim tried to pretend she was interested in the movie's plot, but she only found herself paying attention when Marisa appeared on screen for the first time. She came out of a surgical theater, her mask pulled down to reveal her lips - did all surgeons wear bright red lipstick during operations? - as she berated the doctor who had been observing. Apparently he was taking risks with patient's lives and she was, naturally, sick of it.

According to the back of the box, Marisa played Dr. Sarah Genovese, a brilliant surgeon battered down by hospital administrators. Her plans to quit are put off by her mother's medical bills, and the fact she doesn't know what she would do with herself if she wasn't a surgeon. Rather than focus on Marisa portraying a beaten-down woman, she focused on how damned good she looked in those surgical scrubs. About a half hour into the movie, Dr. Genovese met with a new patient - an older man in need of a kidney transplant. She assured the man that they would find a kidney in time, and everything would go perfectly. And then she met the man's son.

Kim was struggling to stay awake as Genovese and the patient's son, Kevin, flirted in front of the coffee machines. Kevin bought her a candy bar, and told her she would look beautiful if she smiled more. Kim rolled her eyes and said, "Who watches these movies? She's going to remember how to love and she'll rediscover the joy of being a doctor. Seriously."

Genovese and Kevin kept running into each other, since there was a problem finding a matching donor for his father. Before long, Genovese was looking at life in a - yawn - brand new way. She was almost skipping into surgery, for God's sake. Kim told herself that it wasn't Marisa's fault that the writing was clichéd and the director didn't know how to be subtle. It wasn't her fault that this candlelit dinner scene had been done a thousand times before.

Kim was so busy mocking the movie and finding reasons to forgive Marisa's participation that she almost missed what was happening. Genovese and Kevin were dancing after dinner, and then kissing. The living room was lit by the fireplace and, when the kiss broke, Kevin moved his hands to the top button of Genovese's blouse.

"Whoa," Kim said, grabbing the remote and quickly jabbing the pause button. The screen froze on a close-up of Marisa's face, her lips parted in anticipation of another kiss. Kim dropped the remote on the couch and stood up, pacing toward the kitchen. She could see the TV reflected in the microwave door, so she paced toward the stairs. She went back to the coffee table and grabbed the movie case, looking at the rating.

"'Rated R. Language, sexual situations, and nudity.' Of *course* it is." She tossed the case onto the couch and began pacing again. She kept her body twisted so she wouldn't accidentally see Marisa on-screen, horny and willing. She had watched sex scenes before. Hell, she had been in one. In the movie *Back Nine*, when the female lead backed out at the last second, she had volunteered to be a body double. It was just her ass, and it gave her a nice bump in her paycheck. So she understood that sex scenes in movies like this were just as choreographed as the fight scenes, with exactly as much emotion behind them.

There was nothing wrong with watching the sex scene.

She went back to the couch, sat on the edge of the cushion, and stared at the remote. How could she possibly face Marisa tomorrow if she watched it? Her thumb hovered over the stop button. Of course, given her reaction today, maybe she needed to see it and get it out of her system. Once she saw Marisa naked, she would be able to focus on the work. Her thumb moved up to the play button.

"Stop being a baby," she said, and she pressed the play button. She dropped the remote, retreated as far as the couch would let her, and covered her eyes with both hands. She split apart her middle and index fingers and peeked between them as the love scene commenced.

She half expected the scene to be as poorly filmed as the rest of the movie, but it actually wasn't bad. Kevin took off his shirt and kissed Marisa - no, it was Genovese - as he undid the buttons of her shirt and spread the halves apart. Her bra was black and lacy, and her breast yielded under his hand as he explored.

Kim wondered why her mouth was suddenly so dry.

They undressed slowly, mood lighting and romantic music playing as the clothes slowly came off. Kim wanted to slap away the bastard actor's hands as they touched Marisa all over her body. He pushed her skirt up and settled between her legs. Marisa arched her back and he reached up the back of her blouse to undo her bra.

Kim's face was burning. She bit her bottom lip and reached for the remote, having a change of heart, but then Marisa was topless and it was far too late to do the right thing.

"Just breasts," Kim said, frozen with the remote stretched toward the TV. "Wonderful breasts." She swallowed hard and dropped the remote back to the cushion.

Some thrusting, some cheesy elevator music playing over quiet moans, and close ups of Marisa's face lit from the left by firelight. It was almost wrong to have a scene this beautiful in such a crappy movie.

The movie faded to the next morning in the middle of a kiss. Somehow, Genovese and Kevin made it to bed at some point. They spoke while cuddling, and then the movie continued with the search for a match for Kevin's father. Near the end of the movie, a match was discovered and Genovese successfully performed the surgery. Before the father was put under for the operation, he took Genovese's hand - in the operating theatre, contaminating her gloves, but who cares about little details like that? - and told her that whatever happened, she was a good doctor and she should make things work with Kevin.

The obligatory wedding ended the film, with Papa Kidney sitting front and center at the church. While the credits rolled, Kim took the time to list movies she had hated more, or were bigger wastes of her time. The only thing she could think of was that horrible robot war movie a few years back, but only because it had been terrible *and* given her a headache. It would take a lot to top that one.

She ejected the movie from the machine and took it downstairs. She knew that having the movie in her apartment, having that sex scene available to watch over and over again, would keep her from getting any sleep. She put the movie into the return slot behind the counter and glanced toward the racks. A streetlight outside shone through the window, casting strange geometric patterns around the movie posters in the window.

What was the other movie Mabel said they had? Something about thieves. She looked down the dimly lit aisles and then decided not to bother. It was already midnight, and she had a big day in the morning. Besides, if the movie was anything like *Special Operations*, it would just make her feel bad about Marisa's career choices. She headed back upstairs, leaving the thief movie lying in wait on the shelves behind her like a time bomb.

## Chapter Five

Kim woke after a night tossing and turning, trying not to think about Marisa's sex scene. When she finally dragged herself out of bed and through the shower, she was awake enough to pretend the movie had just been a dream. A really, really nice dream. Breakfast was Fruit Loops and milk, eaten on the window seat that looked down at the street that ran in front of Reel Heroes.

The store didn't open until nine, but she knew Mabel always came in a few hours early to check in any movies that had been returned during the night, replace them on the shelves, and get the store ready for another day of customers. She liked everything to be perfect the moment she opened the doors, and then the rest of the day was free for knitting and manning the computer. Kim kept expecting the foot traffic to trail off, for people to abandon the store for various streaming services, but apparently the neighborhood was loyal and reliable.

Kim still remembered sitting on the stool behind the counter, propped up by phone books for the first few years, and checking in the returned movies from the bin. She didn't mind the work; the movies she got to watch more than made up for it. Before she started elementary school, she was in love with Clint Eastwood's unnamed cowboys, Paul Newman's scoundrel Luke, and Carrie Fisher's princess. She hated when she was forced to go to school. Eight full hours where the only movies she could hope to watch were educational films.

She finished the cereal, checked her watch, and grabbed her satchel off the back of the couch and carried it downstairs.

Mabel was vacuuming, but she shut the machine off when Kim appeared. "Saw you returned the movie. How was it?"

"Sucked."

"I could have told you that."

"Would have saved me two bucks."

Mabel shrugged. "I gotta make a living, too."

Kim waved over her shoulder as she left the store. When she got in the Jeep, she started the engine and let Pink sing to her to get the strength to start her day. Nothing got her mind off unwanted thoughts quicker than hard music with a good voice. She drummed her fingers on the steering wheel, eyes closed and bobbing her head in time with the music. Her day was going to be largely spent with Marisa, close quarters, grappling with her. Full physical contact. What the hell was she thinking, watching that love scene? Now all day she would have Marisa's breasts stuck in her head. Her breasts, and her dark nipples, and the way she looked when she...

Kim jabbed the stereo button and advanced the CD to a hard, angry song. She turned the volume up until she could feel the vibrations in her chest, and finally pulled away from the curb as Pink rattled the windows of her Jeep.

Kim had a power pack hooked to her belt, wearing earphones to listen to the actors from wherever she wandered. At the moment, Thomas Templeton was sitting behind the wheel of a car with Simone Lethe in the backseat. Lighting boards blocked the front of the car from view, and a backdrop mimicked nighttime through the back windows. Simone had a gun aimed at the back of Templeton's head.

"Why should I trust you?" Simone asked.

"Because I want the same things you want. I'm willing to help you get those things." He twisted in the seat and looked at the gun. "But we have to trust each other."

Simone kept her eyes locked on Temple for a long moment, a thousand emotions passing over her face before she finally lowered the weapon. She leaned back in the seat and, the curtain lifted, said, "What do you know about Esteban Trujillo?"

Kim was riveted. She was seated on a nondescript black trunk, one of the props for a later scene. She could just barely see the car through the web of wires and cameras and people swarming back and forth to get the perfect angle, but she saw enough on the monitors to be impressed. She knew Marisa was an amazing actress, far better than the shitty surgeon movie implied. An actress of Marisa's caliber could, and should, be in Hollywood raking up awards, not wasting her time on some TV show.

Kenneth shouted cut, and the lights changed. Marisa climbed out of the car and handed the gun to a prop master before stepping off the stage. Kim hesitated before she stood up, the image of Marisa's naked body once again flashing in front of her eyes before she pushed away from the trunk and moved to intercept her.

"You were great out there."

Marisa glanced up, smiled, and said, "You keep sneaking up on me."

"Sorry. Maybe I'll start wearing a bell around my neck."

"Don't. It's nice to be surprised sometimes."

Kim was thrown off guard, but decided to go with it. "Well, hopefully it's a nice surprise."

"That remains to be seen."

Kim gestured at the stage and said, "When you get a half hour or so, let me know and we can start working on your fight scene."

Marisa nodded. "Okay. Actually if you're ready now, I'm game."

"Oh. Sure." She turned and looked toward the front of the soundstage. "There's actually a space right over here. Follow me."

Marisa fell into step next to her. "I'm kind of nervous, to tell you the truth. I get the feeling you and Kenneth will both decide to just let you do it. I've tried to do stunts in the past and they never go very well. I tend to avoid roles that call for a lot of physicality."

"Why did you take this role?"

"I love the books. I thought it was a good opportunity to show what I could do as an actress. I didn't want to turn it down just because it had a lot of fighting and stunts. I knew I'd have someone like you backing me up."

Kim grinned. "Well, I'm happy to do it. Directors like it when their stars do *some* stunts, but it can be a huge hassle. It's not such a big deal if I break my nose or wrist. But if *you* get hurt, well, stop the presses." She winked.

"Well, now I feel bad," Marisa said. "I don't want to think about someone getting hurt in my place."

"Look at it this way, then. You're doing all the heavy lifting, with the memorizing lines and emoting. I get to have all the fun."

"Getting thrown around a movie set is fun?"

"It is if you know what you're doing."

They reached the edge of the set. Between the fake wall of the CIA office and the wall of the soundstage was an empty space about the size of a basketball court. It was filled with props, stage dressing, ladders, and a various accumulation of junk. There was a nice empty space down the center for them to spar. "We can practice here."

"Fantastic," Marisa said. She unzipped her jacket and shrugged out of it, revealing a black tank top that was tucked into her jeans. When she rolled her shoulders, loosening up for the fight, the muscles of her shoulders and biceps flexed and danced under perfectly tanned skin. Kim licked her lips, wondering if the sight would have been more or less distracting if she hadn't seen the movie the night before. Theoretically, now that she had seen everything Marisa had to offer, the appeal should be gone. Still, she mentally reminded herself that Marisa's eyes were Up There. She emptied her pockets and removed her headset, taking off her watch before she moved to the center of the space.

"It's like a dance," she said, explaining her own philosophy. "All you have to do is count. You have to practice your moves well, keep track of your partner's movements, get everything timed just right... it all depends on moving in the right way at the right time. And the rest is just camera tricks."

"Sounds simple when you put it like that," Marisa said. "I just can't put dancing and fighting together in my head."

"It *is* simple," Kim said. She debated against the thought she had then, but decided it was the best way to illustrate her point. She stepped forward and held her hands out. "All right, come here."

Marisa arched an eyebrow. "What are you doing?"

"Starting slow. Here. Put your hand on my hip, your other hand on my shoulder." Marisa smirked, but did as she was told. Kim put her hand on Marisa's hip and began to move. "It's not even a complicated dance. If you trust your partner, it's all just a matter of counting and flow. One, two, three, four. One, two, three, four." She had her hand on Marisa's hip. Marisa was looking down, watching her feet, and Kim stared at the curve of her jaw, the way her dark hair fell across her cheek. Her heart raced, but she couldn't bring herself to stop the dance.

Marisa stopped it for her. "Okay, I think I've got it. But how does that translate to a fight?"

"It's the same principle. Moving your body in a rhythm, matching your partner's movements. Just with fists instead of feet. I swing at you, and you duck out of the way. That's step one. I swing at you with my other hand, you slap it out of the way, two. You grab my arm, hold it, head butt me. Three. I fall back, you kick me so that I fall. Four." She went through the movements again. "All you have to do is remember when to move. And with enough practice, you're the Ginger Rogers of fight club."

"Don't you mean the Fred Astaire?"

"Ginger Rogers did everything he did, but~"

"Backwards, and in high heels." Marisa smiled.

Kim shrugged. "She's an unsung hero."

"Kind of like stuntwomen."

Kim laughed. "Kind of, yeah. Think you've got the moves down?"

"If we go slowly, yeah, I think I can handle it."

Kim stepped back and let Marisa go through the moves on her own. "Good. Excellent. Let's try it a little faster."

"I don't want to accidentally hit you."

"You won't. I'm better at this than you are." Marisa arched an eyebrow and Kim held her hands out. "Just a simple fact. No offense intended." They went through the movements again. "See how it's becoming easier? Muscle memory. You do it enough times, it'll be like second nature when you have to film."

Marisa said, "I wasn't really offended, you know." She grunted as she swept Kim's hand out of the way. "You've trained for years to get where you are. Same with me. So you're better at this sort of thing, and I'm better at..."

"Kidney transplants?" Kim said, the words escaping her mouth before she could stop herself.

"Oh, God. You actually watched that movie?"

"Channel surfing in the middle of the night," Kim lied, striving for nonchalance. "Nothing else was on. I was hoping it would put me to sleep."

Marisa shook her head. "I'd be surprised if it didn't."

Kim realized she had a golden opportunity. She had worked with the big names, but it never occurred to her to use the opportunity to actually quiz them about their work. Now, she was standing toe to toe with the lead actress of one of the worst movies she'd ever seen. "I just have to ask. What were you thinking when you agreed to be in that thing?"

"It was money. I'd never played a surgeon before. I thought I would look cute in the scrubs."

"You did." And, once again her mouth running ahead of her brain, she added, "Didn't look half bad out of them, either."

Marisa laughed and said, "Well, thank you very much, Kim."

Marisa's fist suddenly connected with Kim's cheek. It was a light tap, but Marisa jumped back as if Kim had been floored. "Oh, my God..."

"It's fine..."

"I just punched you!"

"You tapped me," Kim said. "Barely even felt it. I should have been paying closer attention. I'm fine. Promise."

Marisa relaxed slightly. She fell back into fighting position and looked down at her feet, making sure they were positioned correctly. "Okay, I think I have the first combination. What's next?"

Kim took a step back and shook her head to clear any cobwebs before they continued. One tiny mistake was acceptable. Her getting hurt was fine, and the punch really hadn't been anything to be concerned about. But it never should've happened. Marisa only made contact because Kim hadn't been a hundred percent focused on her job. She wasn't going to let it happen again.

She brought up her fist and nodded. "Let's go again."

## CHAPTER SIX

BREAK STEPPED into the dark apartment, looking at the mail in his right hand as he reached for the light switch with his left. He was lit from behind by the streetlight, and he caught just a hint of movement out of the corner of his eye before the man in black grabbed his wrist. Break reacted immediately, swinging his arm straight up to extend the attacker's own arms, then twisting forward. The man in black tumbled and hit the ground hard, releasing Break's arm.

Someone came from deeper in the apartment, and Break placed a boot in that person's gut, kicking them away. The first attacker swung, and Break jumped back, but it wasn't enough. The Taser crackled, and Break's body went rigid. His hands and legs twitched before he went to the ground, defenseless. The two intruders swarmed him, cramming a black bag over his head and securing his wrists with zip ties. One of them grabbed his legs, while the other hooked his hands under Break's armpits. The lifted him from the floor and shuffled him out of the apartment, neglecting to shut the door behind them.

"Cut! Beautiful!" Kenneth said.

The men in black gently put Break down, released his wrists, and pulled the hood off his head. They both extended their hands, and Break took them both, leaping to his feet and then patting them on the back. "Good men," he said.

Kim came over and said, "Nice twitch."

"Thanks, I practice at home hitting myself with a stun gun."

"Next time give me a call, I'll be happy to lend a hand."

Kenneth clapped his hands to get everyone's attention. "Okay, folks, that's a wrap for today. Ending it a little early because tomorrow is going to be brutal. We're on location; see Paige if you don't know the address or if you need directions. See you all bright eyed and bushy tailed at six in the a.m." He ignored the good natured groans of the cast and crew as they began to disperse.

Kim grabbed her bag off the chair and headed for the door. The parking lot was dark, shadows of twilight creeping across the pavement. She happened to turn and look left at just the wrong moment, spotting Marisa and three other people standing next to a brand new silver Prius. One of them was William Easter, the other two she vaguely recognized from being around on-set. She assumed they were Marisa's assistants.

Marisa laughed at something and opened the car door, waving goodbye to the assistants. She turned to say goodbye to Easter, and he bent down and whispered something in her ear. She laughed and, when he pulled back, he lightly pecked the corner of her mouth.

Kim wanted to scream. She wanted to throw her satchel on the ground and stomp on it. He hadn't even kissed her, not really. A polite peck between actors was no grounds for this kind of reaction. It felt like high school all over again, standing on the sidelines with her fashionably ripped jeans and her hoodie sweatshirt, watching as the cheerleaders skipped off to drape themselves across the football players. It wasn't fair.

She dragged herself to the Jeep, dumped her satchel in the back, and climbed behind the wheel. Before she could back out, Marisa's Prius blocked her in. She rolled down the window, and Kim twisted to face her. Marisa smiled. "I'll see you tomorrow, I guess?"

"Yeah. Guess so."

Marisa looked confused at Kim's tone, but she didn't push. "Okay. Have a good night."

Kim waved dismissively, and Marisa drove on. Kim watched her go, the taillights looking like rubies in the dim early evening light. When she was gone, Kim sighed and leaned forward, resting her forehead against the steering wheel.

"Oh, I heard the princess hit you," Break said, "but don't tell me she actually did damage."

Kim sat up and frowned at Break, who was standing next to the Jeep with his hands on the roof. "What?"

Break tapped his forehead. "She knock your marbles around?"

*In a manner of speaking.* "No," she said. "No, just a little wiped."

"You are not the Kim Greer I worked with three years ago," Break said. He drummed his hands on the frame of the Jeep and leaned in the window. "Come on. Old times sake, we'll go lift a glass and fill up the pockets on some pool tables."

"We have an appointment at six tomorrow morning, Break. An appointment where you and I are going to throw ourselves out of a speeding truck."

"So?"

"I'd rather not do it with a hangover."

Break sighed. "Ah, you're getting old, Greer."

"You're older than I am."

"Physically, maybe. Mentally…"

Kim laughed. "True. You are mentally pre-teen."

Break smiled brightly. "What do you say? One drink. No one gets hungover from one drink." He held his hands together, pleading. "I'll get down on my knees if I have to. Come on, Greer. I don't know anyone else on the set. You'll be my wingman. Woman. Whatever."

Kim shook her head. "Fine. But I am not helping you get laid."

Break clapped his hands and started backing away. "Yes. You drive, I'll follow. You know where all the good spots are, I'm sure. You won't regret this, Kim, trust me."

"One drink," she called after him, but he was already running to his car. Kim groaned and looked through the chain link fence at the traffic speeding by. She remembered the last time she worked with Break, on location in Portland, Oregon. Poker games that went until dawn, emptying the minibar, and being the cause of Break's left ring finger getting broken. She did not function well when beer was involved, and beer was always involved when Break was around. She exhaled, blew her hair out of her face, and backed out of the spot.

She wasn't a child, and she wasn't a lightweight. It was one drink with an old friend. He just wanted to thank her for getting him the job. She would stop after one drink, she would drive home, and then she would get a good night's sleep before heading out to do the stunt in the morning.

She knew the plan was doomed before she even drove off the lot.

Kim lifted the pool cue, rested it on her shoulders and draped her hands over the ends. Break stood at the other side of the table, eyeing the last two balls to be sunk. "All right," Kim said. "I sink these two, you buy me the drink you promised, and I get to go home and get some sleep."

"*If* you sink them," Break said. "Emphasis on the wholly unlikelihood of you actually succeeding."

Kim lowered the cue, bent forward, and sighted down the white ball. She struck it gently, and it nudged the first ball. It bounced off the side, hit the second ball with new, stronger momentum, and knocked it into the first ball. They both rolled directly to the pocket.

Break slapped both hands on the side of the table and cursed under his breath. "All right. What's your poison?"

"Just give me," she checked her watch and continued, "crap, give me a rain check. It's a quarter past midnight, Break." She tossed the cue onto the table and headed for the door. She turned and aimed a finger at Break. "If you're late tomorrow morning, so help me, I'll fire you. I don't care if we are friends."

Kim headed outside, well aware that Break was just a convenient scapegoat. No one forced to her grab a pool cue and challenge all comers. No one forced her to stay in the bar well past when she knew it would be wise to head home. She checked her watch again as she went outside, confirming it really *was* that late. She got into her Jeep and gunned the engine. She could make it home in ten minutes, seven if she pushed it. If she just yanked off her shoes and dropped into bed, she could be asleep in half an hour. That would give her a good four hours' worth of sleep before she had to be up and leave for work.

"Idiot," she chided herself. She knew this would happen the second she called Break. It was good that she got it out of the way early. Now that she knew she wouldn't be able to pace herself with him, she would be able to resist him in the future. If *Neutral Ground* went on for multiple seasons, there was a very good chance they were going to be working together for a long time. She couldn't risk getting a reputation of staying out late and drinking all night, not at this stage of her career.

The video store was, of course, closed when she pulled up in front of it. She unlocked the door with her keys, went inside, and twisted the latch. There was a note taped to the stairwell door, and she snatched it without reading it. When she got to the top of the stairs, she turned on the light and looked down at the note. From Mabel, of course, written in her tiny precise handwriting.

"Hope you're safe and NOT DRINKING. Remember to lock door when you come in!! See you in the morning (I hope!)! - M"

Kim tossed the note onto the table and went into the bathroom. She had decided against sleeping in her clothes when she realized how attractive her shower looked, taking a few minutes to soak under the hot water before going into the bedroom. She didn't even bother turning on the light to find her pajamas, she just crawled under the blankets and fluffed up her pillow. She closed her eyes against the glow of the streetlight outside her window and tried to force herself to fall asleep quickly.

Instead, her mind focused on Marisa. Maybe she was just fixated because of her recent drought. She hadn't had a steady girlfriend since she and Tina broke up, and that was... God, ten months ago? That couldn't be right. She held her hand up, the fingers dyed with the halogen glow, and counted off the months. "Damn," she muttered.

No wonder she was so obsessed with Marisa. She wasn't in love, she was just horny. The fastest cure for that, she'd always found, was to find a rebound relationship. She didn't have to lie about her motives; she just had to go find someone looking for the same thing. Like a business transaction. Just to get over the hump, as it were.

The problem was, she didn't feel like getting laid. She didn't want just anyone; she didn't want some random encounter with a woman whose name she wouldn't remember after a week. She wanted something more. Something meaningful. She wanted to be with someone who made her heart skip, her palms sweat, her skin flush.

Someone like Marisa Larkin.

She yanked the pillow out from beneath her head and smashed it over her face.

## CHAPTER SEVEN

THE EDGE of the neighborhood gave way almost immediately to a thick forest. Dirt roads snaked through the foliage like worm tracks and, after two or three turns, it was easy to believe you were in the middle of nowhere. Unless, of course, one were to turn and look down the road to see the trailers and trucks lining both sides of the road. Kim parked at the end of a long trail of vehicles, her head only slightly aching as she slipped her sunglasses on and walked deeper into the woods.

It was insane o'clock in the morning, and she had spent most of the night trying to find a comfortable position in bed. She finally gave up around four, stumbling out of bed to go through her exercise routine. It always worked in the past; working out oxygenated the blood and helped pump the bad juice out of her body. She made herself a bacon, egg and cheese sandwich using eggs of dubious freshness and drank two tall glasses of milk.

She had a large bottle of water purchased on her way to the location, and she prayed it would be enough to keep her head on straight.

The wardrobe trailer was full of swarthy men in olive drab uniforms, all of them unshaven. Kim had hired a few of them herself and knew they were portraying soldiers in Trujillo's militia. She nodded to them as she made her way to the back of the trailer. Her costume for the day was a white T-shirt, lightweight khakis and a brown suede jacket. She changed quickly, leaving her personal items behind in a locker. She kept her bottle of water, however. She was on her way out when Marisa walked in.

Despite the early hour, Marisa's hair looked professionally done, pulled back in a ponytail. She took off her glasses as she greeted someone near the door and hoisted her bag to keep from inadvertently bumping someone as she slid past. She spotted Kim standing near the Lethe outfits and her face lit up into a brilliant smile. She brought her hand up, waggling her fingers in greeting.

One of the surreal side effects of staying up all night was that the days seemed to flow together. It hardly seemed that long ago when she had last seen Marisa, standing next to the Prius and getting a fucking kiss from her hunky male lead. Her frustration was still simmering on the surface, and Kim found it hard to force a smile and return the greeting.

"Hey," Marisa said when she was close enough to speak without raising her voice. "Looks like you had kind of a rough night."

Kim shrugged. "I've had worse. I, uh, need to get to hair and makeup."

"Oh. Okay, sure. I'll see you there."

Kim nodded and slipped past Marisa. The sun had just risen, and the day looked gray-purple in the new light. Birds sang to one another in the trees above their heads and Kim craned her neck to look for them. She was still staring up into the trees when someone clapped her shoulder and nearly sent her reeling. She turned and saw Break, looking completely chipper and fresh. She glared at him, and his smile faded.

"Where's the cheer?"

"I left it at the bar about five hours ago. Don't tell me you got a good night's sleep."

"Haven't even been to bed yet." He started walking, and she fell in step next to him. "Figured I'd get this out of the way and catch a nap in an empty trailer."

"You know, Break, if you weren't the best stuntman I'd ever worked with, I would never have hired you for this job."

He held his hands out and said, "What can I say? I'm a stunt savant."

"You're some kind of savant." She took another swig from her bottle. "You know of a hangover cure?"

"I know two. Either keep drinking or never start."

"I'll remember that."

Marisa came up behind them, and Break glanced at her before smiling at Kim. "Man, look at you, ladies. Almost like twins. I used to have this fantasy--"

"Oh, just stop talking." Kim put her hand on his shoulder and shoved him away. "Go get into costume."

Break saluted and bowed to Marisa. "Pleasant morning, Miss Larkin." He winked at Kim and hurried back to the wardrobe trailer.

Marisa watched him go with a smile and crossed her arms over her chest. "He's quite a guy, huh? Never know quite what he'll say next."

"Mm. Makes you want to just cut out his tongue and get it over with."

"Oh, he's not that bad." They started walking and Marisa nodded toward the truck parked in the middle of the dirt road. "So. That's your stage today."

Kim nodded. It was a typical military transport truck, the bed covered by a canvas tarp. Benches ran along both sides of the bed, and it was there that Templeton and Lethe were being held prisoner.

"You're not scared?"

Kim shrugged. "I'm aware of everything that could go wrong. I'm prepared for it. But I'm not scared, no."

"But you're jumping from a truck. How do they teach that in, in stunt school?"

"They don't teach that specifically. But I learned how to fall a long time ago."

Marisa smiled. "Ahh. So you must be pretty good at it."

Kim smiled. "Oh, yeah. I can fall without even thinking about it sometimes. Doesn't always work out."

Marisa chuckled. "Well, you probably have a lot of planning to do. I'll get out of your hair." She touched Kim's arm, letting the touch linger for a moment before withdrawing. "I hope you feel better."

Kim watched her walk away and then closed her eyes, letting the warmth of Marisa's touch slowly fade away. She uncapped her water and took a long drink, swishing it around in her mouth. Against her will, her mind filling in the blanks about Break's little fantasy. A woman dressed exactly like her, yeah, there was a uniform kink element in play there. She looked at Marisa's ass, swallowed her mouthful of water and shook her head. Little did Marisa know that jumping from a truck was the easiest thing Kim had to get through that day.

Kim sat between two of the swarthy soldiers from the wardrobe tent, hands shackled between her knees. Another soldier sat in front of her, with Break seated to his left. Kenneth wanted to let her try one, just to see how difficult it would be to hide her face. The fight would be so hectic that he thought it was possible. She heard Kenneth call action, and the truck began to rumble down the road. Another truck with a camera mounted on it followed a few feet away. Kim swung her elbow up into the face of the man next to her, and then swung her arms down in the other direction, burying her elbow in the other soldier's stomach.

Break wrapped the chain of his handcuffs around his guard's neck and pulled, and Kim fumbled with the keys on his belt. *Come on*, she thought, willing her fingers to work properly. She got the keys free, and pulled the guard's gun from the holster. Break let him go, and they moved to the back of the truck. There was no time for hesitation, no room for error. She let herself drop from the back of the truck, immediately tucking herself into a ball. The impact still rattled her bones.

She rolled, got to her feet, and brought the gun up. She fired three times at the back of the truck, grabbed the back of Break's jacket, and hauled him into the trees with her as the truck shuddered to a stop. The guards who were still conscious jumped from the cab and gave chase.

"Cut!"

Kim stopped running and slumped against a convenient tree, her hands on her temples and trying to rub away the insistent throb. The world seemed to expand and contract around her. Break put his hand on her shoulder and said, "You okay?"

She grunted. "Yeah, I'll be fine." She turned and shoved him away from her. "No more late nights with you. Ever."

"Hey, I didn't put a beer in your hand."

"Yeah, but you kept losing and buying me beers to pay your debt. If you were just a slightly better pool player…"

Break hissed and touched his side. "Ooh. Ouch. Hit me where it hurts."

They made their way back to a prop master. He took the gun from Kim and unlocked the handcuffs. Kim rubbed her wrist and then looked down at herself. "My wrists don't hurt. I just always feel the need to do this when someone takes my handcuffs off."

"The media is poisoning us."

Kim shook her head. "What an industry to be in."

"Better than being an investment banker."

"Hey, I'd trade jobs in a second," Kim said. "If I knew how to do math, I'd be more than happy to rake in the cash those assholes get."

"You don't have to know math to do that job. Just make it up as you go along."

Kim snickered and left Break to go find Kenneth. She found him by craft services, tossing a bottle of orange juice from one hand to the other. She whistled to get his attention and said, "You want me to go through the warehouse fight with the stunt guys?"

"They're waiting for you out by the trailers." He frowned. "You okay? You don't look so good."

Kim snatched another bottle of water off a table as she passed. "So people keep telling me." She sang, "Say a prayer, if you've got one..."

Somehow, she made it to lunch. Despite the rising temperature of the day, despite the day players who couldn't follow her directions to save their lives, she survived.

Craft services had set up a tent in a meager attempt to keep the bugs away, and Kim dragged herself inside and stretched out on a bench near the entrance. She draped her arm across her face and breathed in the scent of the food, fresh fruits and vegetables that would likely settle her stomach and relieve some of the pain if she only had the strength to make her way over to it. She just needed to rest for a few seconds, she was sure, and she would be fine.

Ten minutes later, she sensed someone standing near her. She moved her arm and cracked one eye, looking up at a battered and bloody Marisa. Kim feigned shock. "Holy hell. What happened to you?"

Marisa looked down at herself. "Running from militiamen in the Florida Keys. You?"

"Nothing quite that exotic." She forced herself up and gestured at the bench beside her. "Have a seat."

"Thanks." Marisa sat down, keeping a comfortable space between the two of them so their thighs wouldn't touch. Kim appreciated and resented the gesture at the same time. Marisa held out her paper plate. "I got you some food, but I wasn't sure you were awake. I didn't want to bother you."

"It's fine," Kim said. "Thank you very much." She took one of the cantaloupe cubes and popped it into her mouth. It almost melted on her tongue and she closed her eyes as she bit into it. "Oh, God. You can always wake me up for ambrosia like this."

Marisa chuckled. "So, um... I guess jumping from a truck wasn't as easy as you remembered."

"Oh, it was easy. It's just better to do it when you're not hungover."

Marisa whistled. "Oh. Yeah, I bet that's not advised."

Kim arched an eyebrow and took another cantaloupe. She was still wearing a costume identical to Marisa's, but it was completely intact save for a small tear on the shoulder and some dirt. Marisa, on the other hand, looked like she had been beaten to a pulp. Her face was smeared with dirt, and what Kim hoped was fake blood was drying on her temple. The jacket was gone, leaving her arms bare, and one sleeve of her T-shirt had been ripped almost completely off. Kim had to stop herself from reaching up and cleaning the blood away.

"This afternoon, we're shooting the last big stunt of the pilot, right? The fight in the warehouse?"

"Yeah," Kim said. "I'll do whatever doubling you need, but~"

"Right, Kenneth wants as much of me as possible again."

"Have you been practicing?"

Marisa laughed. "Oh, yeah. I nearly took my boyfriend's head off last night doing one of those kicks."

The cantaloupe was suddenly rotten in Kim's mouth, but she didn't want to spit it out. She chewed it slowly, swallowed with difficulty, and said, "Oh?"

"Yeah. I think he likes it better when I just step aside and let the stunt double do everything. In fact, he'd probably buy you a car for saving me from jumping out of that truck."

*I don't want him to give me a* car. *Son of a bitch.*

"Well. It's all part of the job description."

Marisa looked at her watch and sighed. "Well, I have to get back out to the Florida Keys. Bad men with guns want to kill me. You know how it is."

Kim managed a smile as Marisa stood up.

Marisa stood over her for a moment, looking down and examining Kim's face. "Are you sure you're okay?"

"I must really look like shit," Kim said. "People keep asking me that."

Marisa shrugged. "I don't know. I think you look pretty damn good for having jumped out of a truck this morning." She held out the plate, offering Kim the rest of the fruit. Kim nodded her thanks and took the plate. "I'll see you at the fight."

"Yeah."

Marisa stuck her hands in her pockets and walked out of the tent.

Kim looked down at the fruit. She felt a sudden tightness in her jaw, tension from holding back the tears that wanted to come. *Boyfriend. Damn it, of course 'boyfriend.'* She stood up and dumped the rest of the fruit into the trash as she left the tent.

## CHAPTER EIGHT

THREE QUARTERS of a mile up the road stood the shell of an abandoned warehouse. It was little more than a concrete shell, resembling the hollow face of a skeleton as the trucks approached. Someone had gone ahead and opened the rusted chain link fence, allowing the crew inside. Kenneth walked straight across the cracked pavement, ignoring the grass growing between the slabs as he eyed the freeway visible in the distance. "We're just gonna have to shoot from this direction." He turned, saw the mountains, and nodded.

Kim was there to observe the final fight and make last minute adjustments as necessary. She doubted she would be asked to stand in for any of the fight, since her costume was still mainly intact while Marisa's looked ready for the scrap bin. When they arrived, Kim ended up walking past Marisa at the garage door. Marisa smiled at her, and Kim noticed a twig caught in her hair. She reached up to brush it away, but Marisa cringed away from her.

"Sorry," they said at the same time.

Marisa pointed at the stick. "The twig?" Kim nodded. "It took them about ten minutes just to get that thing stuck in there. I don't think they would look too kindly on you taking it out."

"Oh." Kim mentally kicked herself. She should have known better.

"Thank you, though. It was sweet. And it is the thought that counts, right?"

Kim shrugged. "Always willing to help a damsel in distress."

She started to continue into the warehouse, but Marisa stopped her. "Wait, Kim... I'm kind of getting cold feet about the whole fight thing."

"You'll be great. Just flow."

"I know. Just like a dance. But... maybe if we could just go through it one more time... just you and me."

Kim glanced toward Kenneth. They were going to be at least a half hour getting everything set up. She touched the corner of her mouth with her tongue, checked the radio on her belt to make sure it was tuned to the right frequency, and motioned for Marisa to follow her. "Come on."

People from the props department moved about the interior of the warehouse like the cobbler's elves, getting everything picture perfect for the scene. They measured and marked, stacked and restacked, stepped to one side and tilted their heads to see how the light hit something before they moved it. "Looks authentic," Marisa said as they crossed the space.

"Seen many militia headquarters on a Florida island?" Kim asked with a bit more snap than she intended. Marisa, fortunately, didn't seem to notice.

"Guess I haven't. But hopefully most of the audience hasn't, either."

"That's the ticket," Kim said.

She led Marisa out to the back lot. A handful of old dumpsters stood against the fence, tops open and swarming with flies and gnats. Patches of oil marked the concrete, and weeds were starting to overwhelm the gravel at the sides of the lot. Marisa squinted past the dumpsters to the freeway in the distance. "God, it's pretty up here."

"If you like cars and fumes."

Marisa chuckled. "I was actually talking about the hills."

Sure enough, past the freeway, there were hills shrouded in the clouds of exhaust. They were a uniform brown, topped with oil derricks lazily moving in their clockwork cycles. It should have looked drab and dull, but it only made the blue sky pop and look unreal by comparison. The sun shone down, and suddenly every car on the freeway shimmered like ripples in a stream. Even with the derricks, it was almost like nature untouched, some kind of living painting, and Kim was blown away by it.

She blinked, half expecting the vision to be gone when she

opened her eyes. "Oh."

"Just have to learn how to look at things," Marisa said. She nudged Kim with her elbow and said, "Okay. I'm so sorry to pester you like this all the time..."

"No, it's fine. My job is to make you look as good as possible. I'm happy to lend a hand. Come around in front of me."

They got into their stance, and Kim slowly went through the moves. Then she changed her position and let Marisa repeat what she had done. The tips of Marisa's fingers brushed over Kim's cheek, and her heart skipped. Their legs tangled briefly, and Kim's mouth went dry. Marisa was good enough that, to an outside observer, it would have looked completely convincing.

"You're better," Kim said. "You really have been practicing." She swung at Marisa's head.

Marisa moved to one side, slapping Kim's arm out of the way. "Well, I had to impress the teacher."

"Well, you've definitely got an A-plus."

Kim faux-punched Marisa in the stomach, stopping herself just before she made full contact, and Marisa bent at the waist. Marisa twisted, grabbed Kim's arm, and pulled her into a wide circle. Kim was forced to go with the movement and went into a controlled fall. She landed on her back, and Marisa scrambled on top of her, straddling her waist. She put her hand in the middle of Kim's chest and poised her right arm to punch Kim in the face. Then she smiled.

"You obviously didn't need this refresher course," Kim said.

Marisa was slightly out of breath. She shrugged and relaxed her right arm. "Well, maybe I just wanted to dance with you again."

Kim blinked. Why the hell wasn't Marisa getting off of her? Her hair was in her face, and it was all Kim could do not to brush it away. Caress her face. Let her hand drift down to her shoulder, her arm, her breast... Why was it suddenly so hard to catch her breath?

"Mar~" The radio crackled, and Kim jumped. "Shit."

Marisa reached down; it had been her radio. "Yeah, Ken."

"We're ready for you and William down here."

"No problem. On my way."

She finally got up, and it took Kim a moment to find the strength to get on her feet. She glanced at Kim and said, "Oh. Crap, your twig."

Marisa touched her hair to find the small piece of wood was missing, and then looked at the ground around her feet. Kim helped her search and found the errant twig first. "Here. I think this is it." Kim picked it up and held it out. "Or close enough, anyway."

"Can you do it? I can't see my own head that well…"

Kim reached up before she could think about it. She placed the twig in Marisa's hair, twisting the strands around it so that it wouldn't move. Marisa's hair was soft, her head dipped forward just a bit so that Kim could see what she was doing. Kim licked her lips before she pulled her hands cautiously away, making sure the twig stayed in place. "There you go. Good as new."

"Thanks."

Kim nodded and stepped out of Marisa's personal space. She stuck her hands in the back pockets of her jeans and followed Marisa back into the building. Marisa held the door for her, stopping her with a hand just above her elbow.

"Listen, I'm having kind of an informal little get together at my house this weekend. Kind of a celebration of getting cast in the pilot, moving on to the actual series. I'm sorry I haven't invited you before, but I wasn't sure it was… your kind of thing, you know. A bunch of actors patting themselves on the back. But you're more than welcome."

Kim wanted to say no. The mere thought of Marisa having a boyfriend was almost too much for her to bear; she didn't think she could actually see them together. But she was intrigued by the invitation to see another side of the woman she was crushing so hard over. She nodded. "Yeah. You know what, sounds like a lot of fun. I'd love to come by."

"Excellent. I'll get you the address before I leave."

They went outside, where the guards and camera crew were waiting. Templeton and Lethe were captured in the woods and finally brought to the militia leader's headquarters. The truck they would be riding in was parked outside the gate.

Kim already regretted accepting the invitation to the party. She would spend the time until the party obsessing about it, so much so that she wouldn't be able to enjoy or focus on anything else. She moved off to the side of the road as Marisa climbed into the back of the truck and shook her head. Maybe seeing her in real life would be good. Maybe it would destroy whatever fantasies she was harboring and force her to see Marisa as a real, fallible human being. Maybe she would find out Marisa had severed heads in her freezer, or she listened to alt-right podcasts. It didn't hurt to hope.

They started filming, and Kim crossed her arms and chewed on her thumbnail as the guards shoved Marisa into the warehouse. "All right, bastard, I'm walking."

Kim was surprised by how Marisa's entire persona seemed to change when she was Simone Lethe. She seemed more dangerous, poised to attack. There was a hardness to her, and Kim was impressed to see how effortlessly she slipped into character.

Marisa and Easter were led toward the metal stairs at the far end of the warehouse. They were halfway there when Kenneth cupped his hands around his mouth and shouted, "Helicopter!" One of the P.A.s began drumming his hands on a clipboard to mimic the chop of a helicopter's rotor. The sound effect would be replaced in post.

"What the hell is that?" one of the guards asked.

"Back up," Marisa said. She threw herself backward into the guard, causing him to fall into the guard behind him in a domino effect. As they fell, Marisa turned to the guard who had been standing with Easter. Kim bit her bottom lip; the moment of truth had arrived.

The guard was a little stiff, and Kim swore she would never use these guys again. But Marisa... it looked as if she had been born throwing punches. She never telegraphed a punch, never anticipated, and it looked fluid and amazing. The script called for Templeton to be "suitably awed" by Lethe's fighting skills, but there was little to no acting necessary. Everyone on set was watching as Marisa put down the guard with seemingly a modicum of effort. She straddled his hips as she had Kim earlier, brought her right arm up, and this time sent her fist into the man's face. He took the punch and went limp.

Marisa pushed herself up and turned to Easter. "What do you say? Need a ride, Feeb?"

Kenneth said, "Cut that, set it, take it to the fucking bank. That is a final take. Beautiful, beautiful, beautiful." He slid out of his chair as the guards got back to their feet. He put his hands on his hips, shaking his head in disbelief as Marisa walked over to join him. "Where exactly have you been hiding those skills, Larkin?"

"New skills," Marisa said. She nodded toward Kim and said, "Thank your stunt coordinator."

Kenneth looked at Kim, looked at Marisa, and threw his hands in the air. "It's official. I am a casting genius. Stay out of my way, folks." He turned and walked back to his seat.

Marisa made her way over to Kim and said, "Okay. The truth.

How did I really look out there?"

"Like the man said. Beautiful."

Marisa may have blushed, it was hard to tell with the makeup, and looked down at her arm. "I think I hurt my wrist, though."

Kim took the wrist and let it rest on her fingers. She probed gently with her thumb and said, "That hurt?"

"A little."

"I think you just twisted it. Let's get you some ice." She guided Marisa toward the front of the building. "It was kind of like watching a kid go off to their first day of school." She reached up and ruffled Marisa's hair. "I'm so proud of you."

Marisa twisted away and said, "Cut that out. Do you have kids?"

"No. No plans for any in the future, either."

"Ditto."

Kim nodded. "Your, uh, boyfriend," she resisted the urge to spit, "have any issues with that?"

"Um, no. No, it's not something either of us have planned. So." She glanced toward the first aid trailer and said, "Want to hold my hand while I get looked at?"

*Yes, please.* "Nah. I think you're grown-up enough. Really great work out there today."

"It was all you. Thanks, Kim." She started up the stairs and then said, "Oh, wait." She came back and pulled a folded piece of paper from her pocket. It was the call sheet for the day. She bent down, pressing the paper against her thigh as she scribbled something down. She ripped off the corner and held it out. "My address, for Saturday. I'll see you there?"

"Yeah, wouldn't miss it." She took the slip and glanced at the address before she put it in her pocket. "Do I need to bring anything?"

"Just yourself. It starts at six. My phone number is on there in case you get lost."

"All right. Thanks. I'll be there."

"Excellent. See you Saturday."

Kim stepped back, waiting until Marisa was inside the trailer before she walked away.

## CHAPTER NINE

KIM SLEPT in Thursday morning, since the shooting schedule only called for talking scenes between the two leads and various guest stars. She woke up sore, her shoulder and back complaining about what she had forced them to do the day before. She took a long hot soak in the bathtub and went downstairs to the video store in her sweats. The store was quiet save for the clicking of Mabel's knitting needles.

Mabel looked up when Kim appeared and feigned surprise. "Well, look who has deigned to make an appearance."

"Sorry. Got in late night before last, left early yesterday morning." She nodded at the swath of yarn. "Is that going to be for me? I think my winter wardrobe is pretty well stocked already."

"Don't get greedy. You have another day of getting punched and kicked, I suppose?"

"Nope. Two days off. I'm going for a run, and then I'll figure out something to do."

"You could help me in the store. Could make a good living at it. And no one would—"

"Punch and kick me," Kim finished in stereo with Mabel. "I'll think about it." She slipped in the earbuds of her iPod, signaling the end of the conversation, and waved goodbye as she left the store.

Today Brandi Carlile was serenading her as she jogged down the hill toward the cross street. She had the route planned out in her head; one of her favorites. It took her down near the harbor, where all the big ships were coming and going. Then down the oak-lined street with its myriad of bookstores and cafés. She would then loop back around, stopping for a light lunch and browsing in the bookstore before she headed home. The whole route would take her about an hour, maybe ninety minutes if she lingered over her lunch.

After that, she wasn't sure. She didn't do well with free time on her hands. Free time meant time to think, to stew, and to put her mind to work on the problem of Marisa. She had two days away from the set, and she hoped the time away would help her get over that queasy feeling she got whenever Marisa walked into the room. Her feelings were just amplified because of her dry spell, that's all. Now that she had identified the problem, she could attack it and eradicate it.

The sun was bright, the day was warm but not hot, and she was ready to get her mind back on track. Marisa Larkin was the furthest thing from her mind as she made the first corner of her path. She tapped the stop sign, the first marker on her trip, and smiled as the metal rang against her fingers. The day was wide open.


She dropped the DVD case on the counter and fumbled with her wallet as Mabel scanned the title. "Another Marisa Larkin movie? I thought the other one, you liked not so much?"

Kim shrugged, keeping her eyes averted. "She's a nice lady. I thought I'd give her another shot before I judged." She was mentally kicking herself as Mabel scanned the movie. Today was supposed to be about getting over Marisa, not watching another movie starring her. And she definitely had no business hoping that this movie had another nude scene. But she couldn't stop herself from feeling a buzz of excitement as Mabel handed the movie back.

"You got a credit for bringing back the last one. Just one buck."

Kim handed over the cash. "Thanks, Mabel."

"You off tonight, too? Got plans?"

"Nothing specific." Translated to: absolutely nothing at all, please save me from having to plan for myself. "Why?"

"I thought you and I could have dinner. Been a long time, kid. And it'll be nice to have a dinner where you're not always running out to smoke those disgusting cigarettes."

Kim smiled. "Yeah, I'd love to. Late dinner, after the store closes?"

"No, I'll have Donny watch the store while I go eat. Needs to earn his paycheck, that one."

"Okay. I'll be down about... six?"

"Six is good."

Kim nodded. "See you then, Auntie Em." She turned and went to the stairs before Mabel could complain about the hated nickname.

Upstairs, Kim kicked off her tennis shoes and left her sweats on the hamper. In the bathroom, she examined her body for bruises or scratches left over from the stunts the day before. There was a small scrape on her back shoulder, but nothing serious. It hadn't even bled. It would be fine. She jumped into the shower just long enough to wash off the sweat, letting the cold water soak her hair and then wrapping it in a towel before she dressed in jeans and a button-down blouse.

She put the DVD in the player and leaned back. "Okay, Marisa. *King of Thieves* is your second chance. Wow me." She hit play.

Benjamin Choate was a career criminal. He hadn't worked an honest day in his life. In Choate's philosophy, if someone was stupid enough to fall for one of his games, then they deserved to lose their money. And Choate deserved to get it from them. He was ready to retire at the age of fifty, after a few too many close calls. He planned one last big score, robbing the home belonging to a captain of industry who wouldn't miss a couple million bucks. He assumed it would be enough to give him the good life until he "passed away in his sleep or, hopefully, in the middle of an all-night lovemaking session with a few beautiful models."

Choate's plan, beautifully executed, fell apart on the day it was supposed to go down. An unexpected security upgrade forced Choate to improvise. The alarms went off, and he was startled by the target appearing at the top of the stairs. Choate fired a flash grenade - he never physically hurt or killed anyone in his entire career. In the darkness, the flash looked like a gunshot. The man at the top of the stairs gasped, his heart seized, and he collapsed. Dead before he hit the ground.

Choate tried to save him, but it was too late. The police were arriving, and he had to make an escape or live out his retirement in a jail cell. As he was running from the grounds, he spotted a woman appear in the guest house doorway like a phantasm. She wore all white, her dark hair mussed from sleep. She looked toward the house, which was now lit up like New Years, and then turned her head to watch the man in black racing across the lawn.

The woman was Corrine Hobbs, as played by Marisa Larkin.

Kim found the movie riveting, despite herself. After the horribly botched job, Choate was racked with guilt. He returned to the scene of the crime impersonating a security consultant, and met Corrine, the lovely daughter he had seen as he fled. She gave him a tour of the house and he pinpointed the flaws in the system - all the flaws he had utilized for his own burglary. By the time the tour was finished, Choate was smitten, and he asked Corrine out for coffee. He offered a sympathetic ear and she agreed.

The tension grew as Corrine hired Choate to improve the mansion's security system. Long days at the house, with only Corrine as company, led to his crush growing. Kim snorted as she watched him fall into Marisa's clutches. "I know how you feel, bud. No use resisting it."

Adding to the drama was the fact that Corrine was unwilling to rely on the police. She had seen the man running from the house that night. She had connections that her father didn't know about. People who could ask the right questions and help her track down the "bastard who murdered her father."

Things came to a head during a thunderstorm. The power went out at the Hobbs mansion, and Corrine called Choate to come be with her. She felt vulnerable, and he made her feel safe. He immediately went over, chiding himself for being the reason she felt vulnerable in the first place. She had Chinese takeout, and they split a carton of rice in the kitchen, surrounded by candles. Corrine was dressed for bed, a robe loosely tied over the nightgown Choate had seen that first night. He told her that he had something to tell her, fully intending to confess, but Corrine beat him to the punch with her own confession. She had fallen in love with him.

Kim didn't hesitate this time. She watched, mouth dry and hand curled into a fist against her lips, as Choate undressed Corinne. He lifted her onto the counter and moved between her spread legs. He ran his hands over her thighs and the camera focused on Marisa's face as he did things to her lower body that were left up to the viewers' imaginations. They kissed, and Kim found herself unbelievably turned on. She squirmed on the couch and looked away, letting the music alert her when it was safe to watch again.

*How can I want her so much?* she thought. *How could I possibly already be this far gone?*

After Choate and Corrine made love, she put on his T-shirt and he spooned her from behind. And then, as apparently the master of bad timing, he confessed his part in her father's death. Corrine was, as could be expected, completely livid. She tore away from him, running deeper into the house. The chase that followed was surprisingly tense. It ended with Choate at the top of the stairs and Corrine below, reversing the position Choate had been in with her father. She has retrieved an antique gun from her father's study and Choate pleads with her to listen to him. He says he loves her, and explains her father's death was an accident.

Corrine was torn, but ready to accept Choate's apology and his explanation. He approached her, reached to take the gun, and thunder suddenly roared overhead. The sound frightened Corrine, and her finger tensed on the trigger. Choate was hit in the stomach, eyes wide, and collapsed. Corrine, horrified, held him and tried to stop the bleeding, but it was useless. Choate managed to smile, his body trembling, and he said, "Guess this place is just cursed."

The movie ended on a shot of Marisa on the floor, cradling Choate's lifeless body, sobbing in the darkness of her home.

Kim stared at the screen as the credits began to roll. She wanted to wonder where the past hundred and twenty minutes had gone, but she knew exactly what had happened. Marisa. She was blown away by Marisa's performance. She was close to tears, her mind racing as she wondered how Corrine possibly dealt with what had just happened. Did she see it as justice for her father? Did the knowledge she killed a man eat away at her? God, how could the movie end that way?

She picked up the remote control and sent the movie back to the menu. Under bonus features, she found several deleted scenes, and a making-of featurette. She clicked on that. She usually ignored features like this; she knew enough about the making of movies that she just wasn't interested. But if Marisa had something to say about the making of the movie...

Kim fast forwarded through the director and costars, and stopped when she saw Marisa. She was seated in a canvas chair, wearing the nightgown from the movie. Her robe was larger and fluffier than the one she'd worn in the film, and her hair was in the midst of being artfully tousled.

"Corrine is a force to be reckoned with, you know? She's not just going to sit around and wait for someone to save her. That's what really attracted me to the character. Corrine has the... cojones? Can I say cojones?" She smiled, winked at the person behind the camera, and continued, "...to go after the guy who killed her dad. She's not a shrinking violet. I love that about her."

Another quick interview with the man who played Choate, and then on-set footage of the director preparing a scene. It went back to Marisa, and Kim hit play.

"Nude scenes, yeah." She laughed. "Well, you know, I'm comfortable with them. Obviously, by now, right?" She laughed again, and it cut to a clip of the scene in question. Marisa perched on the edge of the counter, lit by candlelight, eyes closed as Choate kissed her breast. Her perfect breast, with a hard nipple that... Kim's fantasy snapped apart as the shot went back to Marisa in the canvas chair. "I felt it was important to the scene, and to the character. We had to see how vulnerable she had allowed herself to be with this man so we could understand, you know, her decision to forgive him at the end."

Kim went back to the menu, clicked on the "scene selection" option, and went back to the love scene.

She avoided looking at Marisa's body, sometimes lifting the remote to block certain areas so she could focus on her face. The expressions, the way her eyes slowly closed and then how she turned her head. Slowly, she lowered the remote control. Marisa's body was perfect, beautiful. She was sure a portion of that was lighting and makeup and perfect conditions, but she didn't care. She wasn't falling anymore; she had hit rock bottom. She was completely smitten with Marisa Larkin.

She sank down on the couch, grabbed a cushion, and held it over her face to smother her scream of frustration.

## CHAPTER TEN

THE TERRACE of the Barrens Steakhouse stood at the crest of a hill, the added height allowing diners to overlook the street and focus on the harbor a few blocks to the west. The breeze was cool and smelled of the water, and Kim ate there as often as she could. The steaks were to die for, but people truly came to the Barrens for the view. There were about a half dozen other groups sitting with them out on the terrace, and the dining room's doors stood open so the less fortunate people inside could still get a hint of the beautiful weather.

Kim ordered a beer with her dinner, earning her an ignored tongue cluck from her aunt. While they waited to be served, Mabel carefully draped her lap with a napkin. "So, I notice you've been watching a lot of movies by yourself lately."

"The joy of living above a video store." Maybe she should just sign up for one of those streaming services. Netflix wouldn't judge her or comment on how many of Marisa's movies she watched.

Mabel shook her finger. "It's a shame. A shame, a pretty girl like you sitting at home all the time. And then poker with those ruffians every Friday. You should be out on dates. That nice fellow... what's his name? The one you always work with? Brick?"

"Break?" Mabel pursed her lips until Kim said, "You mean James Ransom?"

"Him. He's very attractive. Single, too."

Kim arched an eyebrow. "Break is single because he's certifiably insane. You really want me marrying someone like that?"

"Marry, what," Mabel said. "No one said marry. I just think you need to get laid."

Kim would never again mock the use of a spit take in movies. Her eyes widened and it was all she could do to swallow before she said, "What?"

"It has been a very long time since Joe."

"It's only been two years," Kim said. She resisted the urge to sigh at the mention of Joseph Danner. He was very firmly closeted, and they provided cover for each other with their family. They would leave together, then go out on their separate dates with others. Then he fell in love and decided to move to Atlanta, leaving her in the lurch. "Look, all right, it's been a while. But I'm fine with that. I'm just, you know... I'm being selective."

Mabel exhaled sharply. "You're thirty four years old, Kim Greer. Apples don't stay on trees for three decades. They get picked early. And then, what, you're left with rotten fruit."

"Am I the apple or the apple picker in your scenario?"

"Both. Neither. Who cares, just find someone." She grabbed the waiter's shirt cuff as he delivered their food. "You look single." She nodded at Kim. "Like the looks of this one?"

The waiter smiled apologetically at Kim and said, "She's very attractive, ma'am. But I'm not single."

Mabel squinted skeptically at him. "You're not wearing a ring."

"No, ma'am, not at work." He winked at her and Mabel withdrew her hand. "Sorry."

"Don't be," Kim said, mouthing an apology to him as he retreated. She made a mental note to add a few bucks to whatever tip Mabel left. "God, Auntie Em."

"Well, I'm *sorry*," Mabel said. "At your age, you have to be a little aggressive. Besides, who takes off their wedding ring for work? Probably gay." She whispered the last word and then glanced to her right, as if she thought he might have been lingering to eavesdrop.

Kim pressed her lips together and looked down at her food. "Yeah."

"Honestly."

"Can you pass the steak sauce, please?"

Mabel handed her the bottle and shook her head at the food on Kim's plate. It was a porterhouse nestled next to a baked potato split open and loaded with sour cream and cheese. "Uck. Such a slab of meat. What kind of girl eats like that? That's what's scaring away all the men, you know."

"Maybe we can just enjoy our dinner, huh?"

"What did I do?"

Kim sighed. "Please?"

Mabel held her hands up as if in surrender and then picked up her silverware.

Kim cut her steak into manageable pieces, a habit she picked up from childhood, moving the pieces until they were swimming like islands in a sea of sauce. She loved her aunt dearly, loved their relationship, but the homophobia was painful to her. It was the reason she was still in the closet, the reason she couldn't reveal who she was *really* interested in. She was mostly out at work, Break and the majority of stunt people in the business knew she was gay, but her personal life was a different matter altogether. It was painful to stay quiet, but she knew it would hurt more to see that disgust in her aunt's face every time they were in the same room.

Mabel seemed to sense Kim's mood and tried to change the subject. "They do a good chicken here, too. Healthier."

"Mm hmm," Kim said. She popped a piece of steak into her mouth and chewed it carefully, looking out over the railing at the cars passing on the street. Even if she did manage to come to terms with her feelings for Marisa, even if by some miracle they ended up together, Mabel would never be happy for her. She would never be able to share her happiness with the most important person in her life.

"Is it too spicy?"

Kim looked at the woman who had raised her from the age of ten. "What?"

"Your eyes are watering. The steak is too spicy?"

"Oh. Yeah, a little." She picked up her glass of water and took a drink, blinking rapidly to dispel the tears that had nothing to do with the temperature of her food.

Kim drove Mabel home to pick up her car. Mabel hesitated before getting out of the car and said, "You're not parking?"

"No. I thought I'd go out. I have another day off tomorrow, so..."

Mabel chewed her bottom lip and said, "Look, I didn't mean what I said, you know? The thing about apples and picking... you shouldn't just grab the first apple you see. You want to be picky, you be picky. You'll end up with a great apple, I just know it."

Kim knew that Mabel had misinterpreted her mood, but she was willing to let it stand. "Thanks, Mabel. But what... what if the apple I pick is one you don't like? What if you think I need a red delicious and I come home with a... a Granny Smith?"

"If you like him, then fine. Who am I to argue? Just find who you want, don't worry about me. It's your life." She took Kim's hand and kissed the knuckles. "Bye bye, Kim. Don't stay out too late."

"I won't."

Mabel unfolded from the passenger seat in a manner that reminded Kim of a marionette being manipulated by a twisted set of loose strings. She straightened her sweater, closed the door, and waved goodbye through the window. Kim watched Mabel unlock her car and get behind the wheel, waved, and pulled away from the curb. She wasn't sure where she was going, she just knew that Mabel would have followed her into the store and talked her into having a conversation. She didn't want to talk to anyone, she just wanted to get away and spend some time with her thoughts.

She parked by the harbor, watching the newly risen moon dance in the water. Boats were still out, lit from within. They reminded her of those candles that floated on lily pads she'd seen at parties. It was a little past eight, and the city seemed to be moving all around her. People going home, people going out, shifts changing and people throwing off their daily lives for their nighttime personalities.

Kim scanned the radio stations until she found something soft and low to fit her mood. All she could think about was Marisa. How had she spent the day? What scenes had they filmed? Was she still hard at work, or dragging herself home? She wondered how Marisa separated herself from the character, how she drew the line between Marisa Larkin and Simone Lethe.

*Am I really falling for her?*

She didn't want to think about that. She wanted to go out to a bar, meet someone moderately attractive, take her home, and get nice and sweaty together. But the idea didn't appeal to her. Her mind flashed on countless other nights, successful one night stands and some that were less than successful. It depressed her to think of going through the whole dance again just to get laid.

Besides, she didn't want just anyone. She wanted Marisa.

*So, yes. I'm in trouble.*

She'd had crushes before, but usually they were just brief flashes of lust that went away after the initial meeting. Celebrities were normal people, just flashier and fancier with an army of hair and makeup people to hide the pesky human parts of being human. But Marisa struck her like no one else. She was impressed by Marisa's talent, her humanity, the way she carried herself. The respect she showed to her fellow actors, and to the crew, was enough to earn Kim's admiration. But it was more than that. This didn't feel like some fleeting infatuation. This felt deeper, almost ingrained. It wasn't love, definitely not, but it had the hallmarks of something that could become... Something.

She wanted to drive to the set, just to see what she was doing. To make sure she wasn't bored. Hell, to sit in her trailer with her and talk.

*But you just said you didn't want to talk with anyone.*

"Well, her," Kim said. "I would talk with *her*."

She rested her elbow against the glass and pinched the bridge of her nose.

The last time she had been in love did not work out well. Phone calls in the middle of the night, insane rambling voice mails on her cell phone, and the piece de resistance: both front tires of her Jeep slashed during the night. Love was barely tolerable when it was good, but when it went bad, it could kill you. Why would she want to put herself through that hell again? The whole thing was a moot point anyway; Marisa was straight. Or even if she was bi, she still had a boyfriend.

*Neutral Ground* had thirteen episodes to produce over the course of the first season. That could mean six months' worth of working alongside Marisa every day. She couldn't quit the job; it was what she had been working toward since she got into the business. But what if Marisa was what she had been looking for since she was fifteen years old?

She finally decided she wasn't going to get any answers from the water, no matter how long she stared at it. The water only had more questions to throw at her, more on every wave. She started the engine and pulled away from the curb, heading for home before she questioned herself into any more corners.

## CHAPTER ELEVEN

KIM DIDN'T get out of bed until noon the next day. Her sleep was disturbed by dreams of Marisa, both erotic and innocent in equal measure. They did nothing to help her state of mind, as she woke frustrated, irritated, and exhausted. A cold shower did nothing for her libido, and a hot shower did nothing to erase her weariness. She finally dressed and went downstairs. She scheduled her departure for a time when she knew the store would be busy, and hurried out before Mabel could flag her down.

She jogged to the gym and spent two hours working out, trying to sweat her way to a clear mind. All it did was make her sore on top of everything else.

On her way home, she stopped by the grocery store to get supplies for the poker game. She didn't much feel like playing cards, but she'd held Friday night poker games every week for the past ten years. She would shoot herself in the foot before she broke that tradition. At least then she would have something to occupy her mind besides Marisa Larkin. She bought chips, pork rinds, beer and pretzels, and stopped by a tobacco shop to pick up some cigars. She may not smoke anymore, but the guys would riot if she didn't provide for them.

Kim got home and moved her furniture out of the way. The table went dead center in the middle of the room, giving everyone access to the snacks in the kitchen and a clear path to the bathroom.

She put away the things she didn't want the guys getting into - her scripts, her books and mail - and dropped onto the couch to nap until the first guest arrived. She loved poker nights, but she couldn't muster up the usual excitement. All she could think about was the long night ahead of her and the clean up afterward.

The players started to show up at a quarter to six, and she pulled herself reluctantly off the couch to let them in. Jonas Barker was the first to arrive, followed by Joshua Lincoln. Barker brought a huge bottle of root beer, while Lincoln had a sub sandwich so massive it required a feat of engineering and all three of the people present to get it up the stairs.

Lincoln and Jonas were both stuntmen she knew from the start of her career. The first time she met them they picked her up and threw her out an open window. Fortunately, cameras were rolling and everything they did was in the script. They had been so reluctant to throw the "frail little girl" out the window that she had been forced to throw herself out first to show them she could handle it. After that, they were so willing to cause damage to her that many directors thought they had a vendetta against her.

Paul "Pluto" Kan, Kim's capoeira instructor, showed up as Lincoln starting cutting his sandwich. Pluto was a whippet thin Asian man, with hair shaved closed to his scalp. He greeted Kim with a crushing hug and slapped Lincoln's shoulder hard enough to knock him off balance. Break was the last to arrive, and he greeted his fellow players with "manly hugs," complete with back patting hard enough to break lesser men's bones.

"Come on, girls," Kim said. "Stop feeling each other up and let's play cards."

She took her seat by the window, well aware that the setting sun would shine into the window behind her and blind the men across the table. Her house, her rules. She shuffled the cards and said, "All right, boys. Break, you haven't been with us in a while, but the rules are the same. Five dollar minimum bet. Cash on the barrelhead, no IOUs, no cars or wristwatches as collateral."

"I don't know if I'd be comfortable carrying all that cash home, Kim," Break said. "I'd prefer if you just gave me your Jeep to settle up."

Kim found the cigar he'd given her earlier in the week and stuck it in her mouth, biting down on the end. "We'll see, Big Talk."

"Thought you quit smoking."

"I'm not going to light it," Kim said. "I'm just going to keep this big phallic thing in my mouth, run my tongue around it a bit... maybe suck on it a little." She popped her lips around the end and eyed the guys at the table, all of whom were staring at her mouth. She smiled, raised an eyebrow, and rapped the cards against the table. "Let's play, boys."

Kim, Break and Jonas were having a standoff, staring each other down over a pot that had grown to fifty bucks in the past ten minutes. Pluto was leaning back in his chair, arms crossed and his eyes darting from one player to another as they measured each other. Lincoln eventually got up and went into the kitchen, returning with another part of the sandwich in his hand. He stayed away from the table, lest anyone think he was cheating, and happened to glance down at the coffee table and stopped to pick up a DVD case.

"Hey, I worked on this."

Kim glanced over and saw he was holding *King of Thieves*. "Oh, yeah?" she said, feigning disinterest.

"Yeah. Some guy breaks into a house, scares the owner to death, and then screws the daughter. It's pretty good."

"What did you do on it?" Jonas asked, still examining his cards.

"All the robbery stuff. Running across this big mansion's lawn, sneaking through the house in the dark." He shrugged and sat down. "You should've seen the lead actress, though." He whistled and shook his head. "Hot little nightgown, clinging in all the right places."

Kim tossed a few more chips onto the pile. She hoped the sound would throw off Lincoln's train of thought and he would drop the subject. "Check."

"Call," Jonas said. "Show 'em."

Break lay down his cards, spreading them across the table in a wide fan. "And the money goes... straight to the king." He smirked.

"Hell," Jonas said, and dropped his cards.

Kim looked down at her cards, spread them in a wider fan and lay them on the table. "Sorry, your majesty. Queen-high flush."

"Screw me sideways." Break tossed his cards down and laced his fingers at the back of his neck. He stretched, grunted, and said, "Well, that about does it for my gambling budget. I think I'm going to have to skip out."

"Ditto," Jonas said as he pushed away from the table. "It's been a very expensive education in how much I still suck at this game."

Break stood up and nodded at the *King of Thieves* DVD as he took out his wallet. "We're working with that actress now. Marisa Larkin, right?"

"Yeah. What's she doing now?"

"TV show. *Neutral Ground.* She plays a spy, Kim doubles for her."

Lincoln said, "Nice. Hopefully it's on one of the pay channels so she can keep on showing her assets."

"Hey, Lincoln," Kim said as she took three twenties from Pluto. "Why don't you try shutting up?"

Lincoln snorted. "Please. Am I offending your delicate feminine sensibilities? The way you talk about the actresses you work with–"

"I said shut up. All right?" She took a hundred from Break and said, "Marisa's a friend. I don't want you talking about her like that."

Lincoln held his hands out in surrender and nodded at the money in her hand. "I'll have to settle up with you next week."

"No problem."

The men started to file out, leaving Break and Kim alone in the apartment. He offered to help her put the furniture back in place, and she gratefully accepted the offer. As they carried the table toward the kitchen, Break said, "Since when are you and Marisa Larkin friends?"

"What? I don't know. She, uh, she invited me to some party tomorrow."

"She invited pretty much everyone on set to that party. It's not like it's going to be some intimate dinner with just the two of you. And you know she has a boyfriend, right? They live together. Have for, like, five years."

"Wow, that's in-depth, Break. Looks like I'm not the only one obsessed with her."

"I Google the people I work with. Sue me. You should see some of the pictures on her Instagram." He whistled and shook his head. "Besides, you were outta line. You can't get bent out of shape when someone says something you yourself have said in the past."

Kim sighed. "I know, I know. It's different with Marisa. I like her."

"Like her, or *like*-like her?"

"What is this, fifth grade? I feel protective of her, that's all."

Break snickered and said, "All right, fair enough." He moved her couch back into place and said, "You're going to give me a chance to win my money back next week. Now that we work together on a regular basis, I'm going to figure out all your tells and then we'll see who rules this game."

"Keep telling yourself that," Kim said. "In the meantime, I'll enjoy spending your money. Thanks for helping me clean up."

"You gonna eat the rest of Link's sandwich?"

"No, please. Get it out of here."

Break went into the kitchen and returned with the remains of the sub wrapped in plastic. "Next week. Go to the ATM, because I don't take checks."

She escorted him to the stairs and shut the door behind him. It was late, but she didn't feel like going to bed just yet. She went to the bedroom and retrieved her laptop, setting up with it in the window seat. She looked down at the street as it booted up. She saw Break on the corner, holding his sandwich under his arm like a newspaper. He stood framed in the streetlight for a moment before hurrying across the street.

She knew Break was right; Lincoln's comments about Marisa were tame compared to some of the conversations they'd had in the past. Comparing various actresses on "faking it" technique, mocking lackluster love scenes and playing "spot the boob job." But she couldn't stand someone doing the same thing to Marisa. She wouldn't stand for it in her house.

"You're definitely off the deep end," she muttered to herself. She took Break's advice and got online, using Google to search for Marisa. She didn't even glance at social media. That seemed like a can of worms she was nowhere near ready to open yet. Google alone had over three hundred thousand results, including a few fan sites and biographical entries that she was sure just rehashed the same information over and over. She clicked on the Wikipedia entry.

The picture used for her entry was nothing special; Marisa on some studio back lot, the collar of a coat turned up to her cheeks, smiling into the camera. The wind was blowing her hair across her eyes, and one hand was raised in the process of brushing it aside. Kim smiled at the photo; it was so candid, so real, and so different from the polished glamour shot she expected to find. She finally tore herself away from the picture to read the biographical information.

Irish and Greek heritage, not bad. Explained her dark features.

She was actually two years younger than Kim, which she hadn't expected. Her first role was at the tender age of sixteen in an episode of a science fiction show, where she played a "precocious alien ruler." After that, she landed two or three roles a year, eventually gaining roles with names. At the bottom of the biographical information was a line that made Kim cringe: "She currently lives with Andrew Close, her boyfriend of several years."

Kim clicked on the boyfriend's name and went to his page. He was also an actor, and seemed to have cornered the market on badass roles. Pretty much every locally-filmed cop or crime show of the past eight years was listed on his credits, always assigning him names like Mr. Pierce, Colonel McBride, Marcos, and identifiers like Gunman and Guard. His picture was nothing special; a strong chin, close-set eyes, and brown hair cut extremely short. His eyes were ice blue and seemed to be looking out of the computer straight at Kim, measuring her. His smile was almost condescending. "Sorry, you were a little too late. Better luck next time."

She did another Google search, this time for Marisa and Andrew together. She found a handful of pictures from movie openings and award shows. Marisa was dynamite, every dress accentuating her many fine features, done up like a princess and smiling as the flashbulbs blinded her. Andrew was always with her, always standing to one side while his lovely partner was adored. He generally wore black suits, fashionably cut, never the same one twice. Marisa was almost always holding his hand.

Hand holding was nothing. And in a lot of the pictures, Andrew had two fingers hooked around Marisa's thumb as she was half-turned away from him. But still, the intimacy of their hands linked that way was hard to look at.

She finally shut down the computer without succumbing to the desire to look for the other pictures Break mentioned. She put the laptop away and turned out the lights, stuck her winnings in a cookie jar to fund next week's game, and went to bed early.

## CHAPTER TWELVE

ON SATURDAY morning, a messenger delivered the script for the next episode of *Neutral Ground* and Kim spent most of the afternoon going over it. No matter how hard she tried to distract herself, however, she kept glancing at the clock and counting down the minutes until the party. The second episode of the series would be relatively stunt-light. The terrorist leader Trujillo had been caught, and the majority of the episode was spent with Lethe and Temple debating who would have the honor of taking custody of him. Their agreement to work together apparently didn't extend to their bosses.

The only big stunt came when Trujillo attempted to escape CIA custody. Lethe and a bevy of soldiers would attempt to cut him off, and Lethe would be blown off her feet by a grenade blast. Kim made some notes in the margin, trying to decide how she would pull it off. It all depended on the director, and how big he wanted the explosion to be. She checked the cover and saw that the second episode would be directed by Solomon Thomas. He was a famous "dialogue" director, and his productions didn't have much in the way of action. Made sense, considering the content of the story.

She leaned back and stretched, looking at the script. Depending on how big they went, she could just walk Marisa through the stunt and let her do it herself. It would probably be a one day job, in and out. She would have to see if anyone else needed a stunt person over the next week, just to fill up her day. Directors were always on the lookout for extras they could throw to the sharks.

An hour before the party was set to begin Kim abandoned work for a quick shower and examined the items in her closet. She wasn't sure how formal the party was going to be, but it was her first party at a celebrity's house. She felt the need to dress up a little. She finally chose a black dress and a long white blouse, leaving the top two buttons undone. She put on her mother's emerald necklace, and actually applied just a touch of makeup.

She refused to do anything fancy with her hair, but she left it down around her shoulders for a change. She stepped back and examined herself, rolling the sleeves of her blouse up to the elbows and decided she looked decent enough to pass for a celebrity. She picked up the DVD of *King of Thieves* on her way out the door and went to the counter to turn it in. Mabel glanced up from the computer as Kim approached, finished what she was doing, and held out her hand for the movie.

"Hey, Mabel. Listen... the other day..."

"Don't worry about it, it's fine. I shouldn't have been pressuring you so much. Served me right." She took Kim's hand and patted the back of it. "You're such a pretty girl. And oh, so pretty today! Do you maybe finally have a date?"

"Uh, no. Just a party tonight. But hey, maybe I'll meet someone."

Mabel kissed her fingers and flicked them at the ceiling. "From your lips, honey, to His ears! You have a good time tonight. Don't even worry about coming in late. I won't make a peep about it."

"I'm going to hold you to that, Mabel. Have a good night."

"You too," Mabel called, using the fingers of both hands to wave goodbye as Kim left the store. The party was set to begin at six; she had twenty five minutes to get across town and locate Marisa's house. Of course, she didn't want to be the first person to arrive; that would just look desperate. First, she drove to the bookstores she passed on her jogging route. Something Marisa had said stuck in her mind, and she wanted to check it out.

The bookstore was somber and well-lit, with a myriad of workers in bright blue shirts moving around the shelves like worker bees. She flagged one down and said, "I'm looking for... I think it's a series of books. They would be about a, um, CIA agent named Lethe working with an FBI agent named Templeton..."

"The Temple series." The kid turned and pointed. "They're shelved under K, for Rebecca Kenny. Let me know if you need anything else." He then hurried off and disappeared down another aisle.

Kim found the Kenny books, and was surprised to see how many there were. They all incorporated the word "Temple" into their titles. She hoped the die-hard fans didn't mind their hero sharing time with a permanent partner. She scanned the titles and picked one of the books at random. *The Body Temple* had a nice ring to it; the cover showed a stretch of desolate tundra, an all-terrain vehicle parked on a slope. The truck's windscreen was shattered by what looked to be a bullet hole, and blood was pooled on the snow next to the driver's door. She flipped the book open and scanned a few pages, her eyes catching on a specific scene near the beginning.

*"I told you in Vienna," Simone said, eyes on the road, jaw tight. "It's not my fault you didn't pay attention. Or maybe you just blocked it."*

*"I didn't block it," Temple said. "I just thought you were teasing me."*

*There was a hint of a smile on Simone's lips, but she said nothing.*

*Temple looked at the woman sleeping in the backseat. "So how long were the two of you together?"*

*"We weren't exactly together. It was more of an informal arrangement we had." She looked in the rearview mirror as she merged.*

*"So when did the 'informal arrangement' begin?"*

*"From the time we first slept together, until the time she went MIA, it was about seven years."*

Kim frowned. 'Together' couldn't mean... She flipped back to the front of the book. She found a scene with Simone wrapped in a "sheet that kept falling off her shoulder, revealing a bit more of the agent than Temple had ever expected to see."

*"Her name is Ophelia Wing. She's spent the last decade as a prisoner in a Russian gulag."*

*"Quite the 'welcome home' you're giving her."*

*"We were lovers," Simone said, refusing to look at Temple. "I thought she was dead."*

*Temple stuttered, "Lovers?"*

Kim said, "My thoughts exactly, Templeton." Another rewind, flipping further back.

*Simone slowly ran her hand over the curve of Ophelia's hip, drawing her fingertips along the pale skin. Ophelia kissed Simone's brow and whispered, "I have missed you so much, my love." Simone closed her eyes and a tear fell from her cheek, falling and tracing a path along the curve of*

*Ophelia's naked breast.*

Kim stared at the book in disbelief. She thought watching the sex scene in the movies was bad. If anyone expected her to watch *this*... well, she probably would. But she would prefer to see it in the privacy of her own home, not from the sidelines in the shadows of a studio. She closed the book and stared at the deceptively innocent cover.

"Great," she muttered. "Just the image I needed in my head before spending the evening with Marisa and her boyfriend." She checked the price of the book, shrugged, and went to the counter to pay for it.

Marisa's house was part of a sprawling development, most of the houses standing at the back of emerald-green manicured lawns fronted by security fences. Japanese lanterns lined Marisa's driveway, already lit with a dull blue glow despite the fact the sun was still up. Kim had to park in front of the neighbor's house, hoping they weren't the kind to call for a tow, and walked up the driveway. She could hear the music as she approached, coming through the open front door and from the back of the house.

She got to the porch and no one appeared to greet her. She knocked on the door frame and Andrew Close peered around the corner. She was irritated to see he was even more handsome in person. His hair was slightly mussed, and he wore a dress shirt open at the collar. She could see why he was always cast as bad guys and military officers; he was built better than the house. "Hi, there. Are you here for the party?"

"Uh, yeah... Kim Greer. Marisa~"

Andrew's eyes brightened and he smiled. "Oh, yeah, Kim. She mentioned you. Come on in." He stepped aside and ushered her into the house. The foyer led directly into the kitchen, relying on ambient light from the living room.

Kim fought back the schoolgirl excitement his comment stoked. *She mentioned me? She's talked about me?* She took off her jacket and he took it from her, hanging it on a row of hangers next to the door.

"I'm Andrew."

"She's mentioned you, too." She took his hand and squeezed.

"Oh. Quite a grip..."

Kim smiled. "Hazards of the job."

Andrew moved into the kitchen and motioned for her to

follow him. "Yeah, stunt double, right? Keeping her from all that dangerous stuff. I owe you a drink for that alone."

"Really? Marisa promised a car."

"Sounds like her," Andrew said with a laugh.

The wall over the sink was a window looking out onto the backyard, although the view was almost entirely hidden behind potted plants. Recessed lighting gleamed off the appliances and fixtures, close to blinding her. Andrew stopped at the counter and picked up a bowl of chips, twisting to hand it to Kim. "Mind helping me carry? I'm not much of a pack mule."

"No, happy to help." She looked past the counter into the living room. She recognized half the partiers from work, the other half from prime time. She had even doubled for a few of the women present. Kim ignored them and focused on the house itself. *This is where Marisa goes at the end of the day. This is where she sleeps and eats.* Andrew held up a bottle of beer and she accepted it, trying not to stare daggers at him. *This is where she makes love.*

The fireplace had a façade of stone, flanked on either side by bookshelves. There were actual books on the left side, but the right was filled with DVDs and framed photographs. The furniture was pushed to the extremes of the room, and every seat was occupied. Kim stayed with Andrew, attached at the hip as they weaved through the crowd. She couldn't help feeling like she was an intruder, like she should be wearing a tuxedo and offering hors d'oeuvres.

"So where is Marisa?"

"Mingling," Andrew said. "She's a social butterfly and I'm stuck playing waiter. But that's no reason to condemn you to the same fate. Go on, I'll catch up with you later."

Kim handed the chips to him and looked for an out of the way spot to be a wallflower. Her plan was to say hello to Marisa, make an appearance for appearance sake, and then duck out as early as possible. She didn't belong in this place, and everywhere she looked reminded her of that fact. Her entire apartment would probably fit in the living room. Hell, it would fit in the pool she could see through the floor-to-ceiling blinds on the sliding back door.

She retreated and found the base of the stairs, stretching up to a loft on the second floor. The refreshment table blocked the stairs and Kim scanned the food available.

"Hey, you made it."

Kim's heart jumped, partly in surprise and partly because of the voice's owner. She turned and saw Marisa coming toward her. She was ravishing. She wore a sleeveless white turtleneck and matching slacks, her hair pulled back in a ponytail.

"Looks like it was your turn to catch me off-guard," Kim said, trying to sound calm over the fluttering of her heart.

Marisa placed her hand on Kim's shoulder to hold her still as she looked her over. "Wow. You clean up well, Kim Greer. I almost didn't recognize you."

"What gave me away?"

"The boots. I love those buckles."

Kim looked down and said, "Ah, well. I'm a slave to fashion."

Marisa grinned. "I'm really glad you made it. Have you had a chance to mingle?"

"Um... yeah. Not really my crowd, though. I'm not sure..."

"Oh, come on." Marisa said. She slipped her arm around Kim's and pulled her close. "They're just regular people. I'm sure you've probably worked with them all at one point or another."

"Yeah, well... working with them and partying with them..."

Marisa smiled and Kim had to look away. She hadn't seen Marisa in two days, but that was enough time to idealize the memory of her. Now, seeing her in person again, the juxtaposition of the fantasy and reality was enough to make her head swim. And, damn, could she be even more beautiful than she remembered? Had her eyes always been so intensely blue? Marisa waved to someone across the room and said, "Hey, I've never thought to ask. Are you single?"

Kim was thrown by the question, but Marisa continued before she had a chance to answer.

"Andrew invited Matthew, this guy he used to work with on *No World's Fair*. He's an actor, but don't hold that against him. He's actually pretty smart. He learned Russian for a role he had a couple of years ago. I'll try to find him..." She started to step away.

Kim reached out, resting her hand on Marisa's wrist. "Marisa... it's okay. I'm not really looking to get hooked up tonight." She let her hand linger, feeling the warmth of Marisa's skin before she finally pulled her hand away.

Marisa said, "Are you sure?"

"Yeah," Kim said. "Thank you, though. I appreciate it."

Marisa smiled and said, "I'm just trying to look out for you. You need someone at home worrying about you like Andrew worries for me."

*I'd worry about you*, Kim thought. She took a drink and said, "Well, I have my aunt. She looks out for me."

"That's great," Marisa said. "Family is..." Someone called her name and Marisa turned away. "Ah, hell. Look, I don't want to abandon you, but..."

"No, please, go," Kim said. "I'll be fine here."

Marisa was already making her way across the room. "I'll come find you later, I promise. Have fun. Mingle. Look for Matthew!"

Kim gave the thumbs up, but she had no intention of being set up with an actor. Not just because he was the wrong gender, but actors always rubbed her the wrong way. There was something phony about everything they did. A person who spent the day wearing someone else's clothes, saying words written by someone else, and answering to a different name was not to be trusted with her heart.

*So why are you so head over heels for Marisa?*

She sighed and swirled the beer in her bottle. "Because I am a very, very stupid woman."

## Chapter Thirteen

THE BEER Andrew gave her was good, imported, but Kim would still have preferred her store-bought brand. She let the bottle dangle from two fingers as she wandered the party. A few people smiled at her, people she'd worked with nodded and acknowledged her presence, but none of them tried to draw her into their conversations. Not that she wanted them to; she would have been absolutely lost in whatever topics they wanted to discuss. Unless, of course, they happened to talk about capoeira or poker, but she somehow doubted it. She made a few circuits of the living room before she decided to hide out on the deck.

The sun had finally gone down, and the shadows proved inviting hiding places. A few partiers had taken off their shoes and rolled up their pants legs to let their feet dangle in the water. The pool was lit from within, and the water sparkled in the dying light of day like some precious jewel. The back yard beyond the deck looked like a miniature park, with rose bushes that were too perfect not to be the result of a loving gardener. There was even a cozy-looking guest house, dark and curtained against anyone who decided to snoop.

Kim found a chaise lounge on the far side of the pool and sat on the edge, leaning forward with her elbows on her knees. She had a clear view of the party through the back door, and Marisa crossed into her field of vision. God, she was radiant. She was speaking to someone on the couch, her right hand clasping her left elbow as she shifted her weight to the opposite foot. She tilted her head as she listened to whoever she was talking to, and then her face broke into a smile. Kim took a sip of beer, aware that she was staring but unable to stop. *See this line? The other side of that line is stalker. You're close enough to make the leap, you know.*

Andrew came up next to Marisa and put his hand on the small of her back. Kim's eyes burned at the sight. He bent down and whispered something to her, Marisa's hair brushing his face. Kim closed her eyes. He was breathing in her perfume, and his breath was washing over her ear, her neck. Was it making her shiver? She opened her eyes and saw Marisa looking at her. She pointed, waved, and then said something to Andrew.

"Shit," Kim muttered. She stood, and Andrew came outside. She forced a smile. "Hey, Andrew. Uh, I was just..."

"No, it's fine," he said. "The pool area is open. Obviously." He gestured at the people around them. "I was just trying to figure out where you disappeared to. One of the guys I worked with on *No World's Fair* is~"

Kim shook her head. "Marisa told me. I'm not really interested. Sorry."

"Oh... she did." He smiled sheepishly. "Sorry. It's just that Mare told me about you, and how great you were. And Matt's been single for a really long time. I just thought it might be nice if the two of you could, you know, maybe keep each other company."

Kim shrugged. "Sorry. I am single, I'm just... not in the market at the moment." She looked toward the back door and saw Marisa had slipped away again.

Andrew nodded. "I understand. And so will Matty." He looked at the pool and said, "Look, I'll leave you alone. No more pestering. This isn't like a timeshare thing, we invite you to a party and then try to sell you one of our friends."

Kim laughed. "Well, if that's the worst thing that happens tonight, I'll be thrilled."

"Try and have a good time." He started for the door, but stopped at the edge of the pool. "And tell Marisa where you bought those boots. She won't shut up about them."

Kim said, "That secret dies with me."

"Now I have to go tell her I failed. Thanks for nothing." He smiled and went back inside.

Kim watched him go, and her smile faded. She wanted to hate

him. More than that, she wanted to steal his girlfriend. It would be so much harder to do either of those things if he insisted on being a good guy.

Kim decided a half hour was a perfect showing, and went back into the house to say her goodbyes. She spotted Andrew in the kitchen and made her way over. "Hey. I wanted to thank you for inviting me. I had a great time."

He frowned. "You're not going, are you?"

"Yeah, you know what they say. Always leave 'em wanting more."

"At least hang out until Marisa reappears. She would literally murder me if I let you go without saying goodbye."

Kim acquiesced. "Okay, then you'll have to point me toward the little girls' room."

Andrew smiled and said, "Um... the downstairs one had a line wrapping around the outside of the house last time I looked." He glanced toward the stairs and said, "Come with me." He went around the counter and put his hand in the small of her back, guiding her through the crowd to the stairs. He walked halfway up with her and pointed. "Go through those double doors, and the bathroom is against the back wall."

"Thanks."

"No problem. Just, if you look in the medicine cabinet, the Rogaine is Marisa's." He winked and gestured at the party. "I'll see if I can track her down for a farewell."

Kim reluctantly went up the stairs unescorted. The upstairs hallway was unlit, relying on ambient light from the living room. She went through the doors Andrew indicated and found a cozy media room. The back wall was filled with books, and a huge flat screen TV hung on the wall opposite the shelves. The wall straight ahead had a door she assumed led to the bathroom, and a pair of French doors hidden behind curtains. Kim continued on into the bathroom, resisting the urge to peek into the medicine cabinet as she went past.

When she finished, she washed her hands and dried them on an embroidered towel. When she went back into the media room, she noticed the French doors were now open. She moved closer and peered out onto the balcony. Marisa was standing in the shadows, lit from below by the pool, with a bottle of beer in her hands. She was looking out past the stone wall that ringed the property to the lights of the city in the distance.

"Hey," she said, knocking one knuckle against the open door.

Marisa turned. "Hey. Drew told me you were looking for me."

"Yeah. I wanted to thank you for inviting me. I had a really nice time."

"It was my pleasure. Do you have to leave right now? I mean, it would be a shame to say goodbye now that we can actually talk to each other."

Kim stepped out onto the balcony. "I guess I could stay awhile." She went to the railing and looked down at the pool. "You guys have a lot of friends."

"A lot of contacts and coworkers," Marisa said. "I love them. Most of them. But I'm not sure I'd call them friends." She smiled. "I'm not much of a party person. I like to pretend I am, all through the planning phase, but when the big day finally shows up?" She shrugged and gestured at the balcony. "I run away and hide until everyone goes home."

"I've been there. Born wallflower."

Marisa toasted her bottle. "Hear, hear. The need to socialize overwhelms the fear of actually making conversation. But you had a nice time?"

Kim smiled, shrugged, and said, "Eh."

Marisa laughed. "I'm really glad you came. I was worried you wouldn't show up, and the whole night would be shot."

"Oh, yeah, I'm the glue that held this thing together."

"For me, you are," Marisa said. "You were the only person I was looking forward to seeing tonight. So, of course, we only got to spend about five minutes together."

Kim was shocked by the emotions that admission caused for her. She looked down at her hands, focused on the glittering of the water in the pool, tried to eavesdrop on conversations below. "Well, I'm glad I came, then." She looked at her watch. "You know, if you're not interested in going back downstairs, I could sneak you out of here."

Marisa gripped Kim's arm. "Don't tease me, woman."

Kim tried to steady her thoughts. "I haven't had dinner yet. If you want, we could sneak out and get some food."

Marisa put her beer down on the balcony. "Let's do it. I just need to get some things from the bedroom. Stay here, all right?" Kim nodded and Marisa smiled as she went back into the house. Kim watched her go with a smile on her face, and then turned and looked out over the city. Her heart was pounding, her hands were sweaty, and she wasn't entirely sure why. It was just a dinner. But it was dinner with Marisa. They were leaving the confines of work and home and going out into the world together. That had to be meaningful, right?

"Okay, ready." Marisa returned with a lightweight coat over her turtleneck, her hair tucked under a baseball cap, and a pair of horn-rimmed eyeglasses in her hand. "My disguise," she explained. "Come on. Hopefully we can sneak out before anyone spots me." She reached out and took Kim's hand, pulling her off the balcony and into the media room.

Kim followed Marisa down the stairs, straight to the kitchen. They managed to get outside to the front walk before Andrew appeared at the door. "Hey, Risa. What's up?"

They turned, and Marisa said, "Kim had something she wanted to show me in her car. I'll be right back."

Andrew glanced at Kim and nodded. "All right. I'll hold down the fort until you get back." He waved to them and went back inside.

"He's cool with you sneaking out?"

"He knows me well enough by now," Marisa said. "He expects this kind of thing. Come on. We've got about an hour."

Kim led the way across the lawn to her Jeep. She unlocked it using the key fob, and Marisa climbed in as Kim went around to the driver's side. As Kim slipped behind the wheel, she saw Marisa holding the bag from the bookstore. "Oh. Uh..."

"Doing a little research?" Marisa asked, holding up the novel.

"Yeah. Seeing what stunts I may have to pull off in the future."

Marisa thumbed through the book, hopefully too quickly to actually read any of the content. "I'm trying to force myself not to re-read the books. I know the Simone of the series will be a different character, so I don't want to muddy the waters. She's just a recurring character in the books. Temple is the main guy. I don't need to know that much about Temple, sorry."

Kim smiled. "So where do you want to go?"

"Well, there is one place kind of nearby. It's a little posh, so you might not like it."

"I'm willing to try anything once."

Marisa arched an eyebrow and said, "Well, then. Drive on, Jeeves. I'll give you directions as we go."

## CHAPTER FOURTEEN

"SO THIS is where the rich and famous go to eat," Kim said, looking over the crowd.

"Best kept secret of the elite." Marisa had her fingers stuck in the pockets of her pants, bouncing on the balls of her feet as she scanned the menu above the counter. The air was thick with the sounds and smells of spattering grease. The shop was small and cramped, but Marisa assured her the ambiance was not the appeal of the restaurant. Kim didn't doubt her. They stepped up to the counter and Marisa said, "Give me an steak burger, with Swiss, and mushrooms." She turned to face Kim, gesturing for her to order.

Kim couldn't make heads or tails of the menu, so she shrugged. "Uh, give me the same."

Marisa chuckled at Kim's expression. "Don't even start. I'll do an extra ten reps of everything tomorrow. This place is a guilty pleasure. Sue me."

"Just pay for my angioplasty and we'll call it even."

Despite Marisa's baseball cap and glasses, a few of the customers still nudged each other and nodded toward her. Kim caught one person surreptitiously using a cell phone to snap a picture. Kim felt offended in Marisa's place, as she didn't seem to notice or care.

When their burgers arrived, wrapped in butcher paper smeared with grease, Marisa paid and nodded toward the back of the café.

She picked up two bottles of soda from a cooler, and then led the way through a door that led out onto a wide boardwalk. Kim suddenly saw the appeal of the restaurant; the harbor spread out in front of them like a shining carpet, still and beautiful, reflecting the night sky perfectly. Music was playing through speakers set above the door, and Marisa guided Kim to the far side of the boardwalk as a singer Kim couldn't identify serenaded them. They found a table near the railing and claimed it for themselves.

"I love this place. Andrew thinks it's a sign of the fall of Western civilization."

"I think I may have to side with your boyfriend on that one," Kim said, examining her sandwich. She caught the disappointed look on Marisa's face and quickly added, "But the view is quickly changing my mind."

Marisa looked over the railing and smiled. "The water is the best part. I'd gladly eat at any restaurant that had a view like this. And if you don't like the food, they have salads..."

"Oh, please. I was just giving you a hard time." She took a big bite of her sandwich, chewed it carefully, and swallowed. "Screw rabbit food. Give me a steak drowning in sauce and shut your mouth about whether it's 'healthy' or not. Odds are, next week, they'll have a recall because there's E. coli in the lettuce and you're doomed anyway."

"Right on." Marisa held out her hand, and Kim slapped it. "But like I said, I have to really attack my exercises tomorrow to make up for it. But if it doesn't make you feel a little bit guilty, what's the point?"

Kim smiled. "Oh, wait. I see what it is. You only brought me here to fatten me up alongside you so I can keep being your double."

"No, but that is a good idea. 'I have to eat it, Andrew, my stunt double has turned into quite a porker. I'm doing it for *her*.'"

"I'd be willing to take the bullet, but they would probably just replace me with someone else if that happened."

Marisa said, "Oh, then never mind."

Kim leaned against the railing. "You know, this already beats the party. In terms of company and enjoyment."

"Well, thank you. I think. I mean, I *did* plan that party, you know. But I'll take the compliment as it was intended." She winked. "I just get so fed up, having to put on a smile and play hostess all night. An hour or two, fine. But these parties tend to go on and on without end." She sighed and shrugged. "The curse of partying with celebrities, I guess."

"You're a celebrity, too, you know."

"In name only," Marisa said. "I still feel like a fake most of the time."

Kim raised her eyebrows and looked down at her burger. "Yeah, I know how you feel."

Marisa looked up, looked at Kim for a moment, and then turned to the water. She rested her chin on her hand. "I can never just be me."

"Well, you don't have to impress me."

Marisa smiled sadly. "Well, it's not all about impressing people. But thank you." She shook her head. "And to be honest, I feel very at ease with you. More at ease than I've felt in... a long time." She sat back. "Did you know my name isn't really Marisa?"

Kim blinked. "No. I had no idea."

Marisa shrugged and said, "Yeah. I officially changed it when I was seventeen, not long after I got bit by the acting bug. I was born Mary Prewitt. Larkin was my mother's maiden name, and Marisa was... well, I just thought it was pretty. It's my real name as far as paperwork goes, but sometimes... I just miss Mary."

"I can understand that." She picked at her burger and said, "I've always wondered how actresses could, you know, take off a character when they went home. I mean, you spend all day being someone else. How can you turn that off, and just go home to be yourself?"

"I hide myself a lot anyway," Marisa said.

Kim couldn't look up into her eyes. "That's a shame. You seem like a pretty good person to me."

Marisa smiled and bowed her head in thanks. "How's the burger?"

"It's good."

"And since I seem to be in confession mode... when I said Andrew was relieved to have you doing all those stunts for me?" Kim nodded. "I lied. He's fine with whatever I decide to do. I'm the one who is grateful you're there for me. I am terrified of a lot of things. I'm fine with heights, unless there's a chance I can fall. I can't even go onto the roof of a tall building without having a panic attack. So having you there to take the fall for me is... a relief."

"I'm happy to do it. It's not that hard to fall for you."

Marisa laughed at that, and turned her head. "Flirt."

Kim cleared her throat. "Yeah." She took a bite of her burger and chewed it carefully. Finally, she said, "I'm gay."

Marisa looked up, eyes wide and eyebrows raised.

"I just..." She gestured at the restaurant. "It's not a huge secret or anything. I'm no celebrity. But a few people know, and then if they see pictures of us out together, it might create some gossip. I should have told you before we came here together." She pressed her lips together and looked up to see Marisa was examining her napkins very carefully. "I just wanted to let you know. And you'd opened yourself up to me so much, I just..." She licked her lips. "I probably shouldn't have said anything."

"No," Marisa said quickly. "I'm glad you did. It's just that I never thought about it. It's not a big deal."

"Are you sure? I could leave if~"

"Don't." Marisa took a drink of her coke. She wet her lips with her tongue, shifted in her seat. "You don't have to worry about me telling anyone. If it's a secret, you can trust me with it."

"I know. That's why I told you. And it goes without saying that your real name is..." She mimed locking her lips shut.

Marisa smiled weakly. "Thank you. So. Big night for both of us, huh?"

"Yeah, pretty much."

Marisa checked her watch and groaned. "Okay, Andrew's probably stalled for as long as he can manage. I should probably head back."

Kim nodded. "Okay."

"Thanks for this, Kim. You don't know how long it's been since I could just sit and talk with someone without a bunch of walls going up."

"It was my pleasure."

They had to go back through the restaurant to get to the parking lot, and in their absence, news of Marisa's presence had spread. Every eye followed her through the room, conversations hushing as she moved. Kim hung back, still worried someone might try to connect the two of them in some tabloid scandal. One brave soul actually asked for a picture, and Marisa graciously posed with him while his friend snapped a shot on his cell phone. Marisa made a quick exit then, waving over her shoulder as she made a bee-line for the door.

The Jeep was parked under a streetlight, and it shone through the windshield like a spotlight when they got in. It reminded Kim of her one year in Drama class, trying to explore her artistic side by being an actor. One relatively tiny speaking role in *Fiddler on the Roof* revealed she had no passion for actually acting.

She reached for the ignition, but Marisa touched her hand and said, "Don't go yet."

"Okay." Kim leaned back in the seat and they sat in silence for a long moment. "Want the radio?"

"No. Well. Sure." She took off her sunglasses and hat, shaking her head to let her hair fall. It was mussed, caught in tangles, and it looked beautiful in the low light.

Kim twisted the key and the radio began to play. It was Iron and Wine, one of Kim's favorites, and the music was soothing enough not to disturb their thoughts.

"Have you ever seen anything Andrew was in?"

"Sure," Kim lied, rather than admit looking him and Marisa up on the internet.

"He always plays a badass. The tough guy, the muscle. He's always the imposing villain. You saw him, I mean, he's built for the role."

Kim nodded, biting the inside of her cheek. She put her hands on the wheel, trying to steady her breathing. *If you tell me he hits you, so help me...*

"He has a reputation to protect. He's worried if it got out that he was gay," Kim's eyes snapped open, "he would start losing jobs. It doesn't matter how he looks or how good he acts, he's afraid the director would pass on him because of the stigmata of being... I don't know, too effeminate. Like that makes any sense, given how he looks. So he has protection."

"You're his beard?"

"Uh huh. And he's mine." She kept looking forward, her jaw set and her eyes focused on the street running in front of the restaurant.

"Yours?" She could barely think over the pounding of her heart.

Marisa smiled. "Half of my movies start with the summary 'boy meets girl.'"

"It's called acting."

"It's not that simple. Straight can play gay, but audiences aren't as accepting with gay playing straight. I mean, it happens all the time. Aliens invade the world ever summer, sure, but directors don't think audiences can suspend their disbelief long enough to watch a gay actress playing straight. But I just... it's just easier." She shook her head. "It's just easier living up to expectations."

Kim's heart was beating a hectic rhythm against her ribs. "You're gay. God."

"I'm sorry. This is a lot bigger than telling you my real name. You cannot tell~"

"No, no one," Kim said. "Trust me, I'm not going to tell anyone."

Marisa nodded and looked down at her hands, folded primly in her lap. Kim let the radio play for a while, Sam Beam singing about a passing afternoon, time slipping through an hourglass, how short life was. Kim couldn't get her brain to work right. Everything had been thrown into her lap at once, and now trying to make sense of it was going to drive her insane. Marisa was suddenly gay and single, and how could she possibly ignore the thing she had been hoping for since meeting her.

"Marisa," she swallowed, suddenly nervous, and said, "Do you want to go out sometime? Get some... dinner? I mean, not... not like what we just... I meant..."

Marisa reached out and put her hand on top of Kim's. Kim stared at Marisa's fingers, the back of her hand, and licked her lips. Finally, Marisa said, "Yes. Sure."

A smile didn't seem to do justice to her feelings at that moment, but banging her fist against the top of the Jeep seemed tacky. She smiled, twisted the key in the ignition, and said, "Well. Maybe we can figure out a time when we're both free."

"Yeah," Marisa said. She nodded again, confirming her acceptance, and said, "Yes. I can't wait."

*Neither can I*, Kim said as she backed out of the parking spot.

## CHAPTER FIFTEEN

THE PARTY was still going on when they got back to Marisa's, but a few cars seemed to have disappeared in the time they were gone. Kim parked much closer to the house than she had earlier and leaned back in the seat. Obviously Marisa wasn't ready for their alone time to end, either, and settled into her seat as well. Kim reached down and turned down the radio, and then scanned until she found something quiet enough to not be distracting. They sat in silence, listening to the music, watching silhouettes move past the windows of Marisa's home.

When the song gave way to a disc jockey, Marisa looked at Kim and said, "I didn't want to say anything earlier because... well, because I've learned to bite my tongue. But I wanted to say that you look really beautiful tonight."

Kim actually blushed. "Well, I wanted to make an impression."

"You did." She leaned across the console and put her hand on Kim's left cheek. Kim felt the warmth of her fingers and held her breath as Marisa leaned in and lightly brushed her lips across Kim's cheek. Just a chaste kiss, but the hand... the hand changed everything. It slid up into Kim's hair, briefly cradling the back of her head before it and Marisa retreated. "Thank you for getting me out of there. You're my hero."

"Anything for a damsel in distress."

Marisa smiled and opened the Jeep door. "Do you want to

come in? I think Andrew is half in love with you already."

"Nah. Andrew's not the one I'm trying to woo."

Marisa bit her bottom lip, ducked her chin, and laughed. Kim tried to cover her embarrassment. *Did I just say 'woo'?*

"I'm sorry," Marisa said. "I didn't mean to laugh. That was a very sweet thing to say. I'll keep it in mind." She looked at the house and said with great sincerity, "Thank you for coming to my party."

"It was my pleasure."

Marisa got out of the Jeep and shut the door, waving one more time before she started up the driveway. Kim watched her go and collapsed forward, pillowing her head against her hands on the steering wheel, eyes closed, trying to convince herself that the moment had really just happened. Convinced it had, convinced that her life may have just taken a very dramatic shift to the better, she sat up and started the engine for the ride home.

Kim's dreams were disjointed. Dark rooms at the top of strangely tall staircases, an Iron and Wine song playing as she floated on a tiny boat, and a quiet study where the din of music and conversation faded to one single voice. The dreams were filled with flashes of Marisa, her face and her eyes, the way she smiled and how she laughed. The firm touch of fingertips on her cheek and the fleeting moisture of a stolen kiss on the opposite cheek. The smell of perfume, unnoticed at the moment but vivid in her subconscious.

She woke a few minutes before her alarm went off with a smile on her face, staring up at the ceiling for a moment before she pushed back the blankets and sat up. She rested her arm across her knees and looked out the window. It was Sunday, and the video store downstairs was closed. The silence coming from below was comforting. She pushed her hair out of her face and finally rolled out of bed. She put on shorts and a T-shirt and went into the kitchen for breakfast.

Kim decided at the last minute to skip the cereal and decided to go all out. She chopped up some ham, cracked some eggs, and cooked an omelet. She felt so good that she hummed while she cooked, tapping her bare foot against the tile of the kitchen floor.

She'd asked Marisa Larkin out on a date.

More importantly, Marisa said *yes.*

Kim bit her bottom lip as she flipped the omelet. She

remembered The Crisis when Tina dumped her. Days when she refused to leave her apartment, nights when she never turned on the lights, sitting in the window seat and staring out at the city and wondering how she could go on living. She had finally gotten back on her feet by promising herself a better time was coming. It had finally arrived. A little later than she would have liked, and there was a lot of pain to wade through, but now here she was. Hope was gleaming on the horizon.

She ate her omelet in the window seat, feet crossed at the ankle in front of her, and looked at the night before under the cold glare of reality. It would be a huge undertaking to be in a relationship with Marisa. First of all, combined they still had three out of four feet in the closet. Kim was semi-out, but she could never tell Mabel that she was dating a woman. And she would never threaten the cover Marisa had so carefully set up for herself. They would still have to work together day in and day out. That shouldn't be too difficult; they were both professionals.

The guest house at Marisa's was an option. She could spend some nights there, perfectly normal considering their budding friendship. And after lights out, if Marisa snuck across the lawn for a little rendezvous...

Kim blinked at her reflection in the window. She had spent so much time lusting for Marisa, and so much time celebrating the fact they were finally going to be together, she hadn't stopped to think about the simple fact that they would most likely be having sex sometime in the future.

Sleeping with someone new was always unnerving and awkward. But when that person was Marisa fucking Larkin, there was a whole new level of panic. She looked down at the remains of her omelet and put it aside. She was going to have to start watching what she ate. And jogging more. Not to mention sit ups, push-ups, pull ups... She had the unfortunate benefit of knowing exactly what Marisa looked like naked.

Kim put aside her breakfast and went down the hallway to change into her sweats. Maybe she would spend the rest of the weekend in the gym.

Kim spent most of Sunday working out, training with Pluto, and trying to keep thoughts of Marisa from overwhelming her. It was just a date. They weren't going to jump into bed together on the first date. But considering how much they enjoyed spending time with each other, she knew it was definitely in their future. She didn't know if she could handle that knowledge, so she did her best to bury and block it somewhere deep in her psyche.

She spent Sunday evening blocking the stunt for *Neutral Ground*. It was pretty straightforward; a squib would explode on the wall, and either she or Marisa would be in a harness that her assistants would yank back at just the right moment. She would land on a pad, and the bungee cord would be painted out in post-production. She went to bed and dreamed again, this time putting herself in the nude scenes from Marisa's movies. She decided upon waking that even if she didn't have a perfect body, it was highly doubtful Marisa would point at her and laugh.

On Monday she woke up, still buzzing but not smiling, as she thought about her impending relationship with Marisa. She was due on the set at seven, so she arrived downstairs just as Mabel arrived to open the store. Mabel unlocked the door and said, "Oh, there you are. I didn't see you once yesterday! How was the party on Saturday?" She paused and wagged a finger at Kim. "Oh, I don't even need to ask. You met a man, I know!"

Kim froze, a deer in the headlights. "What?"

Mabel's grin threatened to split her face. "You're glowing, dear, glowing!"

Kim was thrown. "Uh... I-I have to go to work. I'm running a little late."

"Just tell me his name, dear, that's all I need!"

"Matthew," she said, grabbing the first name she thought of. "I really have to go, Auntie Em. I'll tell you all about him later."

Mabel clapped happily as Kim rushed to her Jeep. "Great. Now I guess Marisa will really have to introduce me to Andrew's costar."

She drove to the studio and parked near the makeup trailers. People were already moving about; production companies tended to rise with the sun and fall with the moon. There were only so many hours of daylight to catch the magic hour. Kim hauled her gear from the back of her Jeep and spotted Marisa's Prius on her way to the door. She shook her head at the way her body reacted to the sight. "Yep," she muttered. "Just like high school."

Except this time, she was actually going to get the girl.

Kim unloaded her things and located Solomon Thomas, the director for the episode. Thomas was a meager man, swimming in his fashionable shirt and trousers. The cuffs of his shirt sleeve formed wide rings around small wrists, and his hook nose brought to mind Ichabod Crane. He nodded as she spoke, and then said, "Good, good, that'll be good, let me know when you're good to go." He smiled, folded his hands together, and turned back to the assistant trying to get his attention.

Kim gave a thumbs up to the back of his head and then went in search of her team. She needed a few good men willing to yank her backward a hundred yards.

She was in the middle of the CIA offices when Simone Lethe stepped through the door of an office. Kim smiled at the transformation; the awkwardness of Marisa was gone, replaced by Agent Simone Lethe's firm jaw and all-business stare. She had a script in her hand, focused on her lines, but glanced up when she realized someone was standing in her path. When she recognized Kim, Simone melted away and Marisa returned. "Hey."

"Hi. I wasn't sure if you would... if it would be awkward."

Marisa said, "There's no reason for it to be awkward. Even if I felt weird about telling you what I did, which I don't, I know enough to bury you. Mutually assured destruction."

"Oh. I didn't think of it that way. I should probably call the tabloids and tell them to cancel the story."

Marisa grabbed the collar of Kim's shirt and pulled her forward. "I've crushed smaller women than you, Greer."

Kim tried not to notice how close their faces were. "Sounds like a lot of big talk, Larkin."

Marisa arched an eyebrow. "Want to try me?"

Kim looked down at Marisa's hands, extremely mindful of all the people who could wander through at any moment. She cleared her throat and said, "Ahh... Marisa..."

Marisa released her shirt and took a step back. "I was just thinking the same thing. I'm so sorry."

"Don't be sorry." Kim straightened her blouse and looked around to make sure no one had seen them. "I was just looking for my team. Have you seen any of them? Break?"

"Yeah. Break was working with me and William earlier on the fight scene at the end of the episode. But that reminds me. C'mere." She took Kim's hand and guided her into the office of Simone Lethe's superior. All Kim could think about was the fact that Marisa was holding her hand. Her fingers were hooked around two of Kim's fingers, just like they'd been hooked around Andrew's in the pictures she looked at online.

Marisa closed the door. The office had four walls, but no roof, so they could still hear everything going on outside. An unlit backdrop showed an eerily shadowed parking lot. Marisa turned to face Kim and gestured at the script with her free hand. "You're going to be doing the big stunt today? The grenade thing?"

"If there's time for it. I think Solomon was planning to have it this evening."

Marisa chewed her bottom lip. "Can I tell you I don't want you to do it?"

Kim frowned. "It's my job. I~"

"I'm not asking you not to do it," Marisa interrupted. "I just want to say I don't want you to do it. I want to say I'm scared for you, and I wish you wouldn't, even though I know you will. And I would never honestly ask you not to. I just... want the credit for saying I wish you wouldn't do this dangerous thing."

Kim couldn't stop the smile from rising on her face. "Okay, then. You can say that."

Marisa looked down at Kim's hands, running her thumb over Kim's knuckles. "I spent all day yesterday thinking about our dinner together. It's been a long time since I felt that way just sitting and talking with someone. And now you come to work and get thrown into a wall because I'm too much of a chicken to do it."

"The studio wouldn't let you do it anyway. You're too valuable to them."

"You're valuable to me."

Kim stepped forward and said, "I'm a stuntwoman. This is what I do. I'm trained to do it so I won't be hurt. Well, not badly. Stunt people have a different relationship to pain than most people. If your shoulder is dislocated, you go to the hospital. Me, I set it myself and go on with my day."

"God."

"I know my body, Marisa. You don't have to worry."

"Can I, though? Just a little?" She smiled. "I'm sorry. I felt something when I met you. And it took me until Saturday night to figure out what it was. And now I feel like I'm going to fall apart every time you do something dangerous. I swear to God, I am not this clingy or this pathetic. I'm just..."

"Nervous."

"Yes."

Kim reached up and touched Marisa's cheek. Marisa turned her head into the caress and Kim lost her breath. She licked her lips, already choreographing their first kiss when there was a burst of static. "Larkin?"

"Shit," Marisa said. She pushed away from the desk and Kim took a step back as Marisa pulled the radio from her belt. "Yeah. I'm here, Solomon."

"We need you outside the CIA set, please."

"I'll be right there." She hooked the radio back on her belt and kept her eyes on the floor. "I should get out there."

Kim nodded. "Yeah."

Marisa touched Kim's arm and said, "Thank you for putting my mind at ease."

Kim smiled and said, "Any time. Go. I've heard Solomon has quite a temper."

Marisa said, "What you were about to do..."

"Don't worry about it."

"I was going to say 'hold that thought.'"

Kim pressed her lips together and said, "I'll do that." Marisa slipped past Kim and left the office. Kim looked out the window at the flat landscape, ripples in the fabric running through supposedly solid buildings. "I'll definitely hold that thought, Ms. Larkin."

## CHAPTER SIXTEEN

THEY FILMED three scenes in the hallway before doing the stunt, all of them talking scenes between Simone, Templeton, and a representative from the Department of Defense. In the second scene, it was just Simone and Templeton debating which of them truly had jurisdiction over Trujillo. While they filmed, Kim went to wardrobe and makeup and transformed into Simone herself. The hairdresser had to adjust Kim's hair, since Marisa was wearing it slightly different for this episode.

When she returned to the set, she found Break and he helped her suit up in her harness. Simone was dressed in a white blouse and a gray blazer. The harness went over the shirt, and the wire was attached to the middle of her chest. She had elbow and knee pads, both of which were thin enough to be hidden by the jacket and her slacks.

Kim tested the catches and made sure everything was secure. "Okay, think you can handle it?"

"I don't know. You weigh a lot more than the last time I did this."

Kim swung at him, but Break easily ducked it.

"Everyone ready?" Solomon asked.

Kim led Break onto the set. The wire threaded through a pulley, one end at the junction of the two corridors, the other draped over the top of a ladder. The floor was covered by several thick mats, giving Kim a safe place to land. Solomon said, "Okay, let's run through this a couple of times."

Kim took her position, and Break hooked up the wire. She leaned back, pulling the wire taut and tugging on the catch to make sure it stayed in place. Break went to the ladder, climbed up four steps, and wrapped his hands around the wire. "Ready?" he asked.

"Go on your cue," Kim said. She pressed herself against the corner of the wall, facing away from the ladder. The wire rested comfortably against her side. She raised her right arm, mimed shooting toward the escaping villain, and braced herself for the tug. "Grenade!" she said, and turned. Break leapt from the ladder and landed solidly on his feet. The wire pulled tight, and Kim went off her feet. She swung her arms, as if in freefall, and landed face first on the mat. She skidded a bit, but rolled onto her side and pushed herself up immediately.

"Looked good," Solomon said. "Let's go one more time."

Kim reset, shouted the cue, and Break jumped from the ladder. This time, Kim hadn't quite turned all the way around when the wire yanked her off her feet. She flew almost sideways, arms raised to protect her head, and hit the mat with her shoulder. She tumbled, ended up on her hands and knees, and took a moment to regain her bearings before she stood up.

"You okay?" Break said.

"Fine," Kim said. "That one actually looked a bit more natural. Let's try it again." She adjusted the harness and glanced toward the back of the set. Marisa was standing near one of the cameras, eyes wide and chewing her thumbnail. She smiled nervously when she caught Kim's eye, and Kim nodded. Marisa made her way over and Kim said, "You okay?"

"Am *I* okay? Are you?"

Kim smiled. "I'm fine. I've done this a thousand times before. So has Break. It's fun for me."

"If you say so." She looked Kim up and down. "It's a little weird, talking to you when you're dressed like that."

"Is it a little *Single White Female?*"

Marisa laughed. "Yeah, a little. But not as creepy."

"Good to know. Listen, I have to do a few more pulls before we shoot it..."

"No, go ahead. I don't want to keep you. Just... be safe, all right?"

Kim nodded. "Always." She went back to take her position,

leaning around the corner. She shouted the cue for Break, turned, and saw him leap from the ladder. Kim went flying again and hit the mat with her shoulder.

She rolled onto her back as Break approached, twisting his head to peer down at her.

"S'all right?"

"S'all right," she said, and held out her hand. He grasped it and hauled her to her feet. The director approached and Kim said, "We're all ready to go."

"Excellent." Solomon turned to the crew and clapped his hands twice. "Let's set it up, people."

The cameramen moved into position, and the actor playing Trujillo set up at the far end of the corridor. Kim took her position, now holding a gun loaded with blanks. Solomon said, "Ready... action!"

Trujillo came out of the holding cell and fired twice in Kim's direction. She ducked back, then leaned out and returned fire. Trujillo yanked something from his belt and tossed it underhand down the corridor.

"Grenade!" Kim shouted, and twisted away. A section of the wall exploded, showering her with debris and dust, and Break leapt from the ladder and sent her flying through the air. She hit the mat, rolled, and ended up with the wire wrapped around her waist. She managed to get untangled as the director yelled cut and came onto the set to help Kim to her feet.

"Nice fall."

"Thanks," she said. She brushed herself off and stepped aside as the crew began removing the pads from the floor. Marisa appeared and Kim waved her over. "Do you want my help going over your landing?"

Marisa looked at the pads as they were dragged away. "Maybe the CIA leaves big safety pads lying around in their hallways in the event of an emergency."

Kim smiled. "Come on, you'll be fine. You'll have a back pad, elbow pads, the works. You won't be hurt at all. Promise."

"Well, if you say so."

Kim put a hand on Marisa's arm and guided her around the corner. As they walked, she picked up a back pad and a pair of elbow pads. "Here. You can put these on under your blouse. They'll take the brunt of the blow. I'll make sure no one peeks at you."

Marisa untucked her shirt and said, "Who'll keep *you* from

peeking?"

Kim turned her back and said, "I was raised better than that. Frankly, I'm offended by the implication."

Marisa chuckled and Kim smiled, watching the crew spread concrete dust on the ground that had been covered by the mat. "All you really have to do is jump forward and roll. It's perfectly safe. Not unlike, ah... sliding into second."

"Not big on baseball, really," Marisa said. "Okay, you can turn around."

"The principle is the same." Kim turned as Marisa finished buttoning her blouse. She got a glimpse of her flat stomach crossed by the strap of her back pad. *You've seen her naked; a strip of flesh above her belt shouldn't turn you on this much.* Still, she licked her lips and said, "I could run through it a few times if you want."

Marisa shook her head. "No, I think I can handle it. Thanks for the offer, though."

Kim shrugged and led Marisa back out to the set. Solomon saw her coming and said, "We all ready?"

"Ready as I'll ever be," Marisa said. She closed her eyes as someone applied concrete dust to her back and hair. She went onto the set and stepped onto the apple crate they had put out for her. She crouched slightly, and Solomon moved toward the monitors. "And... action!"

Marisa threw herself forward and hit the ground hard, sliding across the concrete and coming to a stop against the far wall. She scrambled for her gun and brought it up with her left hand, aiming down the corridor. Trujillo didn't appear, so she grabbed the radio off her belt and shouted into it, "Temple, Trujillo is making a break for it! He's coming your way." She got to her feet and raced back to the corner, checking to make sure Trujillo wasn't waiting for her before she gave chase.

"Cut!" Solomon said. He moved forward and said, "All right, let's reset for the Temple scene. Corridor C, right?"

As he crossed the set, Marisa returned, holding her right elbow. Kim approached and said, "What's wrong? Are you all right?"

"Yeah, I just banged up my elbow when I hit the wall. It's fine."

"Break, get me some ice," Kim said. Break disappeared and Kim said, "Take off your jacket. Let me check it out." Marisa shrugged out of her jacket, and twisted at the waist to present her elbow to Kim's examination. Kim took off the pad and gently probed the elbow. "Does that hurt?"

"A little. I think the pad might have rubbed me the wrong way when I fell."

"That would make it my fault."

"Or mine, for falling wrong."

Break appeared with an ice pack. Kim thanked him as she took it and pressed it against Marisa's elbow. Break crossed his arms and said, "Got an injury, huh? We might make you an official stunt person yet."

"Yeah. I get a boo-boo on my arm, and you guys have to call the paramedics. Kim, meanwhile, repeatedly throws herself to the ground and gets right back up. I think I'll leave the heroics to you guys."

"Probably for the best."

Break led the way across the set to where the new scene was being set up. Kim fell into step beside Marisa and said, "You sure you're okay?"

"Oh, yeah. I've gotten worse than this. Thanks for taking care of me, though."

"It's kind of my job," Kim said. "Besides, I have to make sure you survive until you make good on that promise you made me."

"Play your cards right, I might make good on it sooner rather than later."

Kim grinned as they came out on the other corridor set. It was wider than most of the corridors, and built to be transformed into whatever they might need on any given episode. Today, it was the front hallway of the CIA holding facility. Marisa handed the ice pack to Kim, mouthed, "thank you," and went onto the set. William Easter was standing with the actor playing Trujillo, both of them in costume but chatting casually. The director was giving some last minute instruction to the lighting team and clapped his hand on a clipboard. "Everybody here? Everybody ready?"

Trujillo took his position, and William took on the Thomas Templeton persona. He stepped in front of the door, pulled his gun, and rolled his shoulders. Marisa and Trujillo went around the corner, tucked into the shadows of a small alcove. The director yelled action, and Trujillo ran around the corner with a stolen gun held high. Temple stepped forward and shouted, "Stop right there, Trujillo."

The terrorist leader skidded to a stop, obviously torn. He only had two options; recapture or suicide. Suddenly, Simone Lethe came around the corner and gave him a new option. He grabbed her before she could react, moving behind her and pressing the gun to her forehead. Simone struggled and growled, "Oh, you son of a bitch..."

"Let her go," Temple said.

"I think I am the one making demands here, Agent Templeton. You put your weapon down."

"Don't do it, Temple," Simone said.

Temple hesitated, but then held his hands up to show he was giving up. "Can't let him kill you, Lethe."

Trujillo wrapped his hand in Simone's hair, pulling her head back and thrusting the gun under her jaw. "We will take this nice and easily, yes? No one has to get hurt."

"If you get out of here, you're going to kill hundreds of thousands of Americans."

"Show me some respect, Agent Lethe. I will kill millions." He chortled and pushed Simone forward. When they were almost even with Temple, Simone suddenly shifted her weight backward. Trujillo fired - the quiet, anticlimactic pop of a prop gun - and Temple lunged for him as he tumbled off balance. Lethe grabbed his arm and tore the gun from his grip, spinning on one foot and turning the gun on him as Temple wrestled him to the ground.

"You should have taken the shot," Simone said, hair in her face and gun trained on Trujillo as Temple pinned him to the ground.

"I couldn't risk hitting you."

"Sentimentality will get you killed."

Temple rolled his eyes and hauled Trujillo to his feet. "Come on. Let's get you back in your nice, safe cell."

They led him around the corner and, once they were out of sight, Solomon yelled, "Cut, it's good! Excellent work everybody."

Trujillo came back out with his hand on Marisa's shoulder, his head tilted to look at her chin. She said, "You didn't hurt me, Emanuel. It's fine." She smiled, patted him on the back, and broke away from him. William and Emanuel went toward craft services and Kim intercepted Marisa as she crossed the set. "Hey," Marisa said. "Emanuel was worried he cut me with the gun sight. See anything?" She lifted her chin, giving Kim permission to stare at her perfect neck.

"Uh, no. Nothing."

"I told him he was being too sensitive."

"That was quite a fight scene. And you claim you're not a

stuntwoman."

"Please. That was just shifting my weight."

Kim said, "What do you think ninety percent of stunt work is? Shifting your weight at the right time. You did great today."

Marisa smiled. "We have a few more talking scenes to shoot. Lots of fun. Are you going to be here for those?"

"No, probably not. In fact, this might be my only day here this week."

Marisa's expression wavered. "What?"

"No stunts, no need for a stunt coordinator. It's okay; I'll be back for next week's episode."

"Well, I assumed. But, no… I was just thinking that I really missed you last week, and you were only gone for two days. Now it's going to be another week before I see you again."

Kim was touched, almost an embarrassing amount, to hear that Marisa had missed her. "Um… w-well, if you want, we could go ahead and schedule our… thing."

"Our 'thing'?"

Kim shrugged and watched a lighting guy walk past them with a length of wire. She lowered her voice and said, "What do you want? I'm not the secret agent around here."

Marisa chuckled. "I don't know when my days end around here, so I'm not sure when I'll be free. But we can plan for Thursday or Friday. Can I give you a call when things get more firmly decided?"

"Yeah, sure," Kim said. She took out her cell phone and said, "What's your number again?"

Marisa told her, and Kim dialed it. Marisa's phone rang, and she pressed the ignore button. "There. Your number is automatically stored in mine, and you have my number there."

"Very crafty."

"It's the twenty first century," Kim said. "Who needs numbers scrawled on cocktail napkins?" She smiled and slipped the phone back into her pocket.

Marisa said, "I'll definitely give you a call. Thursday or Friday, but… if it has to be Saturday…"

"I'm open all weekend."

Marisa said, "Ah, so I can keep you up all night on Friday and no one will know you're missing until Monday?" She bit her bottom lip, looked Kim up and down, and said, "Good to know."

Kim coughed and sputtered a bit.

Marisa laughed and started to back away. "I'll see you this weekend."

Kim watched Marisa walk back to the set. She blinked, shook her head, and said, "Hopefully I'll be able to put together a coherent sentence by then..." She sighed and went to find Break in the hopes he was up for some sparring to clear her head.

## CHAPTER SEVENTEEN

KIM HUNG around the set until the end of the day, and then loitered in the parking lot for Marisa to show up. A light drizzle had started and Kim stood under the overhang of the studio with her back against the wall as she watched the water cascade off the eaves. The storm had shattered the humid blanket that had been smothering the city, and Kim wanted to enjoy it while she could. She watched as the rain formed puddles on the asphalt and water droplets hung like diamond earrings on the chain link fence.

When Marisa finally came outside, she paused to look at the rain and adjust her jacket. Kim stepped forward and said, "Marisa." Marisa turned and smiled. "Got a minute?"

Marisa put a newspaper over her head, offering mediocre protection from the weather. "Yeah, but~" She nodded toward her Prius.

"Yeah, of course." They rushed to the car and she unlocked the doors with her keychain so they could both duck inside immediately. Kim settled in the passenger seat and they took a moment to shake off the rain. Kim took a moment to revel in the fact that she was in Marisa Larkin's car. She allowed herself a satisfied smirk, letting the feeling grow within her. *Kim Greer gets to go home with the head cheerleader,* she thought. The rain streaked down the windshield and blurred the world around them. It made Kim feel like she was in a reverse aquarium, on display for fish and sea creatures.

"So, uh," she said, focusing on why she needed to talk with Marisa. "I just need you to help me lie a little bit."

Marisa raised her eyebrows. "Sounds fun."

"I'm not out to my aunt, and she said..." She hesitated. "Sh-she said something this morning, and I had to lie about the party the other night. She was sure that I met someone, so I told her that I'd met Matthew and we'd hit it off."

Marisa smiled. "How'd your aunt know you met someone?"

Kim blushed. "Can we focus on my deception, please? I just need some basic info about Matthew so I can get Mabel off my back. What does he look like?"

"Have you ever seen *Sleepwalker?*"

"I actually worked on it last season," Kim said. "I was a stunt double in a few episodes. Which one was Matthew?"

"He plays Doug, the sidekick. Kind of tall, black hair~"

Kim said, "Goatee?"

"Yeah, that's him."

Kim sneered. "You thought *he* was my type?"

Marisa laughed. "Hey, the fact I tried setting you up with a guy shows I am clueless when it comes to stuff like that."

Kim smiled. "Well, I guess I'm stuck with him for now. What does he do for fun?"

"He likes motorcycles, I think. Drew told me that he has an Indian that he restored."

Kim shrugged. "Okay, I can lie my way through a motorcycle conversation. Thanks."

"No problem." Kim started to get out, and Marisa said, "Hey. Do you want to get some dinner?"

Kim was suddenly famished. She looked at her watch to discover it was twenty to eight, and she had skipped lunch. "Now?"

Marisa shrugged. "Got other plans?"

Kim said, "Nothing quite as appealing. I'll follow you somewhere."

"Okay. What are you in the mood for?"

"I don't care. Surprise me."

Marisa said, "Ah, a blank slate. You might want to be careful handing those out to me, Ms. Greer. We'll talk more about your cover story over dinner."

"Sounds great," Kim waved goodbye and shut the car door, jogging back to her Jeep. She saw William Easter and a few of the other actors from the show hovering around the stage door watching the rain. She ducked her head and allowed herself a satisfied smirk. *That's right, jocks. I'm going to dinner with Marisa Larkin. Have fun sitting out in the rain.*

When she got to her car, she looked in the rearview mirror and decided she had a few issues from high school to work out. But that was fine; she could work them out while she was dating the most popular girl in class. She chuckled and waited until the Prius passed behind her before she backed out of the spot and fell in behind her.

The rain picked up after they left Transom Studios, and Kim's windshield wipers worked overtime to keep Marisa's car in view. The streetlights were reflected off the flooded gutters, and every car's taillights looked bejeweled. Lights were surrounded by halos, making them look ethereal as she passed underneath them, moving carefully through the traffic toward the edge of town. Fifteen minutes after leaving the studio, Kim realized where Marisa was leading her.

Marisa pulled into the driveway of her own house, parking near the front door. Kim parked behind her and reached into the backseat, groping around for an umbrella. She found it, jumped from the car, and hurried to Marisa's door. She opened the umbrella and held it out as Marisa stepped from the car.

"Well, thank you. I may have to keep you around." They walked to the door huddled together under the umbrella. "I called Andrew, and he's out of town until tomorrow night. I thought this might be a nice alternative to spending the night alone. You don't mind, do you?"

"Are you kidding me?" Kim said. "This is the most exclusive restaurant in town."

Marisa laughed as she unlocked the door. "Yeah, it's all in who you know." She pushed the door open and led Kim into the dark entry hall.

The kitchen light helped illuminate part of the living room. A security light in the backyard cast strange shadows across the furniture as Marisa took a dishtowel to her hair. "Make yourself at home. I'm going to go change into some drier clothes." She turned on the living room lights as she passed, and pointed at the bookshelf on her way upstairs. "The stereo is right there. You can find us some music."

"Okay," Kim said. She heard a door close upstairs and then she was absolutely alone in Marisa's living room. It was exactly what she'd been wishing for at the party, but now that she was actually here, she found it a little uncomfortable. But she was always uncomfortable when left alone in a stranger's home, so that wasn't anything new. She walked to the stereo and scanned Marisa's CD collection, letting her fingers brush over the titles until she found a Radiation Canary album.

She put the CD in the machine, pressed play, and wandered to the French doors. The pool looked spectacular in the rain, and she watched its surface ripple and sway under the deluge from above. After a few minutes, she heard the door upstairs open and turned to see Marisa coming down the stairs. She was dressed in a tight blue T-shirt with "rockstar" written across the chest and a pair of baggy sweatpants. Her feet were bare, and she had exchanged her contact lenses for a pair of Buddy Holly eyeglasses. A fluffy robe was draped over her arm, and she gestured at Kim with it as she crossed the living room to her.

"I thought you might want to change, too. We can throw your clothes in the dryer while we eat, if you'd like."

"Uh, thanks." She took the robe and ran her fingers over the smooth material. "You, uh... you look..."

Marisa smiled. "Yeah, sorry. You go home with a movie star and end up with Stephanie Urkel."

"No. I was going to say you look really hot."

Marisa's smile wavered and she ducked her chin. She pointed at the stereo. "Nice choice of music."

"Thanks. I've always loved them."

Marisa nodded and turned to point past the stairs. "The bathroom is in there. You can change while I, ah, see if there's anything here to eat. We may have to order pizza."

"That would be fine. All right, I'll..." She nodded toward the bathroom and Marisa went into the kitchen.

Kim went into the bathroom and laid the robe on the sink. She looked at her reflection in the mirror as she undressed, locking eyes with herself. *This is it,* she said. *No more Marisa Larkin Movie Star talk. You saw her out there. She's a regular person. A beautiful regular person who seems interested in the idea of being with you, but regardless. Stop acting like a fangirl and get your head on straight.*

She left her underwear and T-shirt on, slipping into the robe and cinching the belt around her waist. She gathered her wet clothes in a towel and carried them back into the living room.

"Where's the laundry?"

"Door next to the bathroom," Marisa called back.

Kim found the room and bent to put the clothes in the dryer. The controls were self-explanatory, so she started them running before she went back into the kitchen. Marisa was stretching to get plates from the cupboard, her T-shirt rising up to reveal her hips and the bottom of her belly. She saw Kim. "Pizza is on the way. I kind of doubted you were in the mood for leftover Chinese."

"Well, every now and then. But pizza is good."

"Good," Marisa said. She put the plates on the counter and said, "It should be here in about twenty minutes."

Kim sat on a stool, letting the counter separate her from Marisa. "Thanks for the robe. I didn't realize how cold I was until I got out of those clothes."

"My pleasure," Marisa said. "Do you want a beer?"

"Sure."

Marisa got two bottles from the fridge, popped them open, and handed one to Kim. She took a sip, rested her elbows on the counter and clasped her hands around the bottle in front of her. "I'm really glad you agreed to this. It's been a really long time since I had a real date. I'm not even sure if this is a date."

"I'm sitting in your house in my underwear," Kim said. "That's a date."

Marisa smiled, and Kim noticed how it made her eyes wrinkle a bit.

"You know, if women knew how beautiful you looked without makeup, you might be in trouble." The words were out before she could stop them, and she focused on the label of her beer bottle as she waited for Marisa's reaction.

"Thank you," Marisa said quietly. "But I'm not..." She decided to throw out the humble routine and simply said, "Thank you. So, um... Matthew."

Kim nodded. "What made you think he was right for me?"

"The motorcycles, for one thing. He's an adrenaline junky. He likes danger. I thought it would be perfect setting him up with a stuntwoman."

"I guess that makes sense," Kim said.

Marisa sipped her beer. Radiation Canary was singing a song appropriately titled "Improve the Silence." They listened for a verse and half a chorus before Marisa spoke again.

"What made you decide to go into that line of work, anyway?

Was it just the excitement, the danger?"

Kim tilted her head to the side. "Not... really. Sort of. It's kind of a long story." She licked her lips. "When I was ten, my father was flying home from a family reunion. The plane hit some really bad turbulence, and they dropped fast. The pilots tried to correct, but there was nothing they could do. The plane crashed.

"My Mom had stayed behind to take care of the family video store. The plane crash was all over the radio, and she knew it was his flight. She jumped in the car and raced out to the airport in the hopes that maybe she was wrong, that it was another flight or something, or that it wasn't as bad as they were saying. She only made it a few blocks before someone sideswiped her car. She was killed instantly."

Marisa was staring at Kim, her eyes filled with sadness. "And your dad?"

"No survivors."

"God, Kim."

Kim shook her head. "That day was a very expensive lesson for me. It doesn't matter how well you plan or how much you protect yourself. Things can change at the drop of a hat, and there's nothing you can do to stop it or save yourself. So I decided to live dangerously. I mean, I still wear a seatbelt everywhere I go, and I'll wear safety gear on every single stunt I do. But I'm not going to cloister myself against something just because it might be dangerous. I love the adrenaline."

Marisa grinned. "I wish I could live that way. But I'm always counting and recounting everything that could go wrong. I'm such a wuss when it comes to sticking my neck out."

Kim said, "The turtle that stays in its shell never gets hurt, but it doesn't have much of a view."

"Confucius say?"

"Aunt Mabel."

Marisa grinned and said, "Wise woman."

"So she keeps telling me."

There was a knock on the door, and Marisa said, "Oh, they're early. Be right back." She went to the door and Kim slipped off the stool. She wandered into the living room where she couldn't possibly be seen from the front door; she didn't want to force Marisa to explain a half-naked woman hanging out in her home. Marisa spoke with the delivery person, thanked him, and brought the pizza back into the kitchen.

Kim stared at the box in disbelief. "What the hell is this, benefit of being a movie star? I would have to kill someone to get a pizza delivered this quickly."

"The restaurant is about three blocks away. They don't know I'm a celebrity; I use a fake name when I order." She put the box down on the counter and said, "Anyway, here we are. Half vegan, half sardines."

Kim's eyes widened.

"What? You just said you were a daredevil, willing to try new and strange things." Marisa grinned and opened the pizza box to reveal a sausage and pepperoni pizza. "Then again, some things you just don't mess with."

Kim laughed. "For a second there I was trying to figure out how you could possibly justify vegan *and* sardines on the same pizza."

Marisa laughed. "I guess that's why I'm not a writer. I don't think through my jokes and they end up not making sense."

"But at least they're still funny."

"To an audience of one, maybe."

"How many more do you need?"

Marisa raised an eyebrow and one shoulder. "Touché." She sighed and transferred a slice to one plate. "*Bon appétit.*"

"Thank you." Kim took a bite, chewed it carefully, and watched as Marisa dabbed the top of her slice with a paper towel. "So how long have you and Andrew had this arrangement?"

"Mm, a couple of years. We met when I was doing a recurring role on *No World's Fair.* I was still dating men at the time, just so people would see me out on the town and no one would start asking questions. So I asked him if he wanted to go out, and he just smiled and pulled me aside, and he said, 'Honey, I think my gaydar is a little more acute than yours is.'" She grinned. "He wasn't wrong. After that, we decided we would just be each other's cover. We went on dates, award shows, let people see us in public together, and then we moved in here. We still go out sometimes on double dates."

"How does that work?"

"He picks up the woman, I pick up the guy, and we act like it's a blind date set up."

Kim smiled. "So if I had taken you up on the date with Matthew..."

Marisa said, "Actually, no. Andrew was right. My gaydar is woefully out of tune. I really thought you were straight." She picked at a pepperoni. "I'm really glad I was wrong."

Kim licked her lips and looked down at her plate.

"Andrew tried to tell me that night, right after he met you. And then you came out to me, and... well, I felt like a perfect fool. A blind fool." She shrugged. "Any pings I got from you, I just put off to wishful thinking."

"Wishful?"

"Yeah." Marisa looked up and met Kim's gaze.

Kim cleared her throat, suddenly nervous. "You, um. You look really do look great in glasses."

Marisa stifled a laugh. "Did you say 'look really do look'?"

"Hey, shut up. You're not a writer, I'm not a talker-person."

Marisa let the laugh out, then reached up and touched the frames. "Well, I only wear them on certain occasions. Like when I'm too tired to deal with contacts." She smiled. "You should feel special."

"Trust me, I do."

Marisa took another bite of her pizza. Kim sipped her beer. There was no need for them to speak, so they didn't force the conversation.

The dryer buzzed at the back of the house, startling them both. "Oh," Kim said. "Has the rain stopped?"

Marisa craned her neck to look out the window. "Looks like it."

"I should probably go soon. You probably have an early morning at the studio."

"I..." Marisa started, and then nodded. "Yeah, actually I do. I have to be there at five thirty." She checked her watch and brushed her hair out of her face. "Ugh."

Kim said, "I should probably go after I finish the pizza."

"Yeah," Marisa said sadly.

"It was a nice preview for our next date this weekend. Maybe I can actually wear pants for that one."

Marisa laughed. "Or a skirt. I'm not picky. I know I said it before, but you really did look hot at the party."

Kim arched an eyebrow. "You know, it's still weird to have you flirting with me."

"Should I stop?"

"No. Just keep it up so I can get used to it."

"I'll see what I can do."

They fell back into their comfortable silence as they ate,

occasionally commenting on the show or the other actors. When they had each finished two slices, Kim wiped her fingers on a napkin. "I should probably go see about my clothes."

"Yeah. Listen, I know I said it before, but thanks for coming here with me. I'm really enjoying getting to know you."

"It's not exactly one-sided," Kim assured her. "I'll be right back."

She walked through the living room, well aware of Marisa's eyes burning into her back. She resisted the urge to look over her shoulder and catch her, moving around the stairs to the laundry room. She closed the door behind her and pulled the clothes from the dryer. They were toasty warm, and smelled vaguely of the dryer sheet. She dressed quickly and left the robe folded neatly on top of the dryer before she went back into the main room.

"I think everyone should spend their first date in their pajamas," Marisa said when she returned. "It really soothes the nerves."

"Underwear or pajamas," Kim said. "Works for me."

Marisa chuckled. "I'll walk you out."

Kim followed her to the front door, and they stood in the darkness of the foyer. "So, Thursday or Friday?"

"Do you have a preference?"

"No, but Thursday would be nice. Not as long to wait."

Marisa laughed. "I'll see what I can do."

She stepped forward and put her hand on Kim's shoulder. Kim turned her head to the side as Marisa leaned in, and their lips touched. Marisa pulled back slightly, giving Kim a chance to end the kiss, but Kim leaned forward and met Marisa's lips again. Marisa moaned and moved her hand to Kim's back, splaying her fingers over her shoulder. She smelled pizza on Marisa's breath and suddenly wished they had skipped dinner and just jumped to this point of the evening. But nothing could ruin the fact of Marisa kissing her. Kim's lips parted and she felt Marisa's tongue against her top lip before she pulled back.

Kim was trembling, her eyes closed and her lips still parted as Marisa slowly stepped away from her.

"Drive safely."

"Drive?" Kim asked incredulously.

Marisa smiled. "You could stay here in the guest house."

Kim laughed. "Uh, yeah. That's probably not the greatest idea."

"Think I can't control myself?"

Kim looked down Marisa's body, licked her lips. "I would fear for your safety."

Marisa laughed and leaned in, kissing Kim again. Kim pressed against her, trying to mark every sensation in case it never happened again. The kiss ended far too soon, and Marisa stepped back and glanced at the door. "Well, if you're going to leave, you should probably do it while we're both still capable of rational thought."

"So it's not just me, then."

"No."

Kim smiled. "I'll see you Thursday."

"I can't wait."

Kim opened the door and stepped out into the wet night. The rain had stopped, but the scent of it hung in the air and droplets reflected moonlight from the grass of Marisa's lawn. Every car on the street was diamond, glittering in the darkness. Kim resisted the urge to glance back, but she smiled when she finally heard the door shut. *Spent a few extra seconds watching me go, did you, Miss Larkin?*

She got behind the wheel of her Jeep and looked toward the house. A light was burning on the second floor, and Kim took a moment to watch for shadows against the curtains. She finally gave up on getting one more peek and pulled out of the driveway.

## CHAPTER EIGHTEEN

IN DREAMS, Kim had relived the kiss a good twelve times and was going for the baker's dozen when she was rudely woken by someone banging on the front door of her apartment.

She rolled onto her stomach, burying her face in the pillow and trying to finish out the dream before she was forced to admit she was awake. Unfortunately, the banging was quickly joined by Mabel calling, "Kim! I know you're in there, because I see your Jeep downstairs. Come on, open up for your Auntie."

Kim grumbled and pushed away her pillow. The dream gave way to harsh reality and she crawled out of bed to the sound of Mabel continuing to berate her from the front of the apartment. She stepped into her jeans and found a T-shirt, the clothes she had washed at Marisa's draped over the back of an armchair.

She walked barefoot out of her bedroom. "Cut it out, Auntie Em, I'm awake."

The clock over the microwave said it was a quarter to six in the morning. She considered turning on her heel and going back to bed, but she was already up. She unlocked the door and stepped back as Mabel charged into the apartment. She had two bags of breakfast from the take-out diner down the street and she dropped them on the kitchen table.

"Okay. We're going to eat and talk and you're going to tell me everything."

Kim shut the door and stumbled to the table. She still wasn't fully awake. She hadn't gotten home until ten, and then she tossed and turned until after midnight replaying what had happened. When she finally fell asleep, the night replayed in her head like a movie stuck on repeat. It took her a moment to realize Mabel was fishing for information about Matthew, a man she had yet to meet.

"There's not much to tell, Auntie Em. He's an actor who worked with Marisa Larkin's boyfriend on *No World's Fair*. He, uh, he likes motorcycles." She tried to think of anything else Marisa told her about him, but came up blank. Hadn't that been the point of the evening, of going out to dinner with her? How could they have gotten so sidetracked?

*How indeed,* she thought with a smile.

"Oh, it must be love." Mabel rolled her eyes and reached across the table and patted Kim's hand. "I've been so worried about you, dear, worried you'll never find a man. But look at you! Glowing, glowing, glowing." She sighed and relaxed against the back of her chair. "I'm just so happy you've found someone."

Kim smiled and looked at the Styrofoam container holding her breakfast. "Yeah. Well, there's always a chance you won't like him."

"You barely say two words about him and you're smiling like this? As long as he makes you happy and gives me lots of grandbabies..."

Kim's smile wavered and faded, and she looked out the window. "Yeah..."

"Oh, I know they won't actually be grandbabies, but close enough, right?" She clapped her hands together. "But don't rush on my account. I can wait, as long as I know they're coming. I can be a very patient woman."

Kim picked up a piece of bacon and took a bite.

"What's the matter, honey?"

"Nothing, Mabel. It's just... I don't know. I'm not sure this guy is right for me. Not for the long run."

Mabel clucked her tongue and said, "Not right for you. All you have to do is have him in your mind and look. Brightness and smiles. This man is perfect for you. Just look in the mirror and you'll see."

A tear rolled down Kim's cheek and she looked toward the window. Marisa was probably at work, maybe slumped in the makeup chair while the artist chided her about the bags under her eyes. Had she spent the night thinking about the kiss? Kim looked down at her food and picked at the remaining strip of bacon.

"Aunt, do you remember when you came to take care of me, after the accidents?"

"Of course, dear," Mabel said. "It was a very sad time."

"I remember sitting up here and thinking that my whole world had just crashed down on me. And you sat with me on the window seat and told me that even though things weren't going to turn out the way we thought they would, that didn't mean they would turn out badly. Sometimes things happen, and all you can do is accept it, gather your things, and go with the flow of the river."

"Yes, dear, but what does—"

"I'm dating a woman."

Mabel stared at her for a moment and then tilted her head to the side. "But..."

"I made the other guy up. Well, not... technically. He exists and most of the stuff I told you is true. I-I think. But I've never met him. And I'm certainly not going to date him. I have feelings for the woman I double for on the show, Marisa Larkin. We've had a couple of meals together. And it's going to be something else. Something bigger than I've ever felt before. I know I would never be able to hide it from you like I have in the past, and I don't want to."

Mabel fussed with a napkin. "Before? You've..." She made vague hand gestures.

"Yeah. I've had girlfriends in the past."

Mabel closed her eyes and exhaled sharply. She pushed away from the table and walked purposefully toward the door.

"You said it yourself, Aunt Mabel." Mabel stopped, but didn't turn around. "Every time I think about her. Every time she crosses my mind. The thought of her makes me glow. When I'm around her, I don't want to be around anyone else ever again. As long as I'm happy, Aunt Mabel. As long as I'm loved. Even if you can never accept her, accept that I am in love, and I'm loved in return."

Mabel sighed heavily, shook her head, and left the apartment.

Kim leaned back in her chair and crossed her arms, looking out the window as the tears streaked down her face.

After capoeira training, Pluto invited her out to lunch on the boardwalk. Rather than be alone, or go home to face the cold shoulder from Mabel, she agreed. They got two whole wheat pitas with chicken and cucumbers, carrying them toward a bench that overlooked the water.

As they walked, Pluto said, "Okay, spill. You've been distracted and tense all day. What's eating you, kid?"

Kim watched the people on rollerblades, the small boats zipping around in the water. "I told Mabel this morning."

"Told her... that you're gay?" Kim nodded. "Wow. How did she take that?"

"Not well," Kim said. "I decided to tell her because I'm seeing someone now."

Pluto raised an eyebrow.

"You're sworn to secrecy, Pluto. This~"

"Please. How long have you known me?"

Kim sighed. She climbed onto the bench and sat on the back, feet on the seat. Pluto sat next to her as she held the pita in one hand and picked at it with the other. Finally, she decided that if she had to tell anyone, Pluto was the most trustworthy.

"Marisa Larkin."

He looked at her, looked away, looked back and leaned in, then finally seemed to decide she was telling the truth. "Huh. How about that."

"I don't even know how it happened. It's just like I was walking down the street and she fell into step next to me. And here we are. Together."

Pluto sat next to her, feet planted on the seat. He looked out at the water. "And now you want some ancient Chinese wisdom to get you over this hump?"

Kim looked at him. "Got any?"

"Fuck no. I'm Korean, racist."

Kim laughed and took a bite of her pita.

"But I can point something out that maybe you've missed. All the relationships you've ever been in, you always thought they were something special. But you never took the extra step to tell your aunt about it. Now, you've known Marisa Larkin for a couple of weeks, and you jumped right off the deep end. That should tell you something about your feelings."

"I know that Marisa makes me feel... I don't know. Warm inside. But I don't know if it's worth losing my relationship with my aunt."

Pluto shrugged. "Maybe that's not important. What's important is that you knew it was too big a deal to keep it quiet."

Kim shook her head. "She's in the closet. Even if we do become a couple, we would have to hide it from everyone else in the world. Why should Mabel be any different?"

"Because she's your aunt, and she loves you. You wanted her to know you were happy."

Kim had some mayonnaise on her thumb and licked it off. "I don't know. I still think I should have kept my big mouth shut and let her believe whatever she wanted."

"Would you really have been better off in the long run? You're letting her in on the ground floor. It's easier to tell her now, at the beginning, than later."

"But I don't know if I'm in love with Marisa or not."

Pluto smiled. "Then you aren't paying attention." He glanced sideways at her and said, "Kim, I knew you were falling at the poker game last week. I was kind of wondering when you would get around to telling me who the lucky lady was."

"Sorry to keep you in suspense."

"Eh, don't worry about it. Make sure I'm the first to know when you guys move in together, though."

Kim smirked and nudged him with her elbow. Pluto nudged her back and then nodded at someone rollerblading toward them on the sidewalk. "This guy is going to wipe out in five seconds."

The guy was tall and thin, wearing every piece of protective gear known to man. He zipped around pedestrians on the walkway, huffing and puffing with each swing of his arms. Just as he came even with their bench, he suddenly stumbled and twisted. He hit the pavement and actually bounced a step, ending up on his butt with his hands stretched out to prop him up as the people he had just left in the dust whipped around him.

"How do you do that?" Kim asked.

"That's your ancient *Korean* wisdom," Pluto told her. "Can I tell you something else you probably already know, but apparently need to hear from someone else?"

"Please."

"You run into burning buildings, jump off trucks, get shot at, and fight guys twice your size. But you never, ever go into any of that shit blind. You know exactly what you're getting into, no matter what it is or how dangerous it might be. Why would a relationship be any different? You never let yourself get hurt, Kim. That's what we love about you."

She bumped his leg. "Thanks, Pluto."

Kim parked outside Reel Heroes and watched a group of four

teenagers walk through the front door. She knew Mabel didn't trust kids, and everyone under twenty-five was a kid to her, so she would keep an eagle eye on them until they left. If she wanted to get upstairs undetected, now was the time. She got out of the Jeep, hurried across the street, and tried to sneak through the door without opening it wide enough to ring the bell.

She was halfway to the office when she heard Marisa's voice. "When has this family ever mattered to you?" She froze, looked to either side, and then looked up at the TV on the far wall.

Marisa, looking about ten years younger, was arguing with an older man on the shore of a lake. She wore jeans and a T-shirt, her hair pinned away from her face as she shouted at the indifferent man. Her face was red as she shouted, "It was always about your job! Well, your job isn't here anymore. We are! And we need you, you selfish son of a bitch. If you're too blind to see that, then I feel sorry for you."

Kim tore her gaze from the screen and looked behind the counter. Mabel was knitting, her expression stern, her eyes glancing from her work to the kids lurking near the action movies.

"That's her, huh?" Mabel asked.

"Yeah," Kim said. "That... that's Marisa."

Mabel sniffed and shrugged, adjusted her position on the stool, and shook her head. "I don't know. She's pretty. I guess."

"Well," Kim said. "I think so."

There was maybe a hint of a smile on Mabel's lips, but it was gone before Kim could confirm it was there. She sighed heavily and put down her knitting. "You've been like this a long time, I suppose. Why should you change just because I know? Just don't flaunt it in front of me, I don't need to see that."

Kim stepped closer to the counter and lowered her voice. "Well, she's not exactly out. So we'll have to be discrete."

Mabel pressed her lips tighter together. "Okay, then good. I suppose if it makes you happy, then... then I will shut up and let you do what makes you happy." After a moment, in a very quiet and serious voice, she added, "I'll get better. I'll try to get better. I love you more than I care about anything else. Is that... I mean, is that okay?"

"That's okay." Kim had to struggle to keep her voice steady.

She nodded, picking up her needles. "So what are you waiting for? Go on upstairs. I'm running a business here, you know."

Kim leaned across the counter and kissed Mabel's cheek.

When she pulled back, she saw an unfamiliar rental DVD case next to the computer. It was then that she realized Mabel had said the store only had two Marisa Larkin movies, and Kim had seen both of those. This was a different movie Mabel had taken the time to go and rent, just to check out who Kim was dating. "Did you... rent at Blockbuster?"

"Well, I couldn't show R-rated movies on TV screens here, now could I? This is a family business." She snorted and rolled her shoulders. "Always will be family." She locked her eyes on Kim for a minute before focusing on her knitting.

"I love you, Aunt Mabel."

"Yes, I know, I'm terribly lovable." She grabbed Kim's hand and said, "I mean it, Kim. Just be happy. Don't worry about what grumpy old women set in their ways say about it, do you hear me?"

"Loud and clear, Auntie Em."

Mabel swatted her hands in the air. "Not that name, you brat. Go, go, get out of here."

Kim chuckled and backed away from the counter, glancing up at the TV as she went to the office door. The older man was now standing behind Marisa with his hands on her shoulders. She was crying, but apparently she'd gotten through to the old man. Kim smiled and went upstairs with a palatable sense of relief.

## CHAPTER NINETEEN

KIM SPENT Wednesday on the set of *20 Corpses*, a horror movie about monstrous creatures taking over an apartment building. Joshua Lincoln was the stunt coordinator, and he wanted her for a one-off stunt that was being filmed that day. Her job consisted of being yanked off her feet by a wire, and dragged kicking and screaming down a corridor. She did the stunt five times, letting Lincoln make minute adjustments each time. When they finally rolled film, the stunt went off without a hitch. Lincoln thanked her, and she told him that any time he needed a crash test dummy, he knew where to find her.

The script for the third episode of *Neutral Ground* arrived while she was out, and she spent the evening making notes about the stunts they would have to perform. The plot involved Templeton and Lethe going to the Texas border to investigate allegations of people smuggling drugs, weapons, and people into the United States. They discover that illegal aliens are being trained as suicide bombers, promised that their families will be brought into the United States in exchange for their sacrifices. The climax of the episode involves Lethe and Temple blowing up the cache of bombs, and the smugglers' hideout along with it.

"Big, big boom," she wrote in the margin. It was going to be a hell of a stunt, but she was confident she could pull it off. She would give Simon "Sulfur" Gunther a call; he was the best explosives guy she knew.

She was preparing to go to sleep when her phone rang. She picked it up and her heart skipped a little when she saw Marisa's name on the readout. She flipped the phone open and said, "Hey, Marisa."

"Hi. Are you busy?"

"No, I was just looking over the script for the next episode. What's up?"

"I spoke with Solomon, and tomorrow is going to be a heavy day for Will. A lot of Temple scenes, with his girlfriend and his bosses. So I asked if a few scenes could be swapped around so I could get out early and, lo and behold, I can go home at a reasonable time. So I was thinking that thing we spoke about... tomorrow's good for me if it's good for you."

"It's perfect for me," Kim said. "Uh, what time?"

She heard the dinging of Marisa's car door. "Maybe around seven? I like to eat early when I can, but I..."

"No, seven is good. Perfect. Do you want me to pick you up, or... or how do you want to do it? I've never dated anyone famous."

"Well, I'm all kinds of firsts for you. Why don't you meet me here at my place, and we'll figure things out from there."

Kim smiled. "Sounds fantastic."

"I'll see you tomorrow."

"Yeah. Good night, Marisa."

"Night, Kim."

Kim hung up and sat on her bed, staring at her phone and grinning like a fool.

Kim spent Thursday trying her best not to speculate about the night ahead. She jogged for two hours, trained with Pluto, and had lunch with Lincoln and Break. Both guys spent the entire lunch trying to figure out what she was so preoccupied about, but Kim claimed they were insane and imagining things. She claimed she was just looking forward to the weekend. Being with them also reminded her that their traditional poker game would have gotten in the way if Marisa had only been free for a date on Friday. She was surprised to discover she would have dropped the game in a heartbeat in exchange for dinner with Marisa.

She left the guys with repeated assurances she wasn't hiding anything from them and drove across the town to the most shameful appointment she had ever made. She sat behind the wheel of her Jeep for a long time, staring at the shop and deciding whether or not to wimp out. She took a few deep breaths, closed her eyes, and finally left the safety of her car to walk through the door. A bell jingled overhead and a perky young blonde behind the counter looked up and smiled. "Hi!" she chirped. "Welcome to Bliss Salon. How can I help you?"

Kim reluctantly stepped up to the counter and said, "I'm Kim Greer. I have... an appointment to get my hair done."

The girl glanced at Kim's hair and expertly hid her reaction. "Excellent. Someone will be right with you."

Kim went to the waiting area and sat down with her back to the door, knowing that if she kept it in sight she would run fleeing from the establishment the second she got a chance. She picked up a magazine and flipped through it to keep her mind off what she was about to do.

The hair wasn't that bad. As long as she restrained herself from touching it, she could forget that it was even there. And she had to admit, it looked very good. Better than it ever had, in fact. She decided to wear makeup on the date, dictating a trip to the store to buy some lipstick. The salesgirl was very helpful explaining what she needed, and even showed Kim how to apply some of it before she left with her purchases.

When she got home, she applied the makeup, changed into her best outfit - including a skirt, after Marisa's comment. She also wore what Marisa had dubbed her "buckle boots." They didn't really go with the outfit, but Marisa seemed to like them. That was enough for her to commit the fashion faux pas.

She went downstairs at six thirty, hoping to breeze through the store without Mabel noticing. No such luck. She was almost to the door when she heard Mabel snapping her fingers. Ignoring that would have led to a bigger deal than whatever she would have to endure by answering. She stopped and went back to the counter and Mabel put down her knitting needles.

"Let me see," she said. She looked Kim up and down, sighing heavily when she saw the boots. "Girls are not like boys. They won't be fooled by a little lipstick and rouge, you know."

"I know, Auntie Em. I've been out with girls before."

"Eh, don't remind me." She examined Kim's blouse, turned her wrist to inspect the cuffs of her sleeve. "Okay. Okay. I guess you're presentable enough to go out. Be good. Don't stay out too late."

"I'll do my best," Kim said. She took Mabel's hand, brought it to her lips, and kissed the knuckles. "Thank you, Aunt Mabel."

Mabel waved her off. "Go. I have a business to run, I can't be your own personal fashion guru."

Kim smiled. "Sorry to be a bother."

Mabel rolled her eyes and turned to the computer.

Kim wanted to thank Mabel again, wanted to walk around the counter and give her a crushing hug. But she knew that drawing attention to her acceptance would only make Mabel retreat. Kim smiled and left the video store, chuckling to herself as she walked to her Jeep. She thought about the fact that her Aunt Mabel had just given her fashion advice for a date, a date with a woman, and she laughed out loud.

Kim drove to Marisa's neighborhood and killed some time driving down side streets until it was the moment of truth. She pulled into Marisa's driveway two minutes past seven, parking behind the Prius. She walked to the door, still half expecting to discover everything had been in her head and Marisa wouldn't have the slightest idea what she was doing there. She pushed aside her fears, took a few steadying breaths, and rang the doorbell. She looked at her reflection in the window beside the door, nervously touching the hem of her blouse and wondering if she should have worn pants after all. Her legs weren't her best~

The door opened and Marisa eliminated all Kim's thoughts. She wore an untucked navy blue blouse over black jeans. She smiled and raised an eyebrow. "Hi. Wow. You clean up well."

Kim chuckled nervously and said, "And you look... exactly as beautiful as always."

Marisa pursed her lips. "Nice to know I've reached a plateau."

"Oh, no... I didn't... I was just..."

"Relax," Marisa said. "I'm messing with you." She stepped outside and leaned in to peck Kim's cheek before she pulled the door closed. "Do you want to take your car or mine?"

"I think mine is blocking yours in."

"Yours it is," Marisa said. "I've decided on where we'll eat. Have you ever heard of the Tree House?"

Kim thought for a minute and finally shook her head. "I don't think I have."

"I'm not surprised. I'll navigate for you." She went around to the passenger seat, and Kim winced at the thought of her probably-designer jeans on the seat of her Jeep.

She climbed in. "If you want to sit on a towel or something..."

"I'm fine." Marisa waited until Kim shut the door, and touched her arm. "I'm just a everyday normal person, Kim. You don't have to treat me with kid gloves just because a few people might recognize me on the street."

Kim was looking at Marisa's hand on her arm. "I'll try to keep that in mind. But even if you were a gas station clerk, there's no way I'd ever consider you just an everyday normal person."

Marisa withdrew her hand, smiling. "Take a left when you leave the driveway."


The Tree House was aptly named. It stood on a street Kim had been down a hundred times, but she never noticed there was a restaurant behind the tree-lined fence. She pulled through the wide gate of what seemed like a private residence, the actual building nestled at the back of the lot. The parking lot was full of expensive foreign cars and a limo or two took up space at the edges of the lot. Kim's second-generation Jeep, and all the scars and dings it had accrued over the years, stood out like a sore thumb.

Kim pulled up to the front door where a red-jacketed valet appeared to take her keys. "Make sure you put it somewhere safe," she said. "I don't want to be dinged by any of these damn Beamers."

The valet smiled. "I'll do my best, ma'am."

Kim joined Marisa on the sidewalk and leaned in to whisper to her. "Celebrity hideaway?"

"Sort of. You'll see." She led the way inside, and Kim was again impressed with the subtlety. Low lighting from sconces on the wall, accented by lamps on every table, gave the dining room the feel of a blackout party. The glow highlighted small oases of people, all of whom seemed completely isolated from the rest of the room. A hostess in a red dress stood behind a podium and smiled as they approached. "Good evening, ladies. Do you have a reservation?"

"Larkin, two," Marisa said. "And pull up the ladder."

"Very well, ma'am." The hostess took two menus and turned away from her podium. "This way."

Kim frowned at Marisa and mouthed, "Pull up the ladder?" Marisa implied she would explain later as they followed the hostess through the main dining room. An archway led to a second dining room, just as dim as the first. They were led to the back of the room, out of sight from casual passersby.

The hostess turned to them and gestured like a game show hostess. "Will this do?"

"It's perfect," Marisa said. "Thank you."

The hostess lit the lamp on the table and placed the menus with a well-practiced flourish. "Someone will be with you shortly to take your drink order. Have a pleasant evening."

"Thank you."

Kim went to the table and pulled out Marisa's chair for her. "Who says chivalry is dead?"

"Well, you're full of surprises tonight, Kim. Thank you." She took a seat, and Kim sat across from her. She scanned the room and slowly realized every table in their section had a same-sex couple holding hands or gazing longingly at each other over their food.

"So this place is..."

"'Friendly' is the word we like to use," Marisa said. "It's open to everyone, but it's very exclusive, and very private. So the only people who know about it are celebrities. Even if someone sees something, they know the importance of privacy. No one has ever been outted by eating here."

"Good to know," Kim said.

"And by the way, I'm paying. Just so you know."

Kim raised an eyebrow. "Oh, well, in that case, let me flip to the lobster portion of the menu..."

Marisa grinned. "They don't have lobster here. But get whatever you want. You're worth it."

Kim pressed her lips together. "Keep talking, Larkin. I may just get the porterhouse with a side of ribs."

"You're such a girl," Marisa said, which caused Kim to laugh hard enough to draw stares from the next table.

## CHAPTER TWENTY

"MY HAIR was much lighter when I was a little girl, so my first role was actually Annie."

"I didn't know you sang."

Marisa shrugged. "I did back then. I had to, because the theatre department was combined with the music department, so we did a lot of musical shows. *Annie, Fiddler on the Roof, Oklahoma!,* that sort of thing."

"Hey, I did *Fiddler* back when I thought I wanted to be an actress. I played Shprintze."

"Gesundheit."

Kim smiled.

"So you originally wanted to be an actress? What made you change direction?"

"I don't know if I really wanted to be an actress. I was just drawn to the whole idea of the production. My parents owned a video store, so I got to see more movies than any kid probably should. I loved the idea of being on stage, but I never got cast in the big parts. I think if I had gotten one of the big parts I would have frozen and ruined it. Too many lines, too much time to screw it all up. So I focused on working for stage techs. I got hooked. Doing stunts was just an extension of that. There's just enough acting involved to satisfy me."

Marisa shook her head. "I still can't imagine doing that work every day. Have you ever been hurt?"

"Oh, lots of times. Not as much as Break. You don't get a nickname like that by playing it safe." She smiled. "But I've broken bones."

"Seriously?"

Kim smirked. "This isn't going to turn into a scene from *Lethal Weapon 3*, is it? We're not going to start comparing scars or anything?"

"Why?" Marisa asked. "Are some of them in embarrassing spots? We could wait until we get back to my place." She sipped her drink, keeping her eyes locked on Kim. When she put the glass down, and then ran the tip of her tongue over her lips and smiled seductively.

Kim leaned back in her chair and stretched out her right arm. She pointed just below the elbow. "I've broken this arm here." She switched arms, pointing at her left forearm. "And this one here. I broke the right one doing a fall. It was my own fault. I was off the mark and I missed the pad. The other arm got broken in the middle of a fight scene. I kept fighting, and they worked it into the script."

"I can't imagine going to work knowing you might get injured like that."

"That's why I don't think about it," Kim said. "But I don't mind pain. Pain just reminds you that you're alive. Same with doing something scary like bungee jumping. The surge of adrenaline and the rush you get from knowing that you did something dangerous and survived."

Marisa held her hands up. "You will never see me on a bungee cord. That's why I have you, to do all the scary stuff for me."

Kim reached across the table and took Marisa's hand. She squeezed and said, "I don't mind keeping you safe."

Marisa's eyes sparkled in the lamp light and she returned the squeeze. They eventually withdrew their hands and focused on their meals. Marisa tried to fill in her history between courses. "My parents have a video of me standing in front of the living room window reciting a monologue from some silly cartoon movie. They showed it to every person who came into our house for the next five years. I was embarrassed, but it was because I didn't think it was the best showcase for me. So I made them record a different performance. After that, I guess I was just doomed."

Kim smiled. "Even as a little kid, huh?"

"Yeah. Find what you love and do it until someone tells you to stop and get a real job. I'm still waiting for someone to tell me."

"Plan to wait a while," Kim said. "This series is going to be your ticket, trust me."

Marisa shrugged. "One can only hope."

"What would you do if you weren't an actress?"

"Unemployed or miserable." Marisa smiled. "I honestly can't think of another job I would be happy with. I'd most likely be reheating French fries at McDonald's or something like that."

Kim shook her head. "No, I don't see that. Maybe for six months during high school, but then someone would come in and realize you were perfect for their commercial or their ad campaign, and you'd be right back where you started."

Marisa laughed. "Oh, another poor soul fooled by the make-up chair." She shook her head. "No. You should see me in the morning before the dozens of technicians have a chance to perform their miracles."

"Okay," Kim said.

Marisa pressed her lips together and looked down at her plate.

The waitress came back and Marisa requested the check. When it arrived, she placed her credit card in the book and folded her hands in front of her on the table. She looked at Kim as if memorizing her features, her smile growing as Kim grew more uncomfortable.

"Another benefit of stunt work," Kim said. "It's all about making sure people don't look at your face."

"Their loss," Marisa said. The waitress whisked away the book, disappearing into the back room again. Marisa took the opportunity to say, "I had a really nice time tonight."

Kim said, "Well, good. I'm glad it wasn't one sided."

"What are you doing Saturday?"

Kim thought for a moment and shrugged. "Depends. Do you have to work?"

"Nope. I was thinking maybe we could do this again."

Kim smiled. "You know another secretive gay restaurant?"

"Actually, I know of a couple. But I was thinking we could spend the day together. Maybe go out to the country."

"I've never been much of a country girl."

"That's because you've never seen me in cutoff jeans and cowboy boots."

"Oh, did you say country? Love the country. I'm there all the time."

Marisa laughed. The waitress returned with her credit card and receipt, and Marisa checked her watch. "Yikes. We've really let the night get away from us. Shall we?" She motioned toward the exit.

"Yeah, we probably should." They left the private area, with Kim trying to ignore the presence of Mabel's favorite actor sitting a few tables from them. The valet retrieved Kim's Jeep and, in minutes, they were back on the road. "So when am I going to hear you sing on the show? Simone Lethe goes undercover as a cabaret singer?"

Marisa laughed. "Sorry, any singing I do now would more closely resemble croaking. All those misspent years of my youth smoking cigarettes. I wasn't half bad as a kid, though."

"Ahh. That's been known to happen with cigarettes." Marisa's house was dark when she pulled into the driveway. "Andrew still out of town?"

"Allegedly he's here," Marisa said. "He may have already gone to bed."

Kim looked at her watch. "What time do you have to be at Transom tomorrow?"

"I can be a little late," she said as she unfastened her seatbelt. "Tonight was worth it. Do you want some dessert? I think I have a pint of ice cream in the freezer we could share."

"A pint to share? Wow, you *are* an actress, aren't you?" She turned off the Jeep and said, "Sure, why not."

They walked up the driveway together, and again Marisa unlocked the door and led Kim into the darkness. The lights came on and Marisa explored the freezer. She finally withdrew a small tub of Ben & Jerry's and said, "Looks like it's a bit more than a pint. We can both pig out."

"Excellent," Kim said.

Marisa took two spoons from the drawer and motioned for Kim to follow her. "Come on. I know the perfect spot to eat this."

She unlocked the back door and led Kim outside. She went to a panel on the back wall of the house and turned on the lights in the pool and a low humming noise filled the backyard. "Fancy," Kim said.

"It was the selling point of the house," Marisa said. She kicked off her shoes and walked to the edge of the pool. She set down the ice cream and bent down to roll up her jeans. She rolled them past her knees, sat down, and let her feet dangle in the water. "Oooh, it's cold." She looked up at Kim. "Care to join me?"

Kim sat on the edge of the same chaise lounge she had occupied during the party and undid the buckles on her boots. She pulled them off and set them aside, stuffing her socks down inside, and sat next to Marisa on the edge of the pool. She let her feet sink into the water and took in the scenery. From their position, they could just see the hills outside of town. Little pinpricks of light dotted the dark landscape, mimicking the stars visible through the cloud cover overhead.

"God, it's gorgeous here."

"Thanks. I spend a lot of my time out here, reading scripts and memorizing lines. I keep waiting to get tired of it."

"I wouldn't hold my breath." She picked up one of the spoons and dug into the ice cream. "So is this your standard first date template?"

"No," Marisa laughed. "I don't date enough to have a standard template. The problem with being in the closet, being famous, all that stuff that was making you nervous earlier." She waved her spoon at the city. "It's hard enough to have a relationship. But to try and find someone you like without broadcasting what you're looking for... Every woman I'm interested in has the potential to be one who is willing to ruin my life for a couple bucks from a tabloid."

"Maybe you could use it to your advantage. Come out now, get some publicity for *Neutral Ground*. It's not like they're setting you up for a romance with Temple."

"Season two."

Kim made a face. "God, you're not serious."

Marisa nodded. "They told me from the beginning. They're going to build up to it, and then have the big sex scene right before the summer hiatus."

"Did none of these people watch *Moonlighting?*"

"A show from eighties? None of these people have even *heard* of it."

"Those who don't learn from the past..." She took another bite of ice cream. "I suppose I have to be your body double for that."

Marisa laughed. "I wouldn't put you through that. I've done my share of sex scenes with boys. I'll be fine."

"All right. Just don't expect me to watch it."

Marisa smiled. "Well, well. We've finally found something that makes Kim Greer cringe. Wonders will never cease. Here I thought you were the kind of woman who danced on the edge of volcanoes, all that crazy stuff."

Kim chuckled. "It's not that crazy, you know. It's fun. And you never know what you're capable of until you step up and do it."

Marisa shrugged. "Maybe in a studio, with every little detail figured out beforehand, with safety gear and mats... maybe then."

"That's not a real thrill. Real thrills are spontaneous."

Marisa said, "Like?"

Kim thought for a minute and pushed herself up. She stood with her toes curled over the edge of the pool, her arms stretched out to either side, and said, "Like this."

"Don't!" Marisa shouted, but Kim was already falling. At the last minute, she pushed both of her feet against the tile and launched herself into a perfectly formed dive. She swam to the bottom of the pool, brushed her fingers across the curved concrete, and swam back up. She surfaced in the middle of the pool, pushing her hair out of her face with both hands.

She treaded in front of Marisa and said, "See? Spontaneous."

Marisa was laughing, but her eyes were wide with fear. "Don't do stuff like that. God, I thought you were going to crack your head on the bottom or something."

"It was a risk. But my heart is pounding, and I can't stop smiling. Come on, you try."

"Uh, no..."

"Come on, Marisa." She swam forward and grabbed Marisa's foot under the water. Marisa pulled it away from her, wrapping her arms around her knees. "You'll never know what you're capable of until you try."

"You're trying to get me killed. Get me out of the way, and they'll cast you as Simone."

"How devious of me. Or maybe I just want to see you in a wet T-shirt."

Marisa smirked and put her ice cream aside before she reluctantly stood up. She exhaled, watching the water as if she suddenly distrusted it. She said, "Okay, but I'm not ruining these jeans." She unbuttoned them and slid them down her legs.

Kim pushed back to the middle of the pool, trying not to stare as Marisa stepped out of her pants. She swallowed and wet her lips. "I'll bet that's an expensive shirt, too."

Marisa pursed her lips and dove into the pool at an angle so she wouldn't hit Kim. The wave she created, however, washed over Kim, splashing in her face and upsetting her delicate tread. Marisa surfaced a few seconds later, her hair twisted and tangled like seaweed. Kim swam up to her and pushed the hair out of her face, taking the opportunity to cup the back of Marisa's head and pull her in for a kiss.

Marisa immediately parted her lips, sweeping her tongue across Kim's bottom lip. Kim tasted the pool water on Marisa's mouth, the warmth of her breath compared to the cool of the water, and let the current press their bodies together. Marisa wrapped an arm around Kim's waist and held her where she was, both of them swaying like buoys.

Kim moved her hands down to the buttons of Marisa's shirt, her fingers trembling as she undid them. How many buttons could a damn shirt have? But finally it came free, and Kim pushed it off her shoulders. She broke the kiss and opened her eyes, discovering Marisa's eyes were already open and locked on her.

"I didn't mean~"

"I know."

Marisa kissed Kim again and tossed her shirt toward poolside. Kim slid her hands over Marisa's chest, blindly exploring the curves through a barricade of lace. Marisa undid the top two buttons of Kim's blouse, and Kim lifted her arms. Marisa tugged the shirt up and off without bothering to work the remaining buttons, and it was tossed to dry land as well. "Come here," Marisa breathed, wrapping her arms around Kim and swimming her to the edge of the pool.

Kim felt the tile against her back, her skirt floating around her lower body like a jellyfish, and wrapped her arms around Marisa's shoulders. Marisa reached out on either side of Kim's head and gripped the edge of the pool, slipping one of her legs between Kim's. Kim gasped as the smooth skin brushed against her, then sank down onto it. Marisa whispered something and kissed Kim again. Kim let Marisa and the water do the majority of the work, Marisa's movements kicking up waves around them both.

"I want to see all of you," Marisa whispered when the kiss broke, her voice breathy and weak.

"Make me come first," Kim said, and Marisa whimpered. She moved her body faster, the waves slapping against their bodies more rapidly now. Marisa let go of the pool's edge and they drifted, legs wrapped around each other, fingernails drawing across wet flesh and getting caught on inconvenient underwear. Kim closed her eyes and moved her head to Marisa's shoulder, kissing her throat as she came, bucking wantonly against Marisa's thigh until finally she was still. She licked pool water from Marisa's shoulder before she pulled back and kissed her cheek, her lips and her chin.

"Come here..." Kim swam Marisa back to the edge of the pool. "Get up on the edge."

Marisa pulled herself out of the water, and Kim was treated to a perfect view of the water tracing down her half-naked body, the underwear turned see through, the muscles of her thighs and arms catching the pool light. She turned around, and Kim pushed her legs apart. "Closer... sit right on the edge."

"You're all about living on the edge, aren't you?"

"Yes, ma'am. But don't be afraid. I won't let you fall."

Kim hooked her fingers in Marisa's underwear and peeled it down, the wet material rolling easily down her legs. Kim tossed it over her head, letting it float away from her in the pool. She kissed Marisa's stomach, feeling the muscles quiver in anticipation. She ran her hands over Marisa's thighs, moving closer and closer to the center.

Marisa finally whispered, "Kim, please."

Kim bowed her head and breathed deep. She closed her eyes, suppressed a groan, and brushed her lips over Marisa's folds.

"Oh, God..."

Kim massaged Marisa's thighs as she pressed her tongue gently against Marisa's labia. Her thumbs moved in slow circles, moving in rhythm with her tongue and lips. She felt Marisa's hands on the back of her head, moving down to her shoulders and then retreating as Marisa leaned back and lifted her hips to meet Kim's mouth. She could hear Marisa's ragged breathing over the hum of the pool's motor, the splash of the water all around her. She curled her tongue and pushed it inside, and Marisa seemed to crumble.

Kim brought one hand up, brushing Marisa with the knuckles of two fingers before slipping them inside. She used her tongue to tease Marisa's clit, drawing it from under the hood and sucking gently as she twisted her fingers. She thrust her fingers forward, sucking eagerly as Marisa's movements grew increasingly erratic. Kim opened her eyes and looked up Marisa's body. She had taken off her bra at some point, her small nipples standing erect. Kim kissed Marisa's stomach, moving her thumb to take care of Marisa's clit, and moved her lips up her body. She swept her tongue over Marisa's stomach, between her breasts, and took one tight nipple into her mouth.

Marisa moaned, "Oh, yes, Kim... I'm close..."

Kim lifted her head and captured Marisa's mouth. Marisa's tongue slipped into her mouth and Kim moved her hand faster. Marisa's muscles clenched around her hand, her fingernails digging into Kim's shoulders, and she arched her back as she came. Kim kissed and licked down the column of her throat, holding her until her body stopped twitching.

Kim moved her lips back up to Marisa's mouth, kissing her gently and lowering her to the tile. She withdrew her hand and stretched out on top of Marisa, fitting their bodies together comfortably until they were both breathing normally. She kissed Marisa and brushed the wet hair from her face, and Marisa opened her eyes and focused on Kim.

She smiled and licked her lips. "Wow."

"Yeah. Now what?"

Marisa twisted and looked across the lawn. She pointed. "Want to finally check out the guest house?"

Kim smiled. "Sounds like a plan to me."

## CHAPTER TWENTY-ONE

THE GUEST house had a small laundry room, and Marisa tossed their clothes into the dryer as soon as they got there. When she returned to the bedroom, Kim was standing next to the bed naked, ignoring the robe Marisa had offered her before taking their clothes. Marisa stopped where she stood, eyes running over Kim's body, her smile fading as she ran her eyes over every curve. "And here I thought you only wanted me for my laundry services."

"Come here," Kim said.

Marisa crossed the room and put her hands on Kim's hips, pulling her forward as they kissed. Kim guided her toward the bed and eased her down, stretching out next to her on the mattress. Marisa pushed her hands through Kim's thick dark hair. "It's been a long time since I was with someone like this. I almost said I forgot what it felt like, but... I know it's never felt like this before."

"Are you trying to tell me something?" Kim asked, her fingers splayed on Marisa's stomach.

"I'm telling you I think the two of us may be in very deep trouble."

"Fine by me." Kim bowed her head and kissed Marisa again. "I've been known to seek out trouble." Another kiss. "Trouble is my..."

"Stop talking," Marisa sighed. She curled her fingers at the back of Kim's head and pulled her down.

Kim woke when the dryer buzzed. She was curled on her side, Marisa's arms loosely wrapped around her. She found Marisa's right hand, threading their fingers together before looking over her shoulder. Marisa was awake, her eyes bright, and she smiled when Kim looked at her. "Hey," Kim whispered. "What are you doing?"

"Watching you sleep."

"See anything interesting?"

"Not yet." She kissed Kim's lips. "You're staying the whole night, right?"

Kim nodded. "You couldn't get me out of this bed if you tried." She licked her lips and looked at the clock. It was a little past eleven. "Shouldn't you be asleep? You have to be up early tomorrow. Or... well, this morning."

"As late as it is, it would probably be easier to just stay awake and catch cat naps in my trailer."

"So you're going to just lay there and watch me sleep?"

Marisa shrugged. "You got a better idea?"

"One or two." Kim rolled onto her back and pulled Marisa onto her.

Marisa did end up falling asleep shortly before three in the morning. Kim held her, listening to the quiet sounds of her breathing. Her eyes slowly adjusted to the darkness of the guest house. The bedroom was part of a larger space, with a living room across from the bed and a kitchen along the north wall between them. Marisa murmured and pressed herself tighter against Kim, and she turned her head into the hollow of Kim's shoulder. Kim stroked her hair, now dry after their tryst in the water, and got used to the feeling of having a woman in her arms again.

In ten months since her last partner, she got used to sleeping alone. She even told herself she preferred it. She touched Marisa's back and brushed her fingers down her curves. If she had to share a bed for the rest of her life, if she had to learn to deal with stolen covers and never again got to sprawl, she felt it was a good trade off. A wonderful trade off.

"Kim... Kim."

"What is it, baby?" Kim asked.

Marisa sighed, shifted against Kim, and settled back to sleep.

Kim smiled, realized that Marisa had been talking in her sleep. She kissed the top of Marisa's head. "I'm here," she whispered. "I'm not going anywhere."

"Marisa," Kim whispered. She ran her hand along Marisa's upper arm until Marisa's eyelids fluttered and she slowly woke. She focused on Kim and, after a moment of confusion, smiled sleepily. "Hey. Sorry. It's almost five."

"Oh," Marisa rubbed her eyes with the heel of her hand and said, "I guess I fell asleep after all. Sorry."

Kim smiled. "You were pretty exhausted."

Marisa chuckled and pulled away from Kim. "God. I really should have just stayed awake." She put her hand on Kim's thigh, rubbing it through the blanket. "I probably would have enjoyed it more." She groaned, pushed her hair out of her face, and said, "I have to be at the studio in half an hour. Damn."

"Want me to call in sick for you?"

Marisa chuckled and stepped out of the bed. She opened the closet door and pulled out a robe, putting it on as she walked around the foot of the bed. She left it hanging open, her body on full display in the dim light. Kim hungrily took in the sight, letting her eyes linger on the important spots. Marisa said, "There's a shower through there... I'm going to get started on breakfast. Come on in once you're presentable."

Kim looked down at her body, draped in the blanket with one naked leg stretching out toward the edge of the mattress. "This isn't presentable?"

Marisa picked up Kim's foot, kissed the ball, and let it drop. "Andrew may be there. So as much as I like the idea of drinking milk off your naked stomach..."

"Tease."

"How do you take your eggs?"

"Over easy. Lots of toast."

Marisa nodded. "I think I can handle that." She stopped at the door. "Kim, last night was..." She bit her bottom lip and looked at the floor. After a moment, she said, "Last night was really special for me. It was something I had given up on. Thank you."

"And all I get in return is eggs?"

Marisa laughed and grabbed Kim's foot, giving it a shake. "Hey, come on. I'm pouring out my heart here."

Kim pulled her foot from Marisa's grip and climbed out of

bed. She cupped Marisa's face in her hands, kissed the corners of her mouth, and then embraced her. She pressed her face into Marisa's hair and said, "I love you. I think I have since the moment I first saw you."

Marisa laced her fingers together in the small of Kim's back, pulled her close, and put her face against Kim's shoulder.

"Marisa? What's wrong?"

"Nothing. No one's ever said that to me before in real life."

Kim smiled. She lifted Marisa's head, kissed away a rolling tear, and then kissed her lips. "Go make me eggs and I'll tell you again."

Marisa smiled.

They parted with a reluctant sliding of limbs, Kim's hands brushing the silk that didn't feel half as luxurious as Marisa's skin. Kim went into the bathroom, and Marisa left the guesthouse to start on breakfast. Kim leaned into the shower stall, turned on the hot water, and went to the mirror to wait for the water to heat up. She bent down to get a towel from under the sink and, as she rose, caught her reflection in the mirror. The bleary look in her eyes countered by the stupid grin on her face. She chuckled at herself, draped the towel over the rod, and climbed into the shower stall.

The walk of shame wasn't that shameful, Kim thought, wearing the same clothes as the night before as she crossed the lawn. The sun wasn't high enough to top the buildings, but its glow was spread all across the eastern sky. She carried her boots in her left hand, her feet sinking into the cool, dewy grass as she went to the back door of the house. She wiped her feet on the mat provided and went inside.

Andrew was in the kitchen when she came in, standing by the stove. He said, "Hey, Mar, are these eggs for..." He froze when he saw who it was, eyes wide and mouth hanging open for a moment. "Oh."

"Uh, hey."

Kim looked frantically for Marisa, for evidence that she had been invited. She chose that moment to appear, coming down the stairs in a scoop neck white blouse and tights. She had put her hair up, a few tendrils hanging down around her face and shoulders as she took the stairs two at a time. She saw Kim, smiled, and then noticed Andrew standing in the kitchen. She hesitated on the bottom step and said, "Oh. Drew."

"I knew you spent the night in the guest house," Andrew said, "but I had no idea you had *company*."

"Didn't know I had to consult you." Marisa brushed Kim's arm as she passed, going into the kitchen to check their eggs. Andrew was still looking at Kim, grinning like a fool. "Next time I'll hang a tie on the door or something."

"Next time?" Andrew said, still looking at Kim with an expression of shock and happiness.

Marisa glared at the back of his head. "Don't you have to be at work?"

"Huh-uh." He crossed his hands over his chest and leaned against the counter. "So this little thing is going full steam ahead, huh?"

Marisa transferred the eggs to a plate, grabbed the back of Andrew's belt, and hauled him backward. He stumbled, and Marisa took his place at the counter. She put the plate down in front of Kim and turned so Andrew was out of her line of sight.

"I just got a call from Solomon. He needs me there bright and early, so I'm going to have to abandon you."

"That's fine." Kim started to slip off the stool. "I can skip~"

"No, go ahead and eat your eggs. I'll call you tonight, okay?"

Kim nodded. Marisa leaned across the counter and kissed Kim on the lips. It wasn't overtly passionate, but the meaning behind the kiss made it stronger, better. She retreated, whispered, "Thank you," and backed slowly away from the counter. Andrew was carefully reading a takeout menu off the fridge, ignoring Marisa when she passed. Kim heard her hiss, "Leave her alone," before she disappeared into the entry hall.

When the front door closed, Kim felt alone for the first time in twelve hours. It was not a welcome feeling.

Andrew slowly made his way over to her. He struck an incredibly casual pose and tilted his head at a totally casual angle. "So..." His tone was not convincingly casual at all.

She poked at her eggs with a fork. "I'm not sure Marisa wants me to kiss and tell."

He held up his hands in an insincere surrender. "Okay. Okay. But be... careful. This isn't a fling, some little..."

"No." There was no hesitation in her voice, because there was no doubt that she was in this for the long haul. "Not even a question."

Andrew nodded. "I don't want to tell stories out of school, and it's not my place to tell you this. But it's been a long time since Marisa trusted herself with anyone. I'm still a little gobsmacked that you're here. Was she okay last night?"

"Seemed fine," Kim said, suddenly tense.

"Okay. Well... Just be careful with her. She's been in a fragile state for a long time."

Kim said, "She told me it had been a while, but I just thought... I thought she was like me. In a dry spell."

Andrew shrugged. "You could say that." He poured himself a cup of coffee and said, "I'm going to be upstairs online. You can let yourself out whenever you're ready to go." He put his hand on top of hers. "I saw the two of you at the party the other night. And the way she's been since she met you. Kim said this, Kim does that, Kim has the coolest jacket. Frankly, I'm a little sick of hearing your name around this place." She laughed and he winked. "Keep that up and I think... I think you might be very good for her."

Kim nodded. "Can I ask you something?"

"Sure."

"Do you know which jacket she was talking about?"

He laughed. "Sorry, kid. You'll have to ask her."

"I'll do that."

He wished her a good morning and went upstairs, leaving her alone. She looked down at her eggs, wondering what had happened to Marisa in the past and how she could help her get past it.

## CHAPTER TWENTY-TWO

DONNY, THE part-time clerk Mabel hired to fill in when she had to be away from the store, was at the counter when Kim got home. She flashed him a friendly smile and fled up the stairs, counting her blessings that she wouldn't have to explain to Mabel why she was just getting home and why she was still wearing the same outfit as the night before. She undressed in her apartment and took a long shower, unable to stop her brain from replaying scenes from the night before. She was fairly sure she and Marisa had made love in their sleep a few times; half-awake movements, awakening briefly to quiet grunts and a body on top of her... it made her shiver.

Kim washed her hair a few times, making sure she had gotten all the chlorine out in Marisa's shower, and wrapped herself in a towel before she went back out into the living room. She sat on the window seat and looked out at the city. She smiled, and tears rolled down her cheeks. She wasn't sure what she was crying about, but as long as they were happy tears she didn't mind. She rested her head against the wall and let the tears come.

She didn't fall in love. She never allowed herself to. There was just too much at stake on both sides for a relationship to be anything but a fling. But somehow, long before she ever clung to Marisa in the pool, they had gone far beyond fling. Marisa's touch was electric, the feel of her breath on Kim's neck sent every synapse into overdrive. It was like nothing she had ever felt before. And the sex... she still could barely believe she'd had sex with Marisa.

Andrew's advice was wholly unnecessary. She was going to do everything in her power to show Marisa how much she was loved. If she got even a fraction of that in return, she wasn't going anywhere.

Break had knocked on the apartment door with his foot, his hands occupied by the cooler full of beer. Kim stepped aside to let him in, but made no move to help him carry it. "Thought maybe if I got you liquored up I would... fare better." He frowned at her as he walked into the apartment.

"Keep dreaming, Break. What's with the sour puss?"

"Nothing." He put the beer on the counter between the living room and the kitchen, then turned and looked at her. "Did you get laid?"

Kim's eyes widened and she said, "What are you talking about?"

"You look different. You either got laid or you're already drunk."

"I'm already drunk."

Break smiled widely, showing teeth. "Now I know for sure. Who was it? Tell me you didn't hop back on the Tina wagon. Please, Kim."

Kim rolled her eyes. "I haven't spoken to Tina in eight months."

"You broke up ten months ago."

"Who are you, Columbo? Let it go, Break."

Pluto knocked on the open front door. "Is this a private party, or can anyone join?"

"Come in here." Break nodded at Kim. "Little Kim got laid."

Kim swung at Break and hit his shoulder.

"You're kidding," Pluto said. "Was it~"

"Someone who is in the closet," Kim said, cutting him off before he could say a name.

Pluto bit down on his next words, nodded, and slapped Kim on the back. "Good for you, kid. I'm happy for you."

"I'd be happy for you, too," Break said, exploring her kitchen for food. "If I knew who the hell it was. Come on, Kim, spill."

Kim said, "I can't betray her confidence, Break. Sorry. She's going to stay in the closet until she's ready to come out."

Break dropped into a seat and put his feet up on the table. "Gonna drive me bonkers."

Lincoln arrived a few minutes later with bags of chips, and Break forgot all about Kim's conquest as he tore into them.

Kim went into the kitchen, and Pluto followed her. He tapped her on the shoulder and, keeping his voice low, said, "The woman we spoke about?"

"Yeah," Kim said, her lips inadvertently spreading into a smile.

Pluto smiled. "Good for you, little girl." Kim blushed and handed him a bowl for the chips, still smiling. He looked at her smile and raised an eyebrow. "Wow. You may want to try keeping that goofy look under control. You'll lose your reputation as a badass."

"Either that or you guys will never know whether or not I have a good hand."

"Trust me, your poker face is inscrutable as it is." He took a bottle of beer, toasted her and went back into the living room. Kim forced her smile down, and followed Pluto out to the table.

"Come on, Jonas, we don't have all night here," Kim said, staring at her cards as Jonas played with his chips.

"What's the rush, you got a hot date or something?"

"Well, actually," Break said.

Kim said, "Shut up, Break." He snickered and fanned his cards out again, having already bet. She sighed and picked up her cell phone to check the time. As soon as she picked it up, the phone vibrated with an incoming call. The unofficial rule was that no cell phones calls were taken at the table, but seeing Marisa's number pop up made her throw the rule out. It was her house, after all, and her game. She dropped her cards and stood up. "I'm out."

"Ahh, speak of the devil. The mystery woman," Break said.

Kim ignored him and waited until she was at the window seat to answer. She lowered her voice so the guys wouldn't overhear, and flipped the phone open. "Hey. What's up?"

"Hi. Can you talk?"

"Not freely." Kim looked at the reflection of the poker game in the window. Break was trying his best to act like he wasn't watching her. "I've been thinking about you today."

"No wonder my ears were burning. Listen, I won't keep you long, but I wanted to know if you'd done anything for dinner."

Kim thought back to the sandwich she ate before the game. "No, not really."

"You could come over and have dinner with me and Andrew,

if you'd like. I'm just leaving Transom right now, so give me a few minutes to call for Chinese…"

"Sounds great," Kim said. "Get me anything with chicken and broccoli, lots of rice. I'll be there in about twenty minutes."

"I'll see you then."

Kim hung up and went back inside. "Guys, I'm going to have to duck out early tonight."

"Whoa, hey…" Break said. "Tradition. You can't just walk out on a game."

"It's fine by me." Jonas tossed his cards down and crossed his arms. "Probably be cheaper for me in the long run."

"Pluto," Kim said, "I'm leaving you in charge. Make sure the place is locked up and everything is just this side of a war zone."

He nodded. "Where are you going all of a sudden?"

"Dinner." Kim ducked into the bedroom before she could hear their jokes. Let them mock. It was just one of the many things she was willing to put up with for having Marisa in her life.

Kim arrived to find Marisa's driveway was almost full of cars; the Prius, a red sports car she assumed was Andrew's, and another black SUV with the back sticking out into the street. She parked next to it and peered in the window as she walked to the door, trying to guess who it belonged to. She knocked on the door and it was answered quickly enough that she assumed Marisa was standing on the other side watching for her. She had already changed into faded blue jeans and a college sweatshirt, wearing glasses instead of contacts. "Kim."

Kim hesitated, unsure of the etiquette. Were they allowed to kiss on the front porch? Were the neighbors trustworthy? Marisa solved the problem for her by kissing her on the cheek and pulling her into an embrace. "Glad you're here. Sorry I'm so frumpy."

"You look beautiful," Kim said. "Rocking the Clark Kent look again. I like it."

Marisa smiled and slid her hand down to Kim's. She guided Kim into the house and shut the door behind her.

Andrew and another man were in the kitchen, standing over a group of Chinese takeout containers. The mystery guest turned, and Kim had to stop herself from gasping. She recognized him from pretty much every movie and television show she had watched in the past decade. His hair was going gray at the temples, but his sparkling blue eyes hadn't lost any of their power. He smiled and

Kim held out her hand to him. She couldn't stop herself from gasping, "Nathan Worth."

"What a coincidence," he said. "That's my name, too." He smiled and shook her hand.

"Sorry. Uh, Kim Greer. What are you doing here?"

Marisa put her hand in the small of Kim's back. "Nathan is *your date*," Marisa said. She arched an eyebrow and Kim remembered their cover.

"Oh," Kim said. "Well, it's nice to meet you. I'm usually not interested in blind dates, but I have a good feeling about this one." She slid an arm around Marisa's waist and pulled her close.

Marisa chuckled. "Andrew and Nathan have been together for quite a while."

"That's an understatement," Andrew said. "I think we're common law by now. Does anyone object to shrimp in their food?"

Marisa explained, "We got a combo platter."

Kim nodded. "Ah. No allergies, open to trying anything at least once."

"Adventurous," Nate said. "I like it."

"Hands off," Marisa said, swatting his stomach as she went past him. "Kim, can you come upstairs with me for a second?"

Kim picked up a piece of chicken with two fingers as she passed Andrew and his creation station. "No problem." She followed Marisa up the stairs to the study where they'd met during the first party. The lights were still off, but extra light was spilling in from the bathroom when Kim stepped inside.

Marisa immediately turned, closed the door, and pressed herself against Kim. Their kiss was deep, hungry, and Kim pressed one hand against the door to keep from falling over. When they broke apart for air, Marisa pressed her forehead to Kim's and said, "I'm sorry. I'm so sorry. But as soon as I saw you downstairs, I..." She licked her lips. "The truth is, I've been wanting to do it all day. I'm just not much of an exhibitionist."

"I understand." Kim smiled, feeling more than a little lightheaded. "I'm not exactly complaining."

"I didn't pull you away from anything major, did I?"

Kim shook her head. "No, just a poker game. Nothing important."

Marisa looked down at Kim's blouse and slacks. "But you're all dressed up."

"That's for you. I was planning to see if you wanted to do

something after the game."

Marisa smiled. "Oh. Well, it's not necessary. We may look Beverly Hills, but I'm just Mary Prewitt from Iowa. I rarely even wear shoes in the house."

Kim looked down at Marisa's bare feet. "Well, with feet that pretty, I can understand. Seriously, is there any part of you that isn't beautiful?"

"Stop it, flirt." She kissed Kim again, and Kim let her. She was getting used to the feel of Marisa's lips against hers and she realized that any other pair of lips would be a disappointment after kissing these. When they parted, Marisa whispered, "Will you stay over tonight?"

Kim's smile faded. "Yeah."

"I don't want to move too fast. I don't..."

"Hey. We can just sleep, if you want. As long as I'm with you."

Marisa smiled and said, "Good."

"And if it will make you feel more comfortable..." She sat down in the nearest chair and undid the buckles of her boots, setting them aside and wiggling her toes in the carpet.

"Don't forget those when you leave tomorrow," Marisa said.

Kim said, "If I do, it'll give me a reason to come back."

Marisa pulled her out of the chair and kissed her. "You don't need a reason."

Kim smiled and they left the study together. As they went back downstairs, they saw that Andrew had managed to sort out all the dinners onto three different plates.

"Three?" Marisa said.

"Nate is already out on the deck with his," he said. "It's such a nice night, I thought we'd eat dinner out there."

"Sounds good," Marisa said.

Andrew looked pointedly at their empty hands and nodded upstairs. "So, did you find whatever it was you were looking for?"

"Yes," Marisa said. She looked at Kim and said, "I'm pretty sure I finally did."

## CHAPTER TWENTY-THREE

NATHAN OBLIGED Kim, a longtime fan of his series *Royal Canadians*, with stories from the set. As they ate, Sheryl Crow sang from a stereo inside the house, wafting through the open doors just loud enough to be heard but not enough to be obtrusive. As the meal went on, the "couples" broke apart. Nathan and Andrew, on their side of the table, turned more toward each other. Marisa and Kim also turned their attention to each other as well. Marisa told Kim about things that had happened on the set that day, and occasionally glanced toward the pool. Every time she caught Kim watching her watch the pool, she blushed and bent over her food.

"Maybe we can go for a swim later," Kim said.

Marisa's blush deepened. Her foot slid sideways and rested on top of Kim's. Kim curled her toes as Marisa's foot slid across hers, and she suddenly understood the appeal of footsie. She let Marisa toy with her for a moment, then turned to face her more completely. She slid the arch of her foot up Marisa's thigh, stroking it through her jeans. Marisa smiled and poked at her food with chopsticks and she touched her tongue to her bottom lip.

It was almost fully dark before they finished eating. Andrew gathered up the plates. "I think I'm going to head on up to bed. You girls going to be okay?"

"Yeah," Marisa said. "I think I'll spend the night in the guest house again."

Andrew nodded. "Okay." He bent down and kissed the top of her head. "I'll see you in the morning for breakfast. Night, you two."

"Goodnight." Kim watched as Nate helped take the dishes into the kitchen and then, without comment, they both headed upstairs.

Kim leaned back in her chair. "Nathan Worth. Wow. You're not the only one with a faulty gaydar. I never would have guessed. I thought he was dating that chick who plays a robot on *A.Eye.*"

"Camouflage," Marisa said. "Like me and Andrew. But she's going to be filming in Europe for a couple of months so we needed an emergency sub."

Kim shook her head. "Are there any straight people in this business?"

Marisa shrugged. "If there are, they play it close to the vest." She wiped her lips and fingers on a napkin and shifted in her chair. "Kim, I don't want to seem... I don't want you to feel like our relationship is just based on sex, but..."

"Do you want me to take you to the guest house?"

"Yes, please."

Kim stood up and held out her hands. Marisa took them, brushed her thumbs over the back of Kim's hands, and stood up. She slipped her arms around Kim's waist and walked her to the guest house, their bare feet making quiet sweeping noises through the dewy grass.

Marisa turned the lights on and twisted back to face her. The light shone off the waves of hair falling across her face. "Do you want anything to drink?"

"No." Kim pulled Marisa to her, kissing her gently as their bodies moved together. She broke the kiss and touched Marisa's hair, breathing heavily as Marisa rested her hands in the small of her back. "We went a little fast yesterday. I want us to take our time tonight."

"Yeah," Marisa whispered. She kissed Kim again and walked her toward the bed. "Do you want to watch TV? Maybe talk about politics?" She tugged on Kim's shirt, untucking it from her pants.

"Who did you vote for?" Kim whispered as she started to unbutton Marisa's shirt.

"The human being," Marisa said.

"Good."

She let her shirt fall to the floor and pushed Kim onto the bed. She straddled Kim's hips and carefully undid each button of her shirt, spreading the halves aside to reveal a lacy bra. Marisa smiled and ran her thumb over the material. "Lingerie."

"What about it?"

"Nothing, I just... didn't expect it from you."

Kim said, "Well, I would hate to become predictable."

Marisa stroked Kim's cheek with the back of her hand. "Never." She kissed Kim and slid a hand inside her shirt, cupping the breast and brushing her thumb over the lace fringe of one cup. Kim arched her back into the caress and pressed her thigh against Marisa's crotch.

"I bought it special," she sighed when the kiss broke. "Just for you."

"Just for me?" Marisa whispered. She slipped her hand around Kim's back and undid the clasp. Kim wriggled from her blouse and Marisa pulled the bra away. She let it drop to the mattress and lowered her eyes, taking in every curve. She licked her lips. "I like it better over there."

Kim breathed a laugh and pulled Marisa to her for another kiss. Marisa settled on top of Kim and slid her hand down, teasing the waistband of Kim's pants, and Kim lifted her hips to invite further exploration. Marisa undid the catch, slid the zipper down, and folded her fingers together and slid inside. Kim's breath caught in her throat and her eyes closed as Marisa's hand moved between her legs, cupping her through her underwear.

"I'm so scared," Marisa whispered.

"Don't be," Kim said. "I'm right here." She kissed Marisa's cheek, tasting a salty tear, and put her arms around Marisa. "Touch me. Please, Mary."

Marisa stilled for a moment.

"Is that okay?"

Marisa nodded. "Yes. I want you to know who you're making love to."

"Then touch me, Mary," Kim whispered. They kissed again, Marisa's tongue pushing into Kim's mouth as her fingers twisted Kim's underwear out of the way. Kim groaned, and Marisa pressed forward with two fingers. She rubbed in slow circles, watching Kim's face, and the sound of their breathing filled the small space of the guest house.

When Marisa withdrew her hand, Kim clutched her arm. "No, don't stop, please..."

"Slow," Marisa whispered. She slipped off the bed and tugged

Kim's pants down her legs, letting them drop to the floor. She dragged Kim's underwear off and dropped it as well, while Kim pushed her already discarded clothing off the foot of the bed.

Kim propped herself on her elbows. "Now you."

Marisa unbuttoned her jeans, eyes on Kim, and let them fall, stepping out of them before hooking her thumbs in her underwear. She was shaking when she straightened back up and reached behind herself to undo her bra, and her breasts shook when she let it slide down her arms. She stood naked in front of Kim, blushing and shy.

"It's not like the movies, is it?"

"No. Thank God." Kim held out one hand, and Marisa took it, letting herself be pulled back onto the bed. They kissed, and Kim flipped them so that she was on top. Their arms crossed, Marisa's hand back between Kim's legs and Kim's between hers. They kept their eyes open, for the most part, whispering to one another as they worked each other slowly to orgasm.

Kim succumbed first, tightening her thighs around Marisa's hand. "Mary," she whispered, throwing her head back and biting her bottom lip. Marisa lifted her head and kissed Kim's neck as she came. Kim sagged against her, still thrusting with her hand, her thumb extended to brush Marisa's clit, and Marisa pressed her shoulders into the mattress and came with a series of long, shuddering sighs. Kim kissed her cheeks and lips, and once Marisa was capable of movement, she returned them and rolled onto her side.

Kim stretched out next to her, sliding her hand up to Marisa's stomach. Marisa put her head on Kim's shoulder, slipped her leg between Kim's, and cuddled against her. "I want to just lay here a minute. Is that okay?"

"Fine by me," Kim said, stroking Marisa's stomach in slow circles. Within a few seconds, Marisa's breathing had grown steady and she was asleep. Kim kissed her forehead, pulled her closer, and tried to drift off herself.

It would have been easier if she had been able to stop smiling.

Kim woke to Marisa nibbling her ear. She stirred slowly and tightened her grip on Marisa's waist. "Again?" she whispered.

"If you want," Marisa whispered back. At some point, the lights had gone out. Kim assumed Marisa had gotten out of bed to do it, which made her wonder just how deeply she'd been sleeping. "That's not why I woke you, though. I need to tell you something."

"Okay."

Marisa shifted on the bed, pulling the blankets up to her chest. "My last real relationship was about six years ago. Before Andrew. We met on some show I was doing, and she worked backstage. She asked me out, and I was so relieved to not have to go through the whole 'is she or isn't she' game, that I jumped on the opportunity. We went out to dinner a few times, and then she invited me back to her place. We had sex. I'll spare you the gory details..."

"Thank you."

Marisa smiled. "It was my first indiscretion as a quote-unquote 'famous' actress. It made me feel good. It showed me that I could have a relationship without sacrificing my career."

Kim stroked Marisa's bare hip. "I assume something happened."

"She showed up a couple of days later with a video on her phone. She played it for me on the living room TV. It was... us. Having sex. She'd filmed it with a little camera on her nightstand. She told me it was the only copy, and I could have it for one hundred thousand dollars." She focused on Kim's stomach, drawing circles over her navel. "I had enough money to cover it. Barely. So I paid, even though I knew the chances of her really keeping quiet were next to nothing. I had to. I couldn't bear the thought of being... pulled out of the closet like that. But she was true to her word. She left me alone after I paid."

"God, Mary. Have you ever seen her again?"

Marisa shrugged. "Once or twice. Sometimes she'll be working on a set. I avoid her and she acts like she's never met me. But every time I think of how vulnerable I let myself be with her, every time I remember how safe I felt in that apartment, I remember what happened afterward. And I flee. Andrew was so surprised to see you spend the night because I haven't had a real relationship in three years."

Kim leaned in and kissed Marisa. When she pulled back, she whispered, "You can trust me completely."

"You don't have to tell me that," Marisa said with a smile. She touched Kim's face. "You keep me safe. You throw yourself on grenades for me. When I'm with you, I know I don't have to be afraid of anything. Ever." She ran her thumb over Kim's mouth and said, "Thank you. I didn't even realize I'd been hiding until you brought me out. I love you. You were the first person to ever tell me that in real life, and you're the first person I've ever told it to."

Kim smiled and kissed her. "I love you, too. I'll never let anyone hurt you, Mary."

Marisa slid her hand down Kim's body, back between her legs. She shifted closer and said, "Can we make love again now? Please?"

Kim smiled and lifted her hips to meet Marisa's hand. "Well... since you said please..."

Kim woke again in the middle of the night, the moon shining in through the guest house window. Marisa was spooning her, hands resting loose on her stomach. She could hear Marisa's quiet breath against her shoulder, the small twitches of muscles caught in a dream. The world was silent and silver, and Kim pressed tighter against Marisa's body. She smiled, fluffed her pillow, and fell quickly back to sleep.

## CHAPTER TWENTY-FOUR

KIM AND Break turned on cue and ran across the sandy terrain, kicking up dust devils behind them as they went. After a handful of steps, the director shouted, "Now!" They both leapt gracefully forward onto the pad as a slew of debris was sprayed over them.

The director called cut, and Break helped Kim back to her feet. They brushed each other off as the director approached. His name was Lenny Stewart, a short and squat man who looked like a tank when he was charging toward you. Regardless of mood, he always seemed moments away from tearing you a new one. "Fantastic," he said, waving at the scene. "Bar none. Accept no substitutes. Just one thing, though. Kim, you dropped your gun."

"Ah, damn it."

"Don't worry, we'll do another take."

Kim picked up her gun and she and Break went back to their marks. Break glanced at her as Stewart returned to his den. "You dropped your gun? Seriously?"

"So I'm a butterfingers today. I wanted to see how you felt all the time."

"Funny. One thing I know for sure now, though. You are definitely getting laid."

"You can tell that from me dropping a gun?"

He wiggled his fingers at her. "Tired fingers."

Kim shook her head and slugged him in the shoulder. "Keep

on believing that. I'd rather you fantasize than think I'm some poor old maid."

"Just give me a hint. Is she married? Famous? Is she someone I would know?"

"Yes and no. It's your mother."

Break stared at her. "My mother?"

"Yep. Me and her, hot and heavy."

Stewart called action, and they broke into another run. This time, it looked more like Break was chasing Kim and she was running for her life.

The shoot was on location in one of the only desert-like areas near the studios. Trailers lined the far edge of the land, draped with a tarp in the color of sand in case they needed to shoot in that direction. A green, lush neighborhood was visible just over the tallest dune, with water in the distance. If the camera panned a little too high into the sky, it would reveal telephone wires stretching from one side of the landscape to the other.

Sulfur, the explosives expert, was setting up the big explosion that would be spliced with Kim and Break's run-and-jump, so the cast was released for lunch. Kim went to Marisa's trailer and knocked just under the sign that had her name. She heard a muffled, "Come in," and pulled the door open.

Marisa was lying on the couch with a script, her costume covered by a fluffy white robe. She smiled when she saw who her visitor was and closed her script. "Hey, there."

"You don't have to stop just because I'm here." Kim lifted Marisa's legs, sat down, and let Marisa's bare feet rest on her lap.

"What if someone comes in?" Marisa asked. Kim started rubbing Marisa's feet, and Marisa sagged against the arm of the couch. "Oh, God. Screw it. I'll barricade the door."

Kim chuckled. "How's the script?"

"Good. I really like Simone. She's one of the strongest characters I've ever played. I really hope the series does well."

Kim shrugged. "The books are all bestsellers. They're up to twelve now, I think. You could be doing this job for a decade."

"I'd welcome it. Save me from a lifetime of being the romantic lead, the batting eyelashes and being saved by big manly men." She closed her eyes and said, "God, that feels good."

"Have you ever had sex in your trailer?"

Marisa chuckled. "No."

Kim slid her hand higher, next to Marisa's ankle. "Wanna?"

Marisa moaned. "Yes. But no, I can't."

"Rain check."

"Definitely." Marisa sat up. "Come here." She slipped her hand to the back of Kim's neck and pulled her in for a kiss. As soon as their lips touched, something outside the trailer exploded. They both jumped, and looked toward the window. Kim smiled and jerked her head toward the window. "The, uh... stunt."

"Are you sure?" Marisa asked, curling her fingers so that the nails lightly scratched the nape of Kim's neck.

Kim said, "No. Not at all." She pushed Marisa down on the couch and crawled on top of her. "If we can't have sex..." she kissed Marisa's bottom lip and slid her hand over Marisa's breast, the shape blunted by costume and robe, "...maybe we can just make out a little."

"Or a lot," Marisa said as she lifted her head for another kiss.

"Research for Simone's bisexuality." Kim's hand slipped under the robe.

Marisa moaned and kissed Kim's jaw. "Being a completely straight woman, I'll need all the help I can get, Ms. Stunt Coordinator."

"Work, work, work," Kim sighed against Marisa's mouth.

While on the set, they maintained a modicum of professionalism. At night, they usually went back to Marisa's house and they spent the night in the guest house. One night, lying in bed post-coital and drowsy, Kim said, "Andy doesn't mind us monopolizing the guest house this way?"

"Mm. No. The guest house is mine." She sniffled, eyes closed, and rolled over in Kim's arms. She pressed her face to Kim's chest and kissed between her collarbones. "When we bought the house, we made a deal. He got the master bedroom, and I got the smaller bedroom with the full use of this place. We share the rest of the house equally. Well, except the upstairs bathroom. That's all him. You would not *believe* how much product that man puts in his hair."

Kim smiled. "So you don't mind me forcing you to sleep out here?"

"I sleep out here a lot anyway. It's better with you."

Kim laced her fingers together in the small of Marisa's back. "I should probably sleep at home tomorrow night." Marisa groaned and pressed tighter against Kim. Kim laughed. "Stop it. My aunt is probably ready to call the cops to come find me."

"Have you spoken to her since...?"

"Yeah. It's fine. She accepts it as long as I don't talk about it very much. But she's starting to change her tune on that, too. It's progress." She stroked Marisa's shoulder and heard her purr. She ran her knuckle down Marisa's spine and Marisa's back arched against her. "I want you to meet her sometime."

"I'd like that." Her voice was slurred with sleep, and Kim could tell she was trying valiantly to stay awake.

She kissed Marisa's hair. "Go to sleep, sweetheart. We can talk in the morning."

"Mm-hmm, 'kay."

Kim stroked Marisa's back as her breathing became even. She looked out the window, where she could see the sparkling water of the pool reflected against the side of the house. The night was still, although she could hear the occasional car on a side street, and she focused on the sound of Marisa's breath. It was like a white noise machine, soothing her thoughts and slowly pulling her into unconsciousness.

Mabel was closing the store when Kim got home the next day. Mabel was inside and watched Kim approach through the glass. Kim smiled, gestured at the doorknob, and waited while Mabel made a show of unlocking the door again. She pulled it open, stepped back as Kim entered, and clicked her tongue.

"Well, well. I guess you *do* still live here. I was starting to wonder, you know, having not seen you in so long."

"You saw me... Tuesday."

Mabel said, "And today being Friday means that you have been out doing God knows what. With God knows who!"

"You know who." Kim pointed at the TV. "Marisa Larkin. You saw her. Are you getting senile?"

"If I was, who would know? No one ever sees me day to day, how would anyone notice?"

Kim cleared her throat and dropped the joking tone. "Marisa wants to meet you."

Mabel shifted and fiddled with her keys. "Oh, does she. Well. Well, I don't know."

"She knows how important you are to me, and everything you've done for me in the past. She just wants to see where I came from."

"Well, you didn't come from *me*."

"I know," Kim said softly. "But..."

Mabel waved at her. "Let me finish. Everything you are came from you, Kim. You did it. You made yourself." She patted Kim's shoulder. "Didn't do a bad job of it, either."

Kim smiled. "Thank you, Mabel. So, will you have dinner with Marisa?"

"No kissy-face."

"Do you mean I can't kiss her, or she can't kiss you?"

"Oh, feh." Mabel waved her hands frantically and shook her head as she stepped outside the store. "Either, neither, go away, you mean girl."

Kim chuckled and waited until Mabel locked the door and was safely in her car before she went through the office to the stairs.

Episode four was a continuation of the plot from episode three. A handful of suicide bombers had already headed out on missions before Lethe and Temple destroyed the base. Unaware their families were safe from retribution, they were going to carry out the bombings unless Lethe and Temple could find them. Downtown was doubling as New York, and production chose a street that could reasonably be mistaken as Manhattan. The street was blocked off and completely redressed with new cars and new trees, going by a photograph someone had gotten off the internet. A barber shop sign was covered by that of a deli, and an extra in a turban stood in front of one restaurant with a broom and waited for his cue to begin sweeping.

Kim was on set because the climax of the scene involved Agent Lethe grappling with a suicide bomber before he could set off the charge. Marisa was going to do it herself, but she wanted to go through the moves before they committed anything to film.

They found an alley between two buildings where they could rehearse. A few people hung around the barricades to watch, and others stood in the windows and peered down, but mostly they were left alone. So many projects, TV and movie, had been filmed in town that most people were jaded to the spectacle.

Kim took the place of the bomber, and Marisa stood a few feet in front of her. Kyle, who was playing the bomber in the episode, stood to one side and watched. "You lunge at me. I bring up my hand to stop you, and you grab my hand." Marisa stepped forward, wrapped her fingers around Kim's fist, and Kim put a hand on her shoulder. They twisted and Marisa's arm went across Kim's chest. "I try to escape, but you hold on." Kim bent forward, and Marisa pulled her back. She clasped her hands together and pinned Kim against her. "He struggles, steps on your foot~"

"He steps on my foot?"

"You'll have steel toed boots."

"Okay." She cleared her throat and Kim smirked. If only the other actor wasn't there, this position would definitely merit a comment.

Kim slipped out of the embrace and said, "Ready to try it with Kyle?"

"Why not. Hi, Kyle."

He stepped into position and they went through the scene slowly. With each repetition, they got faster and faster until it looked like Marisa was actually fighting with Kyle. "Excellent. Very good." She clapped her hands and the two broke apart. "That should do it for stunts right now. Thanks, Kyle."

"I'll see you on set," Marisa said as Kyle walked off. She walked up to Kim and said, "That was kind of nice, rehearsing the fight with you. Up close and personal."

"Careful," Kim said, moving her lips as little as possible. "We have an audience."

"Just an actress going over a stunt with her double," Marisa said as she fussed with the cuff of her shirt. "Could you help me with this button?"

Kim stepped closer and took the highest button. There were three buttons on the sleeve, and all of them were undone. She carefully worked it into the hole and tugged on the material to make sure it was tight before moving on to the next. "Stunt people don't usually deal with costuming."

"They do when the buttons come loose in the process of doing a stunt. And you would hate for an unbuttoned sleeve to ruin a take. Continuity is everything."

"True," Kim said.

"You smell nice."

Kim smirked.

"I missed you last night."

Kim did up the last button and said, "There you go." She licked her lips and said, "I could probably swing by your place after we're done shooting. If you wanted to hang out."

Marisa pretended to consider it. "Sure. I don't have anything planned for tonight."

Kim let Marisa drop her wrist and said, "There you are. Ready for your close-up, Miss Larkin."

"Thank you, Miss Greer."

Kim stepped back and stuck her hands in the back pockets of her jeans. Marisa walked toward the mass of cameras and lighting guys. A few seconds later, with a self-conscious glance at the people watching from the sidelines, Kim followed.

George Bradshaw was a drab little man with thick glasses, his shirt collar standing up so that the corners brushed his chin whenever he turned his head. He had a small tape recorder sitting on the table between him and Marisa's position on the couch, one leg draped over the other at the knee, reclining comfortably in the armchair as he checked his notes. "Okay, so it'll just be a quick little piece for Rebecca Kenny's website. Nothing too groundbreaking. She has a lot of fans who just want to make sure the series is true to the books."

"I totally understand," Marisa said. "We want to make them happy. We're lucky enough to be going into the series with a built-in fan base; we don't want to tick any of them off."

"Okay, so we'll start with similarities to the book series. Have you read any of the novels?"

"I'm a big, big fan. It's why I wanted to play this part. I've been avoiding the later books so I won't be tainted by anything that happens in them. No spoilers in your fan mail, folks." She grinned and Bradshaw chuckled and marked something down on his notepad. "There are some changes, of course, that had to be made for the purposes of, you know, a thirteen-episode television series. But for the most part, things are pretty similar. The pilot and second episode follow the first book pretty closely."

The trailer door opened and Kim stepped inside, saw the reporter, and motioned that she would come back. Marisa leaned forward and said, "No, it's okay," waving Kim in. Kim hesitantly complied, closing the door behind her.

Marisa continued as Kim took a seat next to her on the couch. "The fans don't have to worry. We're playing the same characters they've read about for all these years. I'm very focused on keeping true to what Ms. Kenny has written."

"And who is this?" Bradshaw asked, looking between Kim and Marisa. They were both dressed alike for the upcoming stunt and he was marveling at the similarities.

Marisa put a hand on Kim's knee. "Kim Greer, stuntwoman extraordinaire. She's going to do all the amazing, kick ass stuff that makes Simone Lethe look good while I'm kicking back in my trailer drinking margaritas."

"Wonderful! So, Kim, what stunt do you have today?"

Kim shifted uncomfortably. "Uh... we have an explosive expert blowing up the front door of a hotel. I'm going to be thrown into a mailbox. Well, technically I'm being yanked up against a mailbox."

"Sounds dangerous," Bradshaw said.

Marisa said, "That's why they pay her the big bucks." She winked at Bradshaw, rubbed Kim's thigh, and winked at her. Kim pursed her lips and tried to relax as the interview moved back onto the topic of Simone and the book series. Marisa kept her hand on Kim's leg as long as she could get away with.

Finally, Bradshaw packed up his recorder, tucked his notepad into a jacket pocket, and stood up. He shook hands with Marisa and Kim both, then made his way out of the trailer to find William Easter. Kim sagged against the back of the couch, exhausted from keeping herself under control during the interview.

"God, that was an ordeal."

Marisa turned and put her hand on Kim's hip. "It wasn't so bad."

"He could write about... you know... the touching. Or the fact I just happened to wander in to your trailer in the middle of the day."

Marisa moved her hand under Kim's shirt. "One of my little non-relationships, about four years ago. I was doing an interview at home, and the woman I had spent the night with came downstairs wearing nothing but a half-buttoned blouse and a sleepy smile. She kissed me good morning before she realized there were strangers in the house. Remember seeing that on the tabloid shows?"

"Um... not really."

"They didn't use it. There are trashy tabloids, and there are paparazzi bastards, but for the most part, reporters are respectful of privacy. Trust me. Nothing bad will happen."

Kim slid down on the couch, pulling Marisa down with her. "I'm still not sold."

"What will I have to do to convince you?" Marisa asked, her lips moving against Kim's as she spoke.

"Lots," Kim said. She kissed Marisa, moaned, and said, "I can be very stubborn."

Marisa grinned and settled down to make her case.

## CHAPTER TWENTY-FIVE

KIM WORKED with Sulfur on her first job as a stuntwoman. He stumbled from a garage engulfed in flames, and it was Kim's job to tackle him with a blanket and pat out the fire. She was terrified of working with fire, but he calmed her and explained the entire process to her beginning to end. He walked her through the safety procedures and assured her they would both make it out unscathed or "at least with less than first degree burns."

At the moment, he was rigging the front door of a hotel with explosive charges. She didn't understand the machinations required for a hotel to agree to something like this, but that wasn't her job. She stood to one side with her harness on, draped with her blazer. A bungee cord snaked under the back of the jacket, making her appear to have a long thin tail that disappeared in the den of snakes surrounding the cameras. The explosives would go off in front of her - they would be magnified in post-production - and she would be pulled back into the tall blue USPS box that props had placed on the street.

Solomon Thomas was directing again, and he made his way over as Sulfur finished with the charges. "Everything ready? Kim?"

"Ready to go, boss." She looked back at the mailbox. She was supposed to hit it, crumple, and fall over. No problem.

"Charges?"

"Primed and ready."

"Let's light this candle." Solomon winked at Kim and went back to his position behind the monitor. He hopped into his seat and said, "Ready. Action."

The charge popped and sent up a wave of heat and smoke. Kim barely registered it as Break and another stuntman pulled on the bungee cord and she was yanked off her feet. She knew something was wrong the minute she moved; she was angled wrong, and her right foot was only about an inch off the ground. If she wanted to hit the mailbox correctly–

Her shoulder glanced off the metal box, sending a shudder of pain through her bones. She dropped to the ground, skidded, and slammed into the side of a car. She slumped to the sidewalk, her hands folded in her lap, and took an instant inventory to make sure nothing had been broken. Her shoulder was still numb, but she could tell the pain was coming.

"What the hell was that?" she heard Solomon shout.

"New guy didn't pull hard enough," Break groused as he vaulted over the car's hood. He dropped to a crouch next to Kim and tenderly touched her shoulder. "How's it? Anything broken?"

"Don't think so. Just winged me." She looked past Break and raised an eyebrow. "New guy?"

"New guy," he confirmed, teeth clenched. "Solomon's chewing him out now. Think you can stand?"

Kim held out her uninjured arm and Break helped her stand. She leaned on him, her injured arm cradled against her side as she let him walk her off the curb. "Let's give the medics something to do. Make their lives worthwhile."

"You just wanted to talk to that hot nurse," Kim said. "You set me up, Break."

"If I really wanted to talk to her, I would've broken my leg again. Chicks dig broken bones."

Kim rolled her eyes. She was about to speak again when she heard her name called from the direction of the trailers. She and Break both turned to see Marisa jogging over to them.

"Oh, my God," Marisa said, eyes wide with horror. "What happened?"

"New guy misjudged my weight, didn't pull hard enough. I hit the mailbox wrong. It happens. I'm fine."

Break said, "I'm just taking her to the medic now. She'll get an ice pack and a stern warning not to do anything strenuous for a while. Which she'll ignore. But that just means she's a stuntwoman."

"I feel so guilty." Marisa touched Kim's shoulder and flinched as if she was the one who had been hurt. There were tears in her eyes. "Does it hurt very badly?"

"It's fine. I've been hurt worse."

Marisa shook her head. "Still."

Break looked between them. One eyebrow slowly drifted up. "Ah... Miss Larkin, would you mind taking her the rest of the way for me? I have to go rip off the head of my former protégé."

"I'd be happy to."

They transferred Kim, who protested, "I hurt my shoulder, I'm not an invalid."

"Be quiet. Thanks, Mr. Ransom."

"Call me Break." As Marisa turned toward the medics, Kim glanced back in time to see Break mouth, "You could have told me." He smiled, winked, and backed away.

Kim tightened her grip on Marisa and said, "I really am okay."

"You got hurt because of me."

"Hey, Mary." They stopped and turned so they could face each other. "We're not going through this every time I get banged up. And I'm going to get banged up. It's the nature of the beast. I'm willing to do it to protect you."

Marisa pressed her lips together in a pout. "It doesn't mean I have to like it."

"I'm not asking you to like it. I'm asking you to understand."

Marisa nodded.

"I don't like the idea of you doing sex scenes with men. Kissing them, letting them... touch you." She shuddered and pushed the idea out of her mind. "But that's the nature of the beast, right? Shit happens. If you still feel bad at the end of the day, I'll let you take me home and give me a massage. Oils and lotions and everything."

"Deal," Marisa said with a laugh. She pursed her lips. "I really want to kiss you right now."

Kim lifted her hand and pressed her thumb to the back of Marisa's hand. "Good for one kiss, to be delivered at a later date."

Marisa pressed her thumb to the back of Kim's hand. "What if we lose track?"

"We'll guess, and round up. Come on. Let's find a bag of ice, my shoulder is killing me."

A few days after the accident, Kim was in Marisa's bedroom,

waiting for Marisa to get ready for dinner. She sat on the edge of the bed she had never slept in, taking stock of the little details, clues to Marisa's past and present. There were photos of Marisa as a smiling, lanky teenager, and Kim smiled at each one of them. She had been beautiful, even way back then.

Marisa came out of the bathroom in a lavender-colored slip, head tilted to put her earring in. "How is your shoulder?" Marisa asked.

"It's much better." Kim stood and demonstrated by moving her arm in a wide circle without wincing. "You know, we've been together for three weeks, and I've never seen your bedroom. That seems odd."

Marisa went to the vanity and smiled at Kim's reflection. She started to apply her makeup. "I keep my nicest stuff up here."

Kim walked up behind Marisa, wrapping her arms around Marisa's midsection and watching her apply the war paint. "It's just my aunt, you know. It's not an awards ceremony. She stopped televising her dinners in 1996." She kissed Marisa's neck and rested her chin on her shoulder.

"Still, I want to make an impression. I want her to know that you're important enough to me that I want to impress her. Relationships are based on familial perception of the loved one."

Kim scoffed. "What, did you play a psychiatrist at some point?"

"2009, *Sessions*. Dr. Linda Cardinal."

Kim's hand strayed to the hem of Marisa's slip. "Did you have a nude scene in that?"

"No, but I had a... a lesbian kiss."

"Ooh," Kim said. "I'm going to have to rent it."

"You might get insanely jealous. It's a very hot kiss. I'm surprised no one figured out I'm gay just from watching me make out with my beautiful, beautiful-"

Kim said, "Okay, you can stop now."

Marisa chuckled. She turned around in Kim's arms and pulled her close. "Jealous?"

"Yes," Kim said.

Marisa put her hands on Kim's ass, her fingers warm against the smooth material of the suit pants. "Do you remember your first kiss? That thrill, the pressure of her lips against yours, the 'this is what everyone is always talking about' wonder? How magical it feels?"

"Yes."

"When you kiss me, it's even better than that," Marisa whispered.

Kim smiled.

"My first kiss was on camera. It kind of spoiled the experience for me. When I get kissed, it triggers the memory of that first choreographed kiss, and it lessens it for me. But the second your lips touch mine, I'm gone. I'm melting. I forget every other kiss."

Kim tilted her head and kissed Marisa. Their kiss grew hungrier with each passing moment, until Marisa gently backed away. "Stop. We really shouldn't start anything we can't finish."

"So let's finish it."

Marisa laughed. "You're insatiable. I'll tell you what. If you behave with your aunt tonight, I'll reward you in a very special way."

"Are you implying sexual congress?"

Marisa leaned in and whispered, her lips brushing the shell of Kim's ear. Kim sagged at the promise and held on tight to keep from stumbling. Marisa licked Kim's ear, and Kim sagged against her.

"But only if you're a very good girl."

"What if I'm bad?"

Marisa arched an eyebrow and went back to her makeup.

Kim sighed and put her hand on Marisa's hip. "Great. Now I don't know how to act."

Mabel's home was a small house on a quiet street, a chain link fence around the front yard. The house looked as if it was standing guard for the large apartment building looming behind it, a structure that blocked Mabel's backyard from the sun for most of the day. It was murder on the grass, but Mabel loved it for the ability to sit in the shade on the hottest days of the year without an umbrella or a fan.

Kim parked in the apartment's lot, since it was easier than parking in the street. Marisa had finally settled on a purple dress with thin straps over a pale mauve T-shirt. She wore flats instead of high heels, at Kim's insistence. Kim wore a dress shirt and suit pants, her hair pulled back and held by a clip. She hooked her arm around Marisa's and drew her close. She reached down and laced their fingers together.

Marisa looked down at their joined hands. "Are you sure this is okay?"

"If it's not, better for her to get used to it now." She looked around the parking lot, long shadows thrown by the setting sun obscuring the details of the cars. "Unless you meant... someone will see."

"No." Marisa tightened her grip so Kim couldn't get away. "I just didn't want your aunt to get grossed out."

Kim smiled and led the way around the side of Mabel's house. The front porch needed a fresh coat of paint, but the lawn was well cared for. Kim pushed through the creaky gate, stepped onto the porch, and rang the doorbell. "She's going to love you," Kim promised. "You have nothing to worry about."

Marisa took a deep breath that trembled a bit upon release. "I changed my mind. You have to behave, and you have to keep me calm. Do both of those things and you'll get your reward."

"You mean the strap~" She popped the last letter and stopped herself from continuing as the door swung open.

Mabel stood in the glow of two living room lamps. She eyed Marisa, looked at their joined hands, and looked at Kim for a long moment. She worked her lips against her dentures and said, "Well. I guess you're on time. Come on in." She turned around and walked away from them.

"Wow," Kim said. "She really likes you."

Marisa blinked. "Okay. Behave, keep me calm, and translate for your aunt."

Kim laughed and dragged Marisa into her aunt's house.

The front door led into a cozy living room, furnished spartanly with only an armchair and a TV. The dining room table was under the living room window and lit by the ceiling fan that was slowly turning circles overhead. Mabel walked past the table to the kitchen where she withdrew a meatloaf from the stove. She carried it to the counter and motioned at the table with her chin. "Sit, sit. Don't stand around like beefeaters."

"Beefeaters?" Marisa muttered.

Kim said, "Buckingham Palace guards."

The table was already set with two places in front of the window, and one facing it. Marisa said, "Is she letting us sit together, or am I the odd one out?"

Kim said, "I'm not really sure. Aunt Mabel..."

Mabel said, "Sit together, for Pete's sake. The things you two are already doing together, God knows, but sitting next to each other at dinnertime is hardly the strangest, I think."

They took their seats, and Kim noticed Marisa glance at the

window. The curtains were drawn, and there were no reason to assume the paparazzi knew she was there. Kim squeezed her thigh under the table and smiled reassuringly. Marisa returned the smile and relaxed.

"So, Miss Movie Star. Who are you when you aren't pretending to be someone else, getting all naked for every person with ten dollars?"

"Auntie Em!" Kim snapped.

Mabel, the face of innocence, said, "I'm just trying to make conversation."

Marisa's face was red, but from the effort of trying to contain her laughter. She put her hand on Kim's shoulder, as a thank you for standing up for her and a sign that it wasn't necessary. "I was born in Wichita, Nebraska, and we moved to Iowa when I was seven. My parents were David and Sarah Prewitt. Welder and schoolteacher, respectively. I changed my name when I was seventeen. I don't do drugs, I only smoke occasionally, and I don't drink to excess. Your niece is the first person I've felt comfortable with in a long time. I feel safe with her, which is a rarity for me. And even if you don't approve of me by the end of the night, I'm going to stay with her as long as she'll have me, because I'm crazy for her. And I'm going to treat her like a queen every day of her life to keep her from wanting to leave me. Any questions?"

Kim was looking down at her lap, smiling wide enough to split her face.

Mabel brought the meatloaf to the table and served them both. She carried the pan to the kitchen, took her time taking off her oven mitts, and came back to her seat. She looked at Kim, nodded her head toward Marisa. "She sure is a talker, this one, isn't she?"

Kim laughed.

"Kim doesn't smoke, not even a little bit. She finally broke that nasty habit. You want to be with her, you stop, too. Stop completely, not 'occasionally sneak cigarettes.'"

Marisa nodded. "Okay."

Mabel folded a napkin in her lap, settled in her chair, and looked between Kim and Marisa. Finally, she sighed, threw her hands up, and said, "Eh, why not. Better than you having a man who doesn't really care about you. I approve. As long as she does the dishes. But for now, we eat."

## CHAPTER TWENTY-SIX

KIM SAT on the edge of Marisa's bed, red-faced and struggling to breathe normally. "You know," she said, her fingers laced together with Marisa's. "I kept my promise. I behaved... uh... protected you... and translated Aunt Mabel's moods." She licked her lips as Marisa kissed her stomach. "I believe we had a deal..."

Marisa lifted her head. "Did we?"

Kim grunted and she moved her elbows against the mattress to support herself better. Marisa was kneeling on the floor, her arms around Kim's thighs and her hands flat against Kim's pubic hair. Marisa lifted herself to kiss Kim's cleavage. "I don't remember a promise."

Kim said, "Tease."

Marisa bit her bottom lip and sank back down. One hand stretched out and Kim heard a drawer rolling open. Her heart sped up, and she struggled to catch her breath. In the darkness, her skin looked red, an optical illusion she had been trying to figure out in her brief moments of clear thought. She couldn't see anything that would cast a red light on the bed.

Marisa leaned back. "You, um... y-you might have to walk me through this."

"No problem. It's a lot easier to explain than how to fight." Kim licked her lips, swallowed hard, and frowned at the toy. "Hey, why do you have one of those if you've been celibate for three years?"

"Because I've been celibate for three years."

Kim shrugged. "Good point. Just step into it like a pair of underwear." Marisa disappeared from between her legs, and Kim had a momentary change of heart. She wanted to tell Marisa to forget the toy, forget the game, and just *come back*. She steadied her nerves as Marisa squirmed about on the floor. "Got it, hon?" Kim asked, balling her hands into fists in the sheets.

"Yeah, almost."

"Tighten the... straps on the sides. Until they're comfortable."

After a moment, Marisa reappeared. She was still wearing her mauve T-shirt, but the dress was long gone. As was her underwear, as evidenced by her nipples pressing against the tight material. She climbed onto the bed and Kim scooted back to give her room. She lifted her hips and Marisa reached between them to angle herself properly. Kim exhaled and closed her eyes as the tip brushed against flesh made hypersensitive by Marisa's tongue.

"What's wrong?"

"Nothing, baby," Kim said. "It's good, it's good."

Marisa said, "I've always wanted to do this, but I never... trusted anyone enough." Kim opened her eyes and Marisa slipped inside of her.

Kim's eyes rolled back in her head and she wrapped her legs around Marisa's waist. She found her fingers caught in the hem of Marisa's shirt and held tight, tugging on it to pull Marisa to her. She rolled her head against the mattress and groaned, "You just... have to..."

"Shh," Marisa said. "Shh, I think I got it..."

"Yes," Kim groaned. "Oh, Mary, yes, fuck me..."

Marisa rocked her lower body, her hand resting between Kim's breasts. "Kim," Marisa whispered. "How is that?"

"Good... good..." Her toes curled and she lifted her shoulders off the mattress as she came, her body clenching like a fist. She pulled Marisa to her and they kissed, sloppy and wet, a mashing of lips as their bodies continued to move without their consent. Finally Marisa lowered Kim to the mattress and settled on top of her, panting.

"Mary," Kim said. "Why is my skin red?"

"Maybe you're just that hot," Marisa said. She dragged her thumb along Kim's flank, but then lifted her head and looked around the bedroom. "Mm. Alarm clock. Oh..."

Kim looked and saw an alarm clock on the bookstand. The room was dark enough that the red LCD washed the room in a gentle crimson glow. The bed was far enough at the edge of the penumbra that it made Kim look dark red.

"Oh..."

She frowned and cuddled against Marisa again. "Why did you say 'oh'?"

"Nothing."

"Tell me," Kim said, giving her voice a bit of a whine.

Marisa sighed. "It's not a big deal. But it's after midnight."

"Mm-hmm."

"It's my birthday."

Kim sat up. "What?"

"Please don't make a big deal."

Kim stroked Marisa's hair. "I won't. I just wish I had given you something."

"At the risk of sounding corny, you did give me something," Marisa whispered. She kissed the curve of Kim's left breast, holding her lips against the skin a little longer than necessary. Kim wondered if she could feel her heart beating. Marisa lay her head back down. "So, what's the next thing on your fantasy list?"

Kim smiled. "You might not be into it."

"As long as I'm in it."

"Role play."

Marisa laughed and lifted her head. "Why would you think I'm not into that?"

Kim shrugged. "It's what you do for a living." She brushed a hair out of Marisa's face and Marisa moved her head with the caress. "I just thought you might not be interested in bringing playacting into the bedroom."

Marisa lowered her voice and adopted a southern drawl. "Think again, sheriff."

Kim laughed and stroked Marisa's hair. "I'll keep that in mind."

Andrew's hair was mussed, and he wore a pair of pajama pants and an old T-shirt. He was at the stove, meticulously measuring out batter for pancakes. Kim sat at the counter over the eggs she'd cooked for herself before he came down, waiting for Marisa to shower and change. He said, "So, do you live here now? Because we have a chore wheel."

Kim smirked. "I'm squatting. No responsibilities."

Andrew sighed theatrically and poured pancake batter.

"Can I ask you a personal question about Marisa?"

"Is it about why she never dated much?"

Kim shook her head. "She told me about that. I just wanted to make sure there wasn't some deep dark reason she doesn't celebrate her birthday."

"Oh, that," Andrew said. "When is it, today?" Kim nodded. "No, it's nothing deep seated. It's just that she doesn't like the idea of people making a big fuss over her. Spending money on parties and cakes and presents, rearranging their schedules for a party... it's a hassle, and she doesn't like being the cause of it."

Kim said, "Oh. Well, I guess I can understand that."

Andrew said, "You want pancakes to go with your eggs?"

"I thought I was a freeloader."

"You are. Freeloaders mooch."

Kim chuckled. "Well, I'll pass for right now."

Marisa came downstairs dressed for work and Andrew waved his spatula in greeting. "Happy birthday, Marisa."

"Thank you, Andrew." She brushed her hand along Kim's shoulders as she passed and sat on the stool next to her.

"Do you have time for breakfast? I can make you something."

"Yeah, some pancakes would be fine." She rested her head on the counter and yawned. It was still on the wrong side of six in the morning. "Bankers aren't even awake yet. Farmers are still out partying."

Kim reached over and rubbed her back. "Poor baby."

Marisa whimpered.

"You have to let me do something special for you tonight."

Marisa sat up. "No. Nothing extravagant. I don't like~"

"Andrew told me. But I want to. I swear, I won't go into debt or anything, I won't make a big fuss, but I still want to do something. The day is supposed to honor you, and I don't want to pass up the opportunity."

"Maybe dinner at the Tree House?"

"Sure." She put her hand on Kim's thigh and squeezed. "Thank you."

Kim patted Marisa's hand, brought it to her lips, and kissed the knuckles. "Have fun at work today."

"What do you have to do?"

"Jogging, training with Pluto... I have some errands to run. I think everything in the fridge in my apartment is spoiled."

Marisa frowned. "You jog this early?"

"No, I'll wait until seven or so."

"Then why are you awake?"

Kim said, "Because you're awake. I wanted to have breakfast with you."

Andrew, at the stove, said, "Aw," without turning around.

"Ignore him, he's a cynic," Marisa said. She touched Kim's cheek and leaned in to kiss her. "Thank you. That was very sweet of you. But I'd hate for you to be sleep deprived because of me. You can roll over and go back to sleep after I get out of bed."

Kim smiled. "I'll keep that in mind."

Andrew put two pancakes in front of Marisa and she pulled the syrup closer. "Pay close attention, Kim. It's not often you watch an actress scarf a meal that most lumberjacks would need a doggy-bag for."

Kim rested her chin on her hand and said, "I'm on the edge of my seat."

Marisa looked at her and blushed before she, as promised, tore into her pancakes.

Kim relaxed, cell phone against her ear, and toyed with the edge of the sheet as she listened to Marisa on the other end. "Four takes of the same scene. How many different ways can I follow Temple into an office?" She sighed. "By the fifth time, I'm not even paying attention to what I'm saying. So the performance has got to suck. 'Wooden acting.' I hate seeing that in a review. It's not my fault. Well, not always."

Kim smiled. "You know they'll use the first take anyway."

"Oh, so the last few run-throughs were just a waste of time. That makes me feel better."

Kim laughed.

"Hey, your Jeep isn't in the driveway. Where are you?"

"I'm at my apartment, getting ready for our big date." She crossed her feet on top of the mattress and found a more comfortable position on the bed. She rested her free hand across her stomach. "You're not too tired, are you? We could always postpone it a while and call it a late birthday dinner."

Marisa groaned. "I don't know. It is kind of late, and I am completely wiped out. It might be best to just stay in tonight. I hope you're not all dressed up..."

"No, you said it was just a regular dinner out." Kim looked out the window. The moon was already out, shining bright. "But maybe... well, I'm already at my apartment. Maybe I should go ahead and sleep here."

There was a pause and Marisa said, "Okay... that would probably... be best, I guess. But... well, it is my birthday."

Kim smiled. "You said not to make a big deal. I'm just~"

"I know. I just... it would have been really nice to see you."

"I'm sorry, baby. But if you're tired..."

"Yeah. I know. No, it's fine. You should get sleep in your apartment once in a while."

Kim shifted on the bed. "Hey, you're home, right?"

"Mm-hmm."

"You should go out to the guest house. I left a rose on the pillow for you."

Marisa sighed. "Oh, you romantic. That's so sweet. Hold on." Kim heard the French doors open. "Are you planning to go to bed after we hang up?"

"Probably pretty soon," Kim said. "Why?"

Marisa lowered her voice, obviously crossing the lawn. "I figure if we're both on the phone, in bed, in our pajamas, we might... talk."

Kim grinned. "That could be kind of fun."

"Oh, no 'kind of' about it. You haven't lived until you've had phone sex with Marisa... Larkin." Her voice trailed off as she opened the guest house door.

Kim lay in the bed, feet crossed at the ankles and her legs draped with a long, flowing gown. The shoulder straps were wide, but the front dipped low enough to show off her cleavage. Her hair was curled, down around her shoulders, and she was actually wearing makeup. She had on black strapped high heels, stockings, jewelry, the works. True to her promise, one red rose rested on Marisa's pillow. She looked like a supermodel from fifty years ago, all glamour and glitz, and Marisa was absolutely speechless.

"Kim," Marisa said, her voice breaking.

Kim snapped the phone shut and spread her arms across the pillows. "I've thought about it. I'm not interested in having phone sex right now. Is that okay?"

"Okay," Marisa muttered. She dumped her bag and tossed her phone at it, not bothering to make sure it landed safely.

"How do I look?"

"Beautiful," Marisa said. She closed the door and looked toward the bathroom where three candles were burning. Her lower lip trembled and she said, "What..."

"I wanted to give you a bath."

Marisa blinked and walked to the bed. She held her hands out, and pulled Kim to her feet. "You look so beautiful."

"You deserve it." She kissed the corners of Marisa's mouth, then the spot between her eyebrows. She moved her hands to the collar of Marisa's blouse and began undoing the buttons. "I love you. Happy birthday."

"Kim," Marisa said. She kissed Kim, resting her hands on the hips of the beautiful gown, and said against her mouth, "You look like a dream."

Kim spread apart the halves of Marisa's shirt and lightly touched her breasts. "Well, then. Let's make it a good one." She backed up to the bed and pulled Marisa down on top of her.

## CHAPTER TWENTY-SEVEN

HALFWAY THROUGH filming for episode seven, there was a milestone. Kim felt it coming, heralded by sleepless nights when Marisa tossed and turned until well past midnight, and mornings when she hardly touched her breakfast. One morning when they were alone in her trailer, Kim nudged her leg and said, "What's going on? Are you okay?"

Marisa managed a weak smile and said, "Yes, I'm... I'm fine. Mostly fine. Kind of fine." She sighed and her shoulders sagged. "Tomorrow is Wednesday. The fourteenth."

"What about it?"

Marisa picked up a *Variety* and tossed it to Kim. "Check the grid."

Kim guessed what the milestone was as soon as the guide came out, but she looked anyway. *Neutral Ground*, an all new pilot set to air on TBC. A special ninety minute episode presented with limited commercial interruption. She smiled and said, "Hey, congratulations. It's a big day tomorrow."

"Yeah," Marisa said. "My work gets thrown out there to the wolves and I have to sit around and wait for the reviews to trickle onto the internet. Or worse, it'll be so bad the bloggers can't wait to tear it to shreds. And all I can do it wait."

Kim sat down and pulled Marisa to her. Marisa turned and draped her legs over Kim's lap. "It's like movies, isn't it?" Kim asked.

"No," Marisa said. "Movies have premieres. You can go and see it with a group of people and see that they're laughing in the right spots, or if they get teary-eyed. Even if their reaction is bad, at least you're not left in suspense." She rested her head on Kim's shoulder. "Take me somewhere. Some out of town place where I can forget about being an actress."

"We'll stop at some seedy motel along the way."

"I'll sign in as Mary Prewitt."

Kim smiled and said, "Anything for you, sweetheart." She kissed Marisa's eyebrow and was moving down to her lips when Marisa's radio crackled. They both groaned as she picked it up off the table.

"What do you need, Chet?"

"You, gorgeous," the new director said. "On-set in five. We've got the next-door studio for two hours today, so we're going to use the *Letters from Home*'s gazebo. But we gotta hustle."

"I'll be right there," she promised. She put the radio down and said, "Rain check on the making out?"

Kim kissed her lips. "Deal. I'll see about getting you through tomorrow night."

"Thank you," Marisa said. "I feel relieved already." She swung her legs back down to the floor and pushed herself up. Kim watched her go and began plotting their getaway.

Marisa wore a white turtleneck and a blazer, her hair up and glasses instead of contacts. They went in Kim's Jeep, a less conspicuous vehicle than Marisa's Prius, according to Marisa, and Kim drove them deeper into the city. Marisa toyed with the radio stations before deciding to let the Pink CD play, settling back in her seat and watching the scenery roll by. Work was a half day, giving everyone a chance to get home and watch the first airing of the show they were busting their asses to make. Marisa was eager to get away from the spectacle.

"So where did you decide to hide?"

Kim glanced in the rearview and changed lanes. "I have someplace special in mind. You trust me?"

"Yes."

Kim smiled. "Even if I'm taking you into the slums?"

Marisa watched the buildings go by. "This isn't a slum. This is a real neighborhood. You know? People live here and work here. These buildings all have a history. I'd give all those glass and steel buildings downtown for just one block like this. I love neighborhoods like this."

"Good," Kim said. "Because this is where we're going."

Marisa reached over and stroked Kim's thigh. "Are you taking us to your apartment? Because I've been thinking about how to spend our first night there. I'm the struggling actress who can't pay her rent, and you're the tough landlord who has come to collect one way or another?"

Kim cleared her throat. "Not what I had planned, but I love the way your mind works. File that away for later." She pulled to the curb and stopped the Jeep. "Here we are."

Marisa looked out the window to see if she could guess where they were going. Her eyes skipped over one store and then went back. She knocked her knuckle on the window and said, "Oh, that's your aunt's video store, isn't it."

"Yeah. We can look around in there, if you want before we go upstairs. Stay in the car, I'll go around." She got out of the Jeep and went around the front to open Marisa's door for her. "I thought we'd stop in, say hello."

"Looks like a busy night."

"Wednesdays can be crazy."

They walked across the street together, close but not touching in case anyone recognized Marisa. When they got to the store, Marisa pointed at the sign in the door. "Closed for a private party? Video stores close for that kind of thing?"

"Auntie Em's does," Kim said. She knocked on the glass and, a moment later, Mabel appeared. She unlocked the door, pushed it open, and Kim said, "We're not too late, are we?"

"You're right on time. Hello, Marisa."

"Hi, Mabel," Marisa said. She looked into the store and saw the video shelves had been moved out of the way, forming a seating area in the middle of the store. A few people occupied the dozen or so folding chairs, and Marisa recognized most of them from the set. She looked at Kim and said, "What is this?"

"It's your premiere for *Neutral Ground*," Kim said. "I invited some of the stunt people, a few extras, and Mabel handed out some invites at the store yesterday. I just thought, since you were so nervous about~"

"Can I speak with you in private," Marisa asked, her voice cold, rushed and neutral. Kim felt a stab of dread, suddenly afraid she had done the absolute wrong thing. Marisa grabbed her by the wrist and dragged her toward the office door. Kim cast a fearful look at Mabel, who held up her hands to protest her innocence.

Marisa stormed into the office, and Kim closed the door behind them. "Marisa, I'm sorry. I thought~"

Marisa turned, grabbed Kim's face, and kissed her hard. Kim yelped against Marisa's mouth and then grabbed Marisa's hips, pulling her close. They grappled in front of Aunt Mabel's desk for a moment, hearing the chatter in the store outside, and Marisa finally broke the kiss and embraced Kim.

"Thank you. This is exactly what I needed."

Kim relaxed. "I thought you were mad. Your reaction..."

"I just... I wanted to thank you properly. I wanted to kiss you, but I knew I couldn't do it in front of everyone." She broke the embrace. "Thank you, Kim."

"It was my pleasure. Should we go out and meet your adoring public?"

Marisa exhaled, wiped her cheeks of tears, and nodded. "Yes, let's."

The overhead lights were out, the pilot of *Neutral Ground* playing on the big screen across from the front counter. When Marisa appeared onscreen, the crowd broke into applause and Marisa blushed. She reached down next to the seat, where Kim's hand was dangling, and curled her fingers around Kim's. Mabel provided the snacks - for a fee, of course, since it was still a business - and Marisa shared her popcorn with Kim. Occasionally their hands met in the tub and they both froze, letting the contact last a little longer than necessary.

The episode ended with Simone and Temple being taken prisoner by Trujillo's forces and being rescued by a helicopter. Marisa took out the guard using the fight techniques Kim taught her, and Kim smiled with pride. She tapped Marisa's leg with her hand, and Marisa chuckled. "Feels like a hundred years ago."

Kim looked at Marisa's profile and remembered the day they practiced the fight on the cracked pavement. Every touch of Marisa's body to hers was electric, a part of her mind assuring herself they would never be together no matter how much she wanted it. She said, "It might as well have been."

Marisa looked at her, smiled, and nodded.

"What do you say? Need a ride, Feeb?" Simone Lethe motioned for Thomas Templeton to follow her from the warehouse.

A helicopter was landing on the pavement, and despite knowing exactly where the location was, Kim found it easy to believe they were really on a remote island in the Florida Keys. A man in a suit approached Simone and Temple, eyeing the FBI agent warily. "What the hell is he doing here?"

"Saving my ass," Simone said. "We're taking him with us."

The mission commander hesitated and then said, "What the hell. Come on, both of you." He led the way back to the helicopter and shouted at Simone over his shoulder, "We've already got another passenger aboard already."

They climbed aboard and saw Trujillo sitting in the backseat, handcuffed with two Marines training guns on him. Simone smiled. "Looks like you're going to America after all, *Amir ul-Umara.*"

Temple held his hand out to the CIA agent in charge. "FBI Agent Thomas Templeton. I'd like to be in on the interrogation of this man, if you wouldn't mind."

"Temple's information led us straight here," Simone pointed out. "If not for him, we never would have found this place."

The agent in charge looked at Temple's hand and then crossed his arms over his chest. "We'll take it under consideration."

The shot changed to an exterior, showing the helicopter banking away from a lush tropical jungle. As it rose into the distance, the executive producer credit flashed on the screen and signaled the end of the episode. The audience applauded, not out of etiquette this time, and Marisa ducked her head as Kim added her applause to the mix. Kim whistled, and Marisa nudged her with her leg.

Marisa stood up and said, "Well, uh... that was *Neutral Ground.* I hope you guys all tune in next week. Thank you for coming to watch the show with me."

Another round of applause and Marisa gracefully withstood it. The audience stood up, a few of them passing by Marisa before they left so they could offer their congratulations. One or two had TV Guides turned to the full page ad of *Neutral Ground* that they wanted her to autograph. She signed the glossy photograph of herself, thanked everyone for coming out, and hung around until the crowd emptied out.

Mabel was waiting at the back of the room, and locked the door before examining the remnants of the viewing. "Well? Are you too big of a movie star to help a little old lady put her business back together?"

Marisa said, "Never. Come on, Kim."

"She didn't ask me."

Marisa slapped Kim's hip and started gathering folding chairs. After a moment, Kim sighed and joined them in the clean-up.

Marisa rested one knee on the window seat, leaning forward to look out at the city. They had completed the grand tour of the apartment, and Kim was in the kitchen making dinner on the stove. "Are you sure this is enough?" Kim called. "We could still go out."

"No," Marisa said. She turned and looked at the apartment, letting her eyes linger on the movie posters. "I can't think of anywhere else I would rather eat. I love this apartment. It has so much character. It's... like being in a corner of your mind. I just want to curl up and go to sleep in it."

"Well, hopefully you'll be able to eat first." She came out of the kitchen and said, "The water is boiling."

Marisa gestured out the window. "I love your view."

"Not quite the same as yours," Kim said, standing behind Marisa. She put her hands on Marisa's hips and kissed her neck.

"That doesn't make it less beautiful." She relaxed against Kim's body. "Thank you so much for tonight. If I had known to ask for it, it's exactly what I would have asked for."

Kim kissed up to Marisa's earlobe. "It was my pleasure to do it for you."

Marisa closed her eyes. "I'm going to quit acting. Move to Seattle."

"Okay," Kim said.

Marisa smiled. "You really wouldn't care, would you?"

"I'm assuming I get to go with you to Seattle."

"You're the only thing I'd pack."

Kim smiled. "I love you. I don't care if you're famous or not. And if you're just Marisa Larkin, citizen, we could hold hands in the street. Kiss at dinner. So no, I don't care. But I know you won't. You don't quit something you're born to do."

"And you won't quit throwing yourself off buildings."

Kim said, "Well. Maybe one day. I don't see myself doing this when I'm sixty."

"So I only have to live with it for five years?"

Kim swatted Marisa's ass, hard, and Marisa squealed. "If you can live with that, I can deal with waiting until we're in private to do this." She smoothed her hand over Marisa's ass, soothing the flesh she had just made sting. "It makes it more special. Just mine."

"Mmm. It is all yours," Marisa said.

Kim sighed and said, "But that doesn't change the fact, Ms. Larkin, that your rent is three weeks late."

Marisa hid her smile. "I'm doing the best I can. But headshots and acting classes... I'm going on a few auditions every day, I'm just waiting for the phone to ring."

"I have people calling me, too. I need payment, Ms. Larkin. Surely there's something you can do." She moved her hand to the buckle of Marisa's studded belt. "Do you like living here, Ms. Larkin?"

"Oh, yes, Ms. Greer. I'd do anything to stay."

Kim turned Marisa around and said, "Well, let's just see about that." She undid Marisa's belt and guided her down onto the window seat.

"What about the water?" Marisa asked as her jeans were dragged down her thighs.

"Let it boil," Kim said. She pushed Marisa's legs apart and bowed her head. Marisa leaned back, braced her hands against the window, and groaned with pleasure.

## EPILOGUE

SIMONE LETHE lurched down the aisle of the Greyhound, gripping the back of each seat she passed to keep from falling over. Her hair was down over her face, hiding the blood seeping from her hairline. Her jacket was zipped, hiding the knife wounds and dirt smeared over the cotton. She was dragging her right leg behind her, useless and numb. She finally reached the empty back seat of the bus, dropped into it, and winced as her stitches were pulled. Some hack doctor in Oaxaca had managed to get her put back together, but she had little faith in how long his handiwork would last.

She just needed to find Temple, get back to America, and clear their names. And she had to do it with jihadists chasing her on one side, the American government chasing her from the other. It was a lot to handle, and she was drained. So she leaned her head against the glass and let the rocking of the bus lull her to sleep. She was just going to rest her eyes for a bit, build up strength for the confrontation that she knew was coming.

But for now... she was going to rest. Marisa let her muscles relax and slumped against the bus seat.

A few seconds later, Kenneth Swift shouted, "And cut!" A bell rang, and he said, "That is a wrap for episode thirteen, and thus endeth the first season of *Neutral Ground*, people!" The cast and crew applauded, and Marisa stood up. She accepted hugs and handshakes from members of the crew, hugged Kenneth - veteran director of four episodes, more than anyone else - and made her way slowly toward her trailer. She flexed her muscles as she walked, all of them sore from pretending to have grievous injuries for the past five hours.

She got to her trailer and found Kim sitting at the coffee table with the laptop open in front of her. "Hey," Marisa said.

"Hey." She walked toward the back of the trailer to her changing room. As she passed the table, she bent down and pressed her thumb to the back of Kim's hand, a promise of a kiss later. "What are you reading?"

"The message boards," Kim said. "You have quite a following. Well, you and Simone."

"Really?" She had been avoiding online communities like the plague, well aware of how vicious fans could be.

Kim said, "Yeah. Come see what they call themselves."

Marisa returned in her bra, washing grime from her belly with a moist towel. She sat next to Kim, who angled the laptop so she could read the screen. She smiled. "You made that up."

"I did not. Simone's fans proudly call themselves the Lethebians. They have a website and everything. They, ah, really hope you hook up with Temple's boss, Eva."

Marisa raised an eyebrow. "I could see that."

"Keep your tongue in your mouth, Larkin," Kim said with false anger. "I'm going to slip on all this drool."

Marisa kissed her temple and returned to the back of the trailer. "So what's this 'hiatus' surprise you've been talking about?"

"Still a surprise," Kim said. "We'll leave tonight. You'll find out what I have planned tomorrow."

"Why does it sound so devious when you say it like that?"

"Because you're a very suspicious person. Just trust me. You always love my surprises."

"That's true."

Kim closed the laptop and went into the changing room. Marisa had the bloody and dirty clothes draped over the back of the shower door, standing naked with her back to the door. Kim said, "Need some help with the hard to reach places?"

"Sure. If you wanted to get a couple of easy to reach places, too, I'd be happy to oblige."

Kim smiled and stepped into the changing room with her.

They left that night, after a wrap party thrown by the

production company. They drove until dusk, and checked into a small hotel. Marisa checked in as Mary Prewitt, and the clerk showed no sign of recognizing her when he handed the key across the counter. They went upstairs, made love, and fell asleep in each other's arms.

The next morning, they shared a bath and ate room service breakfast before Kim told Marisa it was time for the surprise. They drove into the wilderness until they reached a crowd of cars parked on either side of the road. Marisa could see some kind of gathering up ahead on the bridge, but she couldn't make out what it was. She frowned and said, "Did you bring me to a movie set?"

"No," Kim said. "Come on."

They got out of the Jeep and walked together toward the bridge. Kim looped her arm around Marisa's and said, "You always talk about how you're afraid to take risks. How you wish you were braver."

"Right."

"Well, I've decided that, having spent a year as your stunt double, it's time for you to make a leap of faith."

They reached the bridge and Marisa realized the gathering was a group of people leaning over the edge of the bridge to look down. The bridge was a sturdy cement construct, spanning a canyon of dizzying depth. There was a steel platform attached to the side of the bridge railing, and a long rubber cord was hanging over the edge. Marisa's heart immediately went into overdrive. "No," she said. "Kim, no..."

"It's okay," Kim whispered. She put her hands on the side of Marisa's head and said, "It's a tandem jump. I'll be right there with you the entire time. You said you trusted me. You said I would keep you safe. I will. No matter how dangerous or scary it gets, I'm going to be right here. Okay?"

Marisa looked at the platform and shuddered. "I'm scared."

"So am I. You have to move past that if you really want to live. You don't have to do this if you really don't want to. I'm not going to force you into the harness, and I'm not going to be disappointed if you can't go through with it. But I want you to know without a doubt that if you *do* find the courage to step up on a ledge and do something stupid and crazy, I'm going to be right there with you, holding your hand. No matter what."

Marisa chewed on her bottom lip. "We can just leave?"

"We can absolutely leave. I'm not going to make you do

anything you're not ready for." She took a step toward the car. "It works just as well as a visual aid."

"Wait." Marisa pulled her back.

"You don't have to do it, Mary."

"I know. Just give me a second to make sure that's what I want." She eyed the people in charge. "This is a good company, I assume."

"The best. And these guys, they're a special group. They're all friends of mine. If you want to kiss me or just hold on really tight, you don't have to worry about it getting into a tabloid. They're good people."

Marisa swallowed and gripped Kim's hand hard enough to hurt. She took a deep breath, let it out slowly, and nodded. "Okay."

"Okay?"

"Okay. Let's go." She took Kim's hand and guided her up to the person running the jumps. "I'm scared shitless, but I think sometimes it's good to be scared. When you're with the right people."

Kim smiled and squeezed Marisa's hand. "Then let's go."

Marisa resisted the urge to triple check the harness, her hands trembling where they rested in the small of Kim's back. They were hooked up, standing on the platform, the rocky canyon floor so far below them that the rocks looked like pebbles. Having her contacts out helped, making everything a bit blurry. But she knew how big the rocks really were, and how hard, and how dangerous, and God, how did she get talked into this? She focused on Kim's eyes and forced herself to breathe normally.

"Just keep your eyes on me."

"Okay," Marisa said.

"I love you, Mary."

"I must *really* love you, too."

Kim smiled and kissed Marisa's bottom lip. "It's okay. It's going to be fine. Are you sure you can do this?"

Marisa said, "With you here? Yes."

Kim looked at the man running the jumps and nodded. They both took a series of deep breaths, and Marisa closed her eyes to steady her nerves. "Three." When she opened them again, Kim nodded at her. "Two." Marisa smiled and felt her fear fade. "One!" With Kim, she wasn't quite so afraid. With Kim, she could do this. She tightened her grip. "Jump!"

Kim fell to the side, and Marisa screamed as they fell off the platform. The wind whipped around her, assaulting her body from all sides. The ground seemed to be coming at her so, so, so fast, and then she looked at Kim's face. Her lips were split in a wide smile, and Marisa couldn't help but laugh. She held tight to Kim as the cord snapped and sent them sailing into the air. It was like flying, exactly like flying, and Marisa looked into the sky as she soared. There was another fall coming she knew, it was the nature of bungee jumping, but that was fine. She would be able to handle it. She would be able to handle anything.

She and Kim both laughed as they fell through the sky.

www.ingramcontent.com/pod-product-compliance
Lightning Source LLC
Chambersburg PA
CBHW070955190726
48292CB00004B/1464